MEGAN'S HERO

This Large Print Book carries the
Seal of Approval of N.A.V.H.

THE CALLAHANS OF TEXAS, BOOK 3

MEGAN'S HERO

SHARON GILLENWATER

THORNDIKE PRESS
A part of Gale, Cengage Learning

GALE
CENGAGE Learning

Detroit • New York • San Francisco • New Haven, Conn • Waterville, Maine • London

GALE
CENGAGE Learning

LIBRARY OF CONGRESS CATALOGING-IN-PUBLICATION DATA

Gillenwater, Sharon.
    Megan's hero / by Sharon Gillenwater.
        p. cm. — (Thorndike Press large print Christian romance)
    (The Callahans of Texas ; 3)
    ISBN-13: 978-1-4104-3935-2 (hardcover)
    ISBN-10: 1-4104-3935-6 (hardcover)
    1. Texas—Fiction. 2. Large type books. I. Title.
PS3557.I3758M44 2011b
813'.54—dc22   2011015089

Published in 2011 by arrangement with Revell Books, a division of Baker Publishing Group.

To Lynn and Mary, sisters-in-law
by title, sisters in my heart.
Thank you for being you!

1

She'd thought things couldn't get any worse.

She'd been wrong.

With the windshield wipers swishing at high speed, Megan Smith eased her mini-van off the narrow two-lane highway into the mud beside the road and turned on the emergency flashers. She peered at the outside mirror in a useless attempt to see behind her. Had the driver of the eighteen-wheeler she'd passed about ten miles back pulled off the road too?

"Better not risk it," she muttered and moved farther to the right, hoping the bar ditch was still as wide and shallow as it had been for the past thirty miles across the West Texas ranch country. When she didn't slide into a man-made mini-ravine, she shut off the windshield wipers and the engine. She couldn't afford to waste a drop of gas.

Megan tried the radio again. Not even

static. Why did it have to quit working today? She tapped her fingers on the steering wheel.

Grumbling at the radio wouldn't ease her frustration. She couldn't blame it for her dumb mistake. It was mid-May, with high temperatures in the nineties. She'd lived in Texas most of her life and knew what a developing thundercloud looked like. She'd just been too disappointed in her mother to pay any attention to it.

"I thought maybe she'd gotten sober, Sweet Baby," she said softly, laying a hand on her round stomach. Why had she driven by her mother's house in San Angelo? What had she hoped for? Flowers in the yard? The grass mowed and the place looking like a well-kept home? *Well, yes.* Or some indication that a miracle had happened in the eight years she'd been gone.

At least she'd had the good sense not to contact her mother. And the disheveled woman stumbling down the porch steps, a bottle of beer in her hand, hadn't noticed the dark green van parked at the corner.

A tiny foot kicked against her palm. Was that little movement simply in response to her voice? Or was Sweet Baby trying to tell her that she — or he — understood that she'd never deliberately do anything to put them in harm's way?

Though she may have done so unintentionally. She hadn't passed a house for miles. Now she was out in open country in the middle of a major thunderstorm. Lightning flashed, startling her. "One-one-thousand. Two-one-thousand. Three-one —"

KABOOM!

Megan gasped as the windows rattled and the thunder continued to rumble. "Oh, Baby, that was too close." A few miles behind her, there had been some live oaks and mesquites in the pastures, but it was raining so hard she couldn't tell if there were any nearby. "What if we're in the highest thing around?" Would lightning strike them? Would they be electrocuted?

A gust of wind shook the van and swept sheets of water at an angle across the windshield. Lightning flashes surrounded them, with mere seconds in between. The thunder boomed and rumbled almost continuously. She patted her stomach to comfort her child. And herself.

After about ten minutes, the lightning and thunder eased up and the torrential rain slacked off a bit. Though it was still heavy, Megan thought she'd be able to drive. As she reached to turn the key, the blast of a truck horn made her shriek. The semi roared by, shifting into the next gear. The trucker wasn't going fast, but the van still rocked violently. "Hey! Get a brain, jerk!"

Slumping against the back of the seat, she took a deep breath, trying to calm her pounding heart. "People just don't think about anybody else, Sweet Baby. You'll need to remember that and watch out for them."

Thunk . . . thunk . . . thunk, thunk, thunk. Baseball-sized hail smacked the top and hood of the minivan and bounced off the road. *Not good. So not good!*

She moved the seat as far back as possible. Reaching between the bucket seats, she grabbed a pillow and laid it across her stomach. As she picked up the other one, a hailstone hit the windshield right in front of her. It didn't come through but shattered the glass into a giant spiderweb of cracks.

With a cry, she leaned forward and tented the second pillow over her head, stuffing it between her forehead and the steering wheel, pulling each side down to shield her face. The hail pounded against the vehicle like a frenzied drummer at a heavy metal concert.

The driver's side window exploded, spraying splinters and chunks of glass over her bare arm and legs. Something smacked her upper back, but she didn't know if it was a piece of ice or glass. A hailstone hit her thigh and another pounded her upper arm. Sobbing in fear and pain, she closed her eyes and hunched forward even more, trying to protect her baby. Glass showered her as the right window burst and a hailstone landed in the passenger seat. Rain whipped through the driver's side window, drenching her.

The earsplitting din tapered off for a couple of minutes, then stopped completely. She carefully straightened, draping the soggy pillow across the steering wheel. Was it over?

Trembling, she felt faint. She took a deep breath, then another, and assessed her situation. Her arm and thigh ached where the hailstones had hit them, but she could move both limbs. Nothing was broken. Rain mingled with small trickles of blood on her arms and legs, but there were no big cuts. The bright red contrasted eerily with the shimmering, glitter-like glass covering her skin.

Something big and hard was wedged between her back and the seat. Not cold enough to be hail. Glass. She set both pillows on the passenger seat, leaned toward the steering wheel, and opened the door.

Staying as far from the seat back as possible, she swung her legs around toward the open door and winced as her bare skin scraped over bits of glass. The wind buffeted her, and when she stepped out into the mud, her feet slipped and her legs almost buckled.

Holding onto the top of the door and the van, she steadied herself. Lightning flashed and thunder rumbled, but it wasn't as bad as before. She pulled an ice scraper from the door pocket and swept the big round chunk of glass, along with several smaller pieces, from the seat. "We're okay, little one. We're gonna be all right."

Megan put the scraper away, straightened, and surveyed the van. The windshield was shattered but still in one piece. All the windows on the driver's side were smashed in, as well as the front passenger side and rear hatch. The two back windows on the right side were intact but cracked. The van was paid for. She could drive it with a gazillion dents, but she couldn't go far without windows. And she had no insurance.

Hearing a roar, she looked behind her — and froze.

Tornado!

She stared at the dark column spinning from the cloud to the ground, ripping across the rangeland toward them. There wasn't time to try to outrun it in the van. The twister was too wide, too close, and moving fast.

Her first-grade teacher's crisp instructions raced through her mind. *Get away from the car. Get in a ditch.* "There is no ditch!"

Megan ran up the highway, slipping but not falling on the ice-covered pavement, desperately looking for a place lower than the surrounding ground. *God help me!* She'd never prayed. Didn't even know if there was a God. She'd always taken care of herself. Had to. But it wasn't just her anymore. *God, if you're real, please save us.*

The bar ditch was deeper there, but it still looked awfully shallow. Gasping for breath, Megan stopped and checked the tornado bearing down on them. It had turned slightly, but they were still in its path. That little dip beside the road was her only chance. "Please, God," she whispered. "Don't let my baby die."

She kicked some hailstones aside and dropped to her knees in the ditch, frantically brushing away huge chunks of ice so she could lie down. Wiggling deeper into the water and mud, she stretched out as flat as possible. She rested her face on a little clump of grass and turned her head to the side to breathe. Covering her head and neck with her hands and arms, she squeezed her eyes tightly shut.

She'd heard people compare a tornado's roar to a freight train. A hundred locomotives was more like it. The wind tugged at her shirt and hair. Dirt and rocks pelted her back, legs, and arms. Something scraped across her hip.

We aren't low enough. Tears slipped from beneath her eyelids, melding with the rain. *I'm sorry, Sweet Baby. I love you.*

If there was a heaven, Megan hoped it had a special place for innocent babies. She didn't figure she'd find out firsthand. Wind, rain, and debris battered her. It hurt, but nothing felt big enough to cause her serious damage. She held her breath until the pressure in her ears made her cry out.

Her heart pounded in terror, and she dragged in another deep breath, waiting to be sucked up into the tornado like Dorothy and Toto. *I don't have any red shoes. And no home to go to even if I did.*

"Hurry up!" she shouted, but the sound vanished in the roar. "If you're going to kill me, do it! Get it over with."

Had she really heard those last few words? She listened as hard as she could above the pulse thundering in her ears. *It's not as loud.*

Nor was the wind as strong. Nothing else hit her. Megan swallowed hard, afraid to move.

She lay there for several minutes as the noise grew dimmer, then disappeared. Shaking violently, she slowly got to her knees. The wind had died down to a breeze; the rain had gentled. The lightning and thunder were miles away.

Resting her hands on her mud-covered stomach, she whispered, "We made it." But her baby didn't wiggle or kick in reply. That probably wasn't unusual, was it? Babies didn't move around all the time. Though Sweet Baby usually responded to activity or noise. Maybe now that things had settled down the poor little thing was trying to relax.

She hoped so. Worry crept into her mind. Could she have harmed the baby by lying on her stomach? Or exposing it to the violent storm? Had her terror somehow affected her child? She'd never heard of such a thing, but she wasn't an expert on babies or pregnancy. It was definitely learn-as-you-go and hope she was doing things right.

In the pasture across the road, the ravaged land marked the tornado's path. The destruction was at least three blocks wide and went as far across the prairie as she could see. The fence on that side was completely gone. Two mesquite trees, dozens of branches, and half of a large live oak lay in the middle of the two-lane road next to her.

The fence to her right was undamaged, though a small mesquite limb hung from the barbed wire. Just beyond it in the pasture, mesquite trees, prickly pear cactus, and purple verbena and yellow buttercups had been ripped out of the ground and tossed aside as if a giant had been pulling weeds. A nearby windmill was twisted like a corkscrew. At that point, the tornado had turned almost northward, running parallel to the highway.

Megan glanced down the road. Her van was flipped over on its side, but it appeared to be in one piece. Astonished relief swept through her. Her belongings were scattered along the road and in the pasture, but she'd expected to see pieces of the vehicle. Or not see it at all. The van shouldn't be there.

Neither should she.

She'd knelt in the only undamaged area of the tornado's path. A tornado sometimes bounced around, but given this one's size, the single, thirty-foot, untouched ragged circle — with her smack dab in the middle — could not be credited to a whim of

16

Mother Nature.

She had experienced a miracle. God was real, and he had heard her plea. He had spared them.

She didn't know why. She was a nobody. There wasn't a single person on earth who cared whether she lived or died. For some reason God did. Maybe it was a mother's cry to save her child that had stirred his compassion. It certainly wasn't because she was worth saving.

"Thank you." She closed her eyes, overwhelmed with gratitude and awe. "Thank you. I don't know much about you, God. But I'll learn about you, learn what you want from me. I'll find out how to repay you for saving us." The promise came from the depths of her soul.

She lifted her face to the rain, letting it wash away the mud. Oddly, she felt as if some of the filth of her past was being washed away too. Fanciful thought. People couldn't erase what happened to them or what they'd done.

But you don't have to wallow in the mud. That had been her motto since she was sixteen. Looking down at the front of her body, she smiled. "Unless you're trying to escape a tornado."

She pushed to her feet and ran her hand

17

over the front of her shirt, knocking off the big chunks of mud. But when she cautiously wiped a small spot on her thigh below her shorts, ground glass dug into her skin. Sucking in her breath, she swiped her hand on a clump of grass. The mud and the glass weren't her biggest problems.

She was soaking wet, chilled, shaken. And about fifteen or sixteen miles from the nearest town, according to a "Callahan Crossing 20 Miles" sign she'd passed earlier.

The rain slacked off to little more than a sprinkle as she walked back to the van. It would be even better when the rain completely stopped. In a perfect world, the clouds would drift away, and the sunshine would warm her up. She glanced at the gray, cloudy sky. The worst of the storm had passed, and that was good enough.

She stopped beside her vehicle and scanned the things scattered on the ground between it and the barbed wire fence. Two cans of pinto beans, a jar of peanut butter, a magazine she'd found by a dumpster, a saucepan, and a full, refillable water bottle.

And her purse. *Thank you.* Would her cell phone work out here? She'd dropped her regular account a month ago and bought a cheap prepaid phone for emergencies.

After she picked up the big brown leather

bag, relief turned to dismay. The bag had two large compartments, each with its own zipper. One side had been open, and the tornado had devoured the contents, including the phone. The items in the other side, including her wallet, were still intact.

She took a long drink from the water bottle, put it in her purse, and set it beside the van. A sweater dangled from a high branch in a mesquite tree in the pasture. The tree had been split in half, but her sweater was at the top of the portion still standing. Something blue, probably a pair of jeans, was tangled in a big prickly pear cactus nearby.

A suitcase lay in the grass between the fence and the tree. She squinted, studying the squashed blue rectangle. No, make that half a suitcase. Which meant at least a third of her clothes were strewn all over the pasture.

She checked the back of the minivan. It had been ransacked and robbed, only not by human hands. She hadn't brought a lot with her — mostly clothes, food, a cooler, a few pans, and dishes for meals. Also some of her baking equipment and recipes. She couldn't bring herself to part with something that brought her so much enjoyment.

Now it was gone anyway. As were all three

suitcases and the plastic storage box with her tax records. The clothes she wore were all she had, and they were pretty much ruined. Hopefully, she would be able to find some more in the pasture later.

With a sigh, she picked up everything beside the road and tossed it into the back of the van through the gaping hatch window. What was beyond the fence would have to wait until someone could help her or she found another way into the pasture. She wasn't about to try to slip between the strands of barbed wire.

Digging through the rubble inside the van, she found a spoon and took a few minutes to eat several bites of peanut butter. The water and food restored some of her strength and all of her determination. The rain had stopped completely by the time she put the spoon, the jar of peanut butter, and another sports-size bottle of water from the van into her purse. She slung the long, wide strap over her head and across her shoulder, letting the bag hang at her side.

"It's a good thing we've been doing lots of walking lately, Baby." Heading north, Megan struck out toward Callahan Crossing, stepping carefully to avoid slipping on the remaining hailstones. Surely a car would come along and give her a ride into town.

Unfortunately, that might be a while. She hadn't seen more than five cars since she left San Angelo.

Trying to ignore the big, aching bruises on her thigh and arm and the dozens of other lesser pains that were reporting in, she marched down the road. Hopefully she'd find a house right around the curve up ahead. If she didn't, she'd keep going.

God had saved her, and she wasn't going to wimp out on him now.

2

Will Callahan pulled out from the Callahan
Ranch onto the two-lane highway and
headed south. He and his family had
watched the tornado for several minutes
before taking shelter in the storm cellar. A
faint smile touched his face. Even though
he was thirty-two years old, when his father
ordered them to get into the cellar, he
obeyed. He argued with Dub on occasion,
but when they might all blow away wasn't
the time.

Thankfully, the twister missed all the
houses in the Callahan compound. That was
what he and his brother and sister called
their cluster of homes around the ranch
house. Since the tornado had run parallel
to the highway, none of the other structures
on the ranch were affected either. The
twister had dissipated before reaching any
of the homes or farms to the north of the
ranch. Will wanted to see what kind of dam-

age it had done in the pasture, mainly whether or not it had destroyed any of the fence.

Cattle were curious animals and always considered the grass greener on the other side of everything. If there was a gap in the fence, they were bound to wander through it, wind up on the highway, and cause problems for the rancher and drivers.

He also wanted to make sure no one traveling along the road had run into trouble from the storm. It wasn't likely, but he'd feel mighty bad if someone needed help and he hadn't bothered to check.

Half a mile down the road, large hailstones dotted the roadway. There wasn't a lot, but it was good-sized hail. The storm had passed through over half an hour earlier, so it had already melted some. They hadn't had any hail at the house.

After pulling his cell phone from the pouch on his belt, he called his dad. "Looks like we had at least baseball-sized hail starting about half a mile south of the gate. I can see patches of white in the pasture far from the road, so we'd better have Buster and Ollie check on the cattle."

"I'll call them," said Dub. "How's the highway?"

"Slick in spots. It hasn't been too bad so

far, but the hail is getting thicker now." He spotted someone in the distance walking along the highway. "I see somebody on foot. I'll go see how I can help."

"Holler if you need us."

"Yes, sir." Will laid the phone in a tray on the console.

The pedestrian was a woman. She was really hoofin' it considering she had to pick her way through the mess on the road. When she saw him, she stopped and waved her arms. He slowed down and pulled off the highway near her.

She was five-two at the most. Maybe in her early twenties. Mud covered her legs, part of her arms, and the front of her clothes — at least what her big brown purse didn't hide. If he were a wagering man — which he wasn't — he'd bet next Sunday's dinner that she'd taken shelter from the tornado in the bar ditch.

It appeared she hadn't made any attempt to wipe off the mud, and he figured he knew why. Somewhere down the road they would find a car with the windows smashed out. As Will shut off the engine, she lifted the long purse strap over her head, and the sunlight glistened in tiny sparkles on her arm. *Glass.*

He opened the door, eased out of the

truck so he wouldn't slip on a piece of ice, and walked around the front of the pickup. She clutched her purse with both hands. He had no doubt that if she sensed danger she'd take a swing at him with that big bag and knock him silly.

Oh, man, she's pregnant! She watched him cautiously and tried to catch her breath. He hoped she was breathing hard just because she'd been walking. He couldn't tell if her top was one of those stretchy things some women wore when they were carrying a baby, or if the rain and mud had glued it to her body. Either way, it clearly revealed her very round stomach. Will was no expert on expectant ladies, but he guessed she was about five months along.

He nodded politely and touched the brim of his hat in greeting. "Ma'am, do you need me to take you to the hospital? I can get you there faster than if we call for help."

She shook her head. "There's a man hurt in a semi about a mile down the road. The tornado blew his truck over and into the pasture. The windshield is gone, so I could talk to him and touch him. He has a nasty bump and cut on the side of his head. It was bleeding really bad, but I found a T-shirt caught in a bush. I folded it up and held it against his head until the bleeding stopped. He thinks his leg is broken, and he probably has a concussion. He's kind of drifting in and out of consciousness.

"His radio isn't working, and he didn't know where his cell phone was. Probably got blown away like mine." Pleading filled her golden brown eyes. "He's a lot worse off than I am. You've got to help him."

"We will. Let's get you into the truck and turn on the heater. You look cold." He gently put his arm around her, careful not to brush against the glass on her arm. Surreptitiously counting her breaths, he guided her toward the passenger side. Her breathing was normal for someone who had been walking as fast as she'd been. She was trembling, but he knew it wasn't only from being chilled.

Dozens of small cuts and trickles of dried blood dotted her arms and legs, along with a lot of tiny glass fragments. He didn't see any bad cuts, but she had a large bruise on her arm and another on her thigh. Smaller bruises were showing up everywhere. They'd probably be a lot darker by tomorrow. "Did you lose your car in the tornado?"

"My minivan flipped over beside the highway. I'd pulled off because of the heavy rain. Then the hailstorm hit. When I saw the twister, I laid down in the bar ditch."

"Good for you. I've heard those instructions all my life but never had to do it."

"Me either, until today. Moving warmed me up some, but I'm still cold." Her clothes were soaked but not dripping, and her short, curly brown hair was only damp. So she'd been walking for a while.

When he opened the door, she laid her purse on the floor. With his hand hovering behind her in case she needed help, she put one foot on the running board, grabbed hold of the handle on the dash and the one above the door, and hoisted herself up, easing onto the seat with a wince. She grimaced when she leaned against the seat back.

"Do you have glass down the back of your blouse?"

"Nothing big, but there must be some slivers caught in the material. Mostly I just feel like I've been beaten up."

Will frowned. Something in the way she said it indicated the comparison came from firsthand knowledge. "You have been." This time by hail, glass, and debris from the tornado. But who had done it before? "Do you mind if I check your pulse?"

"Why?" The guarded expression was back.

"So I can relay the information to the sheriff's dispatcher." He shrugged and smiled, hoping to put her at ease. "I'm a volunteer fireman, and that's what we're trained to do when someone has been hurt."

"Okay." She held out her arm.

Placing his index and middle fingers over the pulse in her wrist, he counted each beat, timing the process with his wristwatch. "Strong and a little fast, but that's understandable." It was also slightly irregular, and that worried him.

When he released her arm and handed her the seat belt, she lifted one brow. "I could have told you that."

"Yeah, you probably could've." He smiled and walked around the front of the pickup and quickly got in. Starting the engine, he turned the heater on high but left the fan off. "It needs to warm up."

He checked behind them and pulled out onto the road, then picked up the phone and dialed 911. "Hi, Lisa. Will Callahan. We had a twister come through out here."

"Dub called to alert us. He said everybody at the ranch was fine." The dispatcher at the sheriff's office was an old family friend. As were a lot of people in Callahan Crossing.

"We are. But I'm told it overturned a semi south of our place. The driver has a probable broken leg and concussion. I haven't gotten there yet."

"Okay. Hang on a minute while I make

the call." He heard her give the radio call, then she came back on the line. "Anything else?"

"I picked up a young woman on the highway. She's pretty battered, bruised, and drenched — and pregnant." He glanced at his passenger. "She got caught in the hailstorm and is covered in glass. No serious cuts, but many little ones. She has a couple of big bruises and a bunch of smaller ones. Her pulse is strong, a little fast, and a bit irregular, but nothing extreme."

That earned him a slight frown. "Respiration sounds clear, deep, and also a little fast. But she's walked a mile or so. The tornado flipped her van over, but she took shelter in the bar ditch. She's the one who told me about the trucker. I'll put the phone on speaker so you can talk to her." He pushed the speaker button and laid the phone on the console.

"What's your name, honey?" the dispatcher asked.

"Megan Smith."

"You were in the tornado?"

"It went right over me. I got away from my van and lay in the ditch."

"You did exactly what you were supposed to do. Do you have any other injuries besides the cuts and bruises? Did any big debris hit you?"

"No, ma'am. A lot of small rocks and dirt. Probably some small branches. I didn't stick my head up to see what was pounding me."

Megan's hand lay protectively on her stomach. The quicker an EMT checked her out the better.

"Are you having any bleeding or contractions?"

"No. I'm just cold, wobbly, and woozy."

Will frowned. Could she be going into shock now that she wasn't focused on saving the trucker's life? He reached over and curled his fingers around her wrist, finding her pulse. She shot him a questioning glance.

"Will, can you check her pulse again?" Lisa asked.

"Doing it right now." He paused until he had taken the count. "It's still strong at her wrist and has slowed down a little, though still irregular. Her skin is cold but not clammy." He lightly ran a finger over her forehead before placing his hand back on the steering wheel. "Not sweating. I don't see any symptoms of shock."

"Good. How far along are you, Megan?"

"Twenty-eight weeks." She took a deep, shaky breath, drawing Will's attention again. Her voice was thick with emotion when she spoke. "Could being in the storm have done anything to my baby? It hasn't moved around or kicked since before the tornado, and Sweet Baby is usually pretty active."

Sweet Baby. So much love in those words.

"I don't think it would have harmed your baby," Lisa said gently. "But we'll have the medics check you out thoroughly too. As for being wobbly, you probably need to eat something. That's speaking as a mother of six, not as a medical authority."

"I had some peanut butter before I started walking. But that was a while ago. I brought the jar with me."

Will interrupted. "I have some energy bars. Would that be good for her?"

"Yes. And lots of water. Maybe some juice if you have it."

He motioned toward the glove box and nodded for his guest to help herself. To his relief, she wasn't shy about following his suggestion. "I don't have any juice, but I've got some bottles of water." He spotted the truck in the pasture beside the road, the path of the tornado extending for at least a mile beyond it. "We're at the semi, Lisa."

"Call Johnny and give him an update on the driver. Dalton and the fire truck are on their way too."

"You'll need a big tow truck." He scanned

the scene as he pulled off the highway again. "And another truck to haul lumber. It's a mess out here. I'll let Dad know what's going on. They can be here directly to help."

Will parked off the road but away from the wreckage. He left the engine idling and cranked up the heater fan. His guest was resting her head against the back of the seat and devouring a chocolate-covered power bar. "Are you okay?"

"Getting better." She glanced at the truck, her forehead wrinkled in worry. "Wave if you need any help."

He nodded and opened the door. "You rest and eat. Have as many of those as you want." He noticed she'd set a half-full sports bottle in the holder in the console. "There's more water in a box on the floor behind your seat. Do you want a bottle?"

"No, thanks. I have another one in my purse. I'm good for now."

Will paused a few seconds and studied her as she folded up the power bar wrapper and tucked it in the small plastic garbage bag hanging from the heater knob. As his grandpa used to say, she had gumption. Grandpa had admired that in a woman.

So did he.

3

After grabbing a pair of leather gloves from a pouch in the door, Will stepped down to the ground and stuffed them in his back pocket. The sun had come out, raising the temperature and melting the hail faster.

He had worked several accidents, though he'd been first on the scene only once. Standing by the pickup, he surveyed the area. No downed power lines. Truck engine off. He sniffed the air — no fuel leaks. They were well off the road, so there was no danger from passing cars and plenty of room for the emergency vehicles when they arrived. No obstacles hanging in the mesquite trees or on the truck that could fall on them.

He removed a first aid kit from behind the backseat and paused long enough to pull on a pair of nonlatex gloves. He called the ranch as he picked his way through the rubble of broken lumber, tangled fencing, mesquite limbs, and debris that came from somewhere else, including a badly dented aluminum water trough. Will quickly explained the situation to his brother, Chance, and ended the call as he walked around the cab of the truck.

The big rig lay on the left side, with the driver lying against the cab door. The cracked windshield had popped out and was about twenty yards away in the pasture. He checked for oil or other fluid leaks. Nothing to cause a problem.

Will recognized the injured man. Ted made regular hauls from San Angelo to Callahan Crossing, delivering lumber for the houses Chance built.

"Cavalry's arrived," the driver mumbled.

"Just the scout. But the cavalry is on the way." Will knelt beside the opening where the windshield used to be and set the first aid kit on the ground beside him. He didn't think he'd need any of the bandages in the kit, but it paid to keep it handy.

The truck had landed hard, breaking off the rearview mirror and crumpling the left fender and bumper. The side of the cab lay on the ground at a slight angle. "How ya doin'?"

"Leg's busted. Ribs hurt. Whoppin' headache."

"It's no wonder, considering the size of that goose egg on your head." His shirt and the door panel between the window and armrest were soaked with blood. "I'm going to open your shirt and see if you're bleeding anywhere."

He quickly but gently unsnapped the front of the western shirt and checked for injuries. "I don't see any big cuts. Just some little scrapes." But he was going to have some nasty bruises. "All this blood must have come from your head."

"A purty little gal stopped it." A faint frown creased his brow. "Or did I dream that?"

The bloody shirt was tucked underneath his head. "You didn't dream it. She's the one who told me about the wreck. She's in the truck, warming up and having something to eat."

"Good." Ted's eyelids drifted closed, and Will wondered if he'd passed out. But he looked at Will again, pain and worry clouding his eyes. "She hurt? Can't remember."

"She got caught in the hailstorm, but I don't think she has any bad injuries. The medics will check her out too. I need to ask you a couple of questions that will give them an idea how you're doing. Can you tell me your name?"

35

"Ted Bentley." He frowned at Will. "You know that."

"Yes, but I wanted to see if you did. Do you know where you are?"

Ted's frown deepened and he glanced past Will at the lumber scattered about. "Goin' to Callahan Crossing."

"That's right. Do you know what day it is?"

"Sunday?" the trucker asked hesitantly.

"No, it's Thursday. Do you remember what happened?"

Ted pondered the question, started to shake his head, and winced.

Will quickly leaned forward, put a hand on each side of the man's head, and held it still. "Don't move your head until the paramedics tell you it's okay." He looked down at Ted's twisted leg. Definitely broken, but there was no sign of additional blood anywhere. "Can you tell me what happened?"

"Thunderstorm. Pulled off the road." He paused to take a few shallow breaths. "Rain let up. Got goin' again." He paused again, frowning. "Big hail. Angel woke me up. In a heap of pain. Did I have a wreck?"

"Yep, with a tornado."

"No kiddin'?"

"You need to lie still so I can check your

pulse, okay?"

"Yeah."

Will was worried. The trucker had grown paler as they talked. He moved one hand and gently placed his fingers on the side of Ted's throat and counted the weak pulse. Fifty-five beats a minute. He sure hoped the medics got there pronto.

"Still tickin'?"

"Yep." Will checked the pulse in Ted's wrist. It was the same. Good. Not sweating, but he was breathing fast and shallow. He laid his hand lightly on Ted's chest, counting his breaths. "Does it hurt when you breathe?"

"Yeah. Ribs. Did I have a wreck?"

"You got hit by a tornado." Déjà vu all over again. Megan guessed right — concussion.

"No kiddin'?"

Two pickups pulled in behind his. "Dad and the boys are here." Will braced Ted's head again to keep him from moving. "I'm just going to hold your head steady."

"Okay." Ted closed his eyes.

His dad and Chance joined him a minute later. His brother-in-law, Nate, stopped by Will's pickup to check on Megan.

"How is he?" Chance asked quietly, squatting down beside him.

37

"Not as good as I'd like. You hold his head while I call Johnny and give him an update." He leaned closer to the injured man. "Ted, Chance is going to stay with you while I call Johnny." No response. Will carefully lifted his hands and shifted back out of Chance's way.

"He's unconscious?" Chance framed the driver's head with his hands.

"He's been talking, but I think he passed out a minute ago." Will moved a few steps away and hit the speed dial for the paramedic. "Johnny. It's Will. The trucker is Ted Bentley out of San Angelo. Leg's definitely broken. Ribs either bruised or broken. Head injury, at least a concussion. He doesn't remember the accident. Short-term memory isn't good. I told him what happened, but he didn't remember it a few minutes later.

"Pulse fifty-five and weak. Respiration twenty-six and shallow. He said it hurts to breathe deep. He was talking up to a few minutes ago, but he's unconscious now. He's lying on his side, still in the seat, against the door. I didn't get a chance to ask about medical history. He works for Best Lumber in San Angelo, so they could put Lisa in touch with his family."

"I'll give her a call," said Johnny. "Don't let him move." The siren wailed, almost drowning out his voice.

"Chance is holding his head steady. What's your ETA?"

"Five minutes. You know Butch. He loves these country calls 'cause he can go warp speed."

"We're about a mile past the ranch entrance. Don't fly past us."

"We won't."

Will hung up the phone and met his father's gaze. Nate had joined them as he was making the call, so everyone heard the report. "They should be here in five minutes." He looked at Nate. All the men in the family were volunteer firemen, so his brother-in-law knew what to watch for too. "How's Megan?"

"She's okay. Getting warmer. Said she felt better after she ate the energy bar." He smiled slightly. "She wanted to know what was up with everybody checking her pulse every few minutes."

"I get the impression she's pretty independent."

"No wedding ring," said Nate.

Will had noticed that too. "Might not mean anything." By the time he'd shared what little he knew about her, the EMTs had arrived. They hauled their equipment around the front of the truck before Butch went to examine Megan.

Johnny took over Ted's care, and the Callahans and Nate moved out of the way. Will shifted so he could see Megan as Butch examined her. He couldn't hear the conversation, but she had a very expressive face. She was worried, and whatever Butch was telling her wasn't easing her fears any.

"She'll need to go to the ER," his dad said quietly.

Will nodded. "Not only to clean off the glass and treat her cuts. Her pulse was irregular, and she felt faint earlier. I'll take her in as soon as Butch gives the go-ahead."

He knew the others could take care of Ted and see to cleaning up the truck wreckage. "Her minivan is down the road, but I don't know how far."

"We'll handle it," said Chance. "I'll run down there and take a look as soon as we get Ted out of here. I'll give Joe's Towing a heads-up that we'll be needing a wrecker."

"Sounds good." Will glanced to see how Johnny was doing with the trucker. He had put a neck brace on him and was starting an IV. When Will looked back at Megan, she said something to Butch and emphatically shook her head. Butch was arguing with her, though clearly in a nice way. "Think I'll go see what the problem is." He caught Chance

40

and Nate exchange a quick glance. "What?"

His brother shrugged nonchalantly. "It's just interesting to see you get all protective of the lady."

"What good is rescuing somebody and not following through to make sure she's okay?" But in his heart, he knew that wasn't the whole truth. Despite her determination and resourcefulness, Will sensed a vulnerability in Megan. He had the feeling she needed a friend, and he intended to be one, if only for today.

As he strolled over to his pickup, Megan asked the medic, "Can't I just go somewhere and hose off the mud and glass?"

"No, ma'am," Butch said patiently. "You need to go to the hospital to be checked out more thoroughly." She turned in the seat, putting her feet out the door opening, and he stepped back. Will stopped a few feet away, wondering why she was against going to the hospital when she'd been so worried about her baby earlier.

"You said the baby's heartbeat sounded okay." She held her arms out away from the inside of the truck and brushed off some of the dried mud. "See, it's coming off and taking the glass too." Will noticed a little wince, though she tried to hide it. The glass wasn't coming off as easily as she pretended.

"I'll just knock all this off and be done with it. Then we can figure out what to do with my van." She slid out of the truck to the ground, forcing Butch to move farther back. He almost tripped over his bag and looked away as he moved it over with his foot.

She took a step and swayed, the color draining from her face. Will jumped forward, swept her up in his arms, and tipped her feet higher than her head. She sure didn't weigh much. When she wasn't pregnant, she wouldn't be bigger than a minute.

She hung limply almost upside down for a few seconds, then grabbed hold of his shirt with one hand and frowned at him. "Put me down."

Her voice wasn't nearly as forceful as he expected she intended. Ignoring her, he glanced at Butch.

"Not yet." The EMT checked the pulse in her throat and wrist again, then wrapped a blood pressure cuff around her arm and pumped it up.

She attempted to glare at the medic, but it was a puny effort. The woman was feisty, which Will admired. But she wasn't showing much common sense at the moment.

Butch took her blood pressure, then removed the cuff. "Okay, you can raise her up now, but no standing. Put her on the seat and take her to the hospital."

Will slowly lowered her knees and raised her shoulders, holding her a little longer than was necessary. "Let us take care of you, Megan," he said quietly. Confusion and a hint of fear clouded her face. He played his ace. "And your child. Let's make sure Sweet Baby is okay."

Tears misted her eyes, and she swallowed hard as he carefully placed her on the truck seat. "I want to, but I don't have any insurance," she said softly. When she looked up at him, her eyes were dark with worry — and shame. "Or the money to pay for a visit to the ER. I don't want to be a charity case."

"I'll cover it."

"I can't let —"

"It's not up to you." He grabbed the seat belt, leaned over her, and fastened it with an emphatic click. "I'll take care of it."

"Then I'll pay you back. As soon as I can. When I find another job."

She didn't need to. His bank account was stuffed full and bustin' at the seams, but he suspected it was very important for her to carry her own load. "Deal."

He shut her door and stopped to check with Butch. "Is she okay?"

"I think so, but I'm concerned about her

almost fainting. Could just be an emotional reaction to what she's been through or something else going on with her pregnancy. I expect they'll want to keep her overnight."

"They should. She's been through a lot today and will have a lot more hassles before things get straightened out with her van." If she didn't have a job or health insurance, she probably didn't have car insurance, either. "She doesn't need to be fighting any health issues too."

Butch grinned. "Being pregnant is enough to deal with all by itself."

Will waved to his dad and got into the pickup. Megan glanced at him, then closed her eyes. He turned around and started up the highway toward Callahan Crossing just as his friend, Deputy Sheriff Dalton Renfro, arrived along with the fire truck and a couple more volunteer firemen. He just waved and kept going. Somebody else could bring them up to speed.

He thought she was asleep, but right after they drove past the entrance to the Callahan Ranch, she turned to look at him. "Callahan Ranch, Callahan Crossing. You're that Callahan?"

"One of them. The rest of the men in my family came to help. You met Nate, my brother-in-law. He's married to my sister,

Jenna. The other two are my dad, Dub, and my brother, Chance."

Her tired smile held a hint of whimsy. "I never had a real cowboy ride to my rescue before."

Will grinned. "Sorry I didn't ride up on a white horse."

"I'm not. Pickup's better." Her smile faded. "Thank you."

"You're welcome."

She kept studying him until he grew uncomfortable. "What?"

"Are you for real? Or is this good guy stuff just an act? What are you going to want in return?"

"Nothing. People around here help each other, Megan."

"Even strangers?"

"Yep."

"Why?"

"That's just the way it is. God has blessed us, so it's only right that we do what we can for other folks."

"So you believe in God?"

"Yes. Do you?"

She nodded, looked out at the passing scenery, then rested her head against the seat again and closed her eyes. "After today I do."

45

4

Megan had never been a patient in an emergency room, and she didn't like being one now. She wore a clean hospital gown, though dried mud and glass remained on her arms and legs. Her filthy shoes and filthy clothes were stuffed in plastic bags and hung on a hook on the wall. Except for her top, which was in the garbage. Miniscule glass fragments had covered a good portion of the back and part of each side. The nurse had cut it off rather than pull it over Megan's head and risk getting glass on her face or in her eyes.

That was my favorite blouse, Megan thought sullenly.

Which she couldn't have used again anyway. But an idiotic anger had her ready to lash out at someone. The past six months had been enough to tick anybody off. She'd gotten pregnant — definitely not planned — then was so sick that she had to give up a job she enjoyed. She'd used up her savings and still lost the apartment. And when she did feel good enough to look for another job, there weren't any. It had been the pits.

But she'd adapted, living in the van and camping in parks for the past three weeks.

Now, her tiny home-on-wheels might be useless. Most of her belongings had been gobbled up by the tornado. Even if the van could be repaired and she could somehow gather up everything, it wouldn't matter. There was nothing of value left to sell.

She didn't want to think about how much this hour or two in the ER would cost. Will had said she could pay him back later, but when would that be? Job openings were few and far between. She'd looked in almost every town between San Angelo and Austin.

And she had exactly fifty-five dollars and twenty-one cents to her name.

Like mother, like daughter, she thought bitterly. The fruit didn't fall far from the tree. Megan never drank, and the only thing she'd ever swiped was a pair of cheap earrings, but obviously she'd inherited Jackie's lousy judgment when it came to men.

She'd messed up her good, comfortable life and ruined everything she'd worked so hard to accomplish. She'd let down her guard and trusted a man who made promises he never intended to keep.

A little tap, flutter, and wiggle sent a wave of relief and love washing through her. Sweet Baby was okay and doing a little boot scootin' in her belly. She patted the little foot that bounced against her hand. Or maybe it was a tiny hand exploring his — or her — world.

Okay, so maybe she hadn't messed up so bad after all. At least now she'd have someone who loved her. And, for the first time in her life, she had someone to love. Quick tears stung her eyes. Stupid hormones. Crying wasn't her style.

She'd get through this. She'd had nothing when she took off at sixteen, but she'd worked hard and built a good life for herself. She could do it again at twenty-four.

"It may take a while, Sweet Baby, but I'll give you a good home," she whispered.

She scrunched up the pillow, raised the head of the bed a little more, and waited for the pleasant but no-nonsense nurse to return. The woman had strapped a fetal monitor around her belly first thing, explaining that it was the kind that sent a signal directly to the nurses' station. It was also portable, so Megan wasn't restricted to the bed by a bunch of wires.

Not that she was interested in getting up right then. Despite the dried mud tightening up her skin, it felt good to rest and hide behind the curtain for a few minutes.

Though it didn't do much to keep out the world. She could hear snippets of conversations in other rooms and almost everything said at the nurses' station. A constant beep came from somewhere that would drive her bonkers if she stayed there long. Every few minutes footsteps went up and down the hall, and occasionally something rolled by.

Will hovered in the hallway. She couldn't see him, but it seemed as if every person who walked by knew him and said hello. He knew them too, speaking in a deep, quiet voice, calling them by name and often asking about a family member. Particularly if they had a kid who played football. The man must know the stats on every high school player in town.

Before long it seemed every woman in the small hospital had found some excuse to wander down to the ER and scope out the handsome cowboy leaning against the wall outside her room.

It didn't matter that his worn jeans were stained with mud from kneeling beside the truck. Or that sprinkles of glass had rubbed off her blouse onto his pale blue shirt when he picked her up. Somehow, the little dirt smudge on his cheek only made him more ruggedly appealing. About six-two, slim but muscular, with dark brown hair and even darker brown eyes, Will Callahan was the kind of man women of all ages fawned over.

And he charmed them all. Three ladies had already stopped and asked about his mama, his sister, and his sister-in-law. He answered them politely — not revealing much, she noticed — and inquired about their families. No one mentioned his wife, so evidently he didn't have one.

Three more women stopped to flirt a bit. He responded with an easy banter that told Megan he was an expert at the game but didn't take any of it seriously — and neither should they.

The nurse bustled in and walked around to the far side of the bed. Everything about her, from her short pixie-style gray hair to the tailored bright blue top and pants and black Crocs made Megan think of competency and efficiency. She glanced at her name tag — Peg Renfro, RN.

"You're looking a bit perkier than when you came in."

"My baby has been wiggling around and practicing his — or her — line dancing."

The nurse smiled. "I expect that eases

your mind some."

"Yes, ma'am."

"This should too. Your baby's heart rate is good, and you aren't having any contractions. We have our twenty-minute baseline, so I can take the monitor off now." She unfastened the wide stretchy straps holding the two electronic disks in place and motioned for Megan to lean up so she could pull them out from beneath her back. "We'll check the baby's heartbeat every thirty minutes, but I can just hold the transducer — the disk — in place for a minute or so to get that reading."

The nurse pressed a button or flipped a switch that Megan couldn't see, and the blood pressure cuff that had been wrapped around her arm inflated, making her wince. The dumb thing was so tight it hurt. That had to send her blood pressure up a few notches. How many times did they have to check it anyway?

"So you don't know whether it's a boy or girl?" asked a female doctor who stepped around the curtain and stopped at the foot of the bed. She appeared to be in her early thirties.

"No, ma'am."

The doctor moved closer and held out her hand. "I'm Dr. Cindy Jarman, though most

51

people around here just call me Dr. Cindy. I hear you've had a wild day."

"That's a good description."

"How are you feeling?"

"Pretty good. I don't feel tired and weak now."

"Do you have a headache?" Dr. Cindy gently pressed here and there on her abdomen. She smiled when Sweet Baby gave her hand a little nudge.

"Yes. Not real bad, though."

"Have you been having a lot of headaches?"

"Several in the last few weeks." But she figured she'd had enough tension to cause them, even when she'd spent a lot more time resting than she would have if she'd been working.

"Butch said you almost passed out after he examined you."

"I don't think I was really going to faint. I was just real dizzy."

"Has that happened other times recently?"

"Twice this past week. I thought it had stopped after I quit barfing all the time."

The doctor hooked the earpieces of the stethoscope into her ears. She checked Megan's heart and lungs, then moved down to her stomach and listened to the baby's heartbeat.

When she raised her head and removed the instrument from her ears, she nodded. "One-hundred-fifty beats a minute. Strong and steady."

She inspected the bruises on Megan's arm and leg and shook her head at the mud and glass. "When was your last tetanus shot?"

"A couple of years ago."

"Good. One less thing to worry about. Both you and your baby are a little small for twenty-eight weeks along. Did we get that number right?"

"Yes. I've been sick most of my pregnancy. When I wasn't barfing, I was still so nauseated that I couldn't eat much. About all I could do was lie in bed or on the couch. It started at the end of my first month and lasted until four weeks ago."

"So you've been eating well only the last month. That would explain it. Are you taking prenatal vitamins?"

"Yes, ma'am." Megan smiled at the thought of the bottle of pills in her purse. "They're one of the few things that didn't blow away."

"That's good, but I'm sorry you lost so many other things." Dr. Cindy removed the stethoscope from where it hung around her neck and tucked it into a jacket pocket. "You didn't want to know whether it was a boy or girl when you had the ultrasound? Or was the baby turned so they couldn't get a good view?"

"I haven't had one."

That brought a frown. "Have you been under a doctor's care for your pregnancy?"

"Yes." Megan shifted, more from mental and emotional discomfort than physical. "But I haven't seen her in two months." She swallowed as heat flooded her face. "Money has been a problem lately. I was so sick I had to give up my job."

"So you haven't had any blood work done lately either?"

"No." Megan knew she should have gone in for it, but two months ago she was saving every penny to pay her rent and to buy what little food she could keep down. Last month, she'd finally felt so good, she figured everything was all right. Her stomach tightened, and she caught her breath. It wasn't painful, but it was new.

"Are you having a contraction?" asked the doctor.

"Maybe. My stomach just got tight. It's gone now, but I've never felt that before."

"You haven't had any Braxton Hicks contractions?"

"No. But I've read about them, and I think that's probably what it was." She hoped, even as worry settled in and wouldn't budge.

"Probably." Dr. Cindy picked up the chart and scribbled on it. "However, after all you've been through today, I'm not taking any chances. I want to keep you tonight so we can monitor you and the baby. I'm ordering some blood work to check your blood sugar and to look for anemia." She nodded at the nurse. "Peg will bring you an icky sweet drink in a few minutes. Then an hour later, we'll do the blood draw. That will tell us how well your body is processing the sugar.

"I don't anticipate any problem with that, but it's a test I normally run about this time in a pregnancy. I expect you're a little anemic. That would cause the weakness and dizziness."

"But my vitamins contain iron."

"It may not be enough for you. Some women need more. I had to take extra when I was pregnant. It's not a big deal. While we're waiting for the sugar to digest, Peg will get this mud and glass off of you."

She started toward the door, then turned back around to face Megan. "In the morning, I want to do a sonogram. That's another name for an ultrasound." When Megan nodded, indicating she knew they were the same, she continued, "Your baby's heart sounds good, and it's moving around fine, but the ultrasound is another tool to evaluate your little one's well-being."

"Do we really need to?" Megan was torn between desperately wanting to make sure the baby was all right and worrying about the expense. Staying overnight would cost a fortune, and an ultrasound wouldn't be cheap.

Before she could figure out how to explain her reluctance, Will spoke up. "Don't worry about the cost, Cindy. Do anything you need to." The heels of his boots tapped on the floor as he walked into the room and stopped on the other side of the curtain. "And you let her, Megan."

She didn't know whether to be annoyed about his interference — and his bossy attitude — or grateful for his help and that he'd respected her privacy enough not to charge all the way into the room. When she shot an exasperated glance at the doctor, the woman grinned.

Before she could think of anything to say, Will spoke again, with a hint of humor in his voice. "If you don't let her take good care of you, Megan, it'll ruin my reputation."

She smiled in spite of herself and adjusted

the sheet up higher as the nurse moved toward the curtain.

When Peg slid it back, Will winked at the nurse, then focused on Megan. He stood there looking a bit mournful. "I'll be plumb afraid to ride to the rescue next time I see a damsel in distress."

"Ha!" Peg said with a laugh. "I'll stand on my head the day you're afraid of anything."

Will laughed, and the deep sound slid over Megan like a warm comforter on a cold, rainy day. She looked at the nurse, then the doctor. "Is he always so bossy?"

The women exchanged an amused glance before Dr. Cindy answered. "Has been ever since I've known him, and that's been since junior high. You'll discover that all the Callahans have a way of persuading people to do what they want, but the rest of them have a bit more tact than Will." She walked toward him and made shooing motions. "Go out in the lobby where you're supposed to be and let Peg tend to our patient. You can visit her again when she's in her room. Give us about an hour."

He leaned around her to look at Megan, his smile fading. "Don't get any ideas about sneaking out of here."

In what? A hospital gown? And on foot? "I think I'm stuck for now."

"Good." He let the doctor grab his arm and escort him out of the room, leaving Megan pondering his expression. Concern, a hint of stubborn seriousness, and something she couldn't quite put her finger on.

5

After his old friend Cindy bullied him away from Megan's room, Will went outside to make some phone calls.

He'd watched Butch and Johnny bring Ted into the ER about ten minutes earlier. Considering they had to extricate him from the truck, they'd gotten him there pretty fast. The town's other physician, Dr. Pharr, was taking care of him, though he expected Cindy would be right in the thick of it. Since Ted lived in San Angelo, Will figured they'd transport him there as soon as it was safe, likely airlifting him.

He called his dad, filled him in on Megan's condition, and asked how they were doing at the scene of the wreck.

"The wrecker is on the way," said Dub. "Ted's company is sending another lumber truck up from San Angelo to pick up what they can of the load. Chance will have his dump truck crew take care of everything else. We've gathered up everything we can find from inside the truck cab that was scattered nearby in the pasture."

"What about Megan's van?"

"Chance and Nate are down there now. Call him and get the info firsthand. I talked to your mom. She wants to know if they need to come back from Abilene earlier. She's already planning for Megan to stay with us, for a few days anyway."

Will's mom, sister, sister-in-law, and his parents' housekeeper had gone to Abilene for an all-day ladies meeting involving several churches. He knew they'd hurry back if he said the word, but they'd really been looking forward to the evening's speaker.

"Cindy is going to keep her overnight, so there's no reason for them to cut their meeting short. But having her stay with y'all, at least until we get her transportation situation straightened out, is a good idea." He hesitated a second. He knew his parents probably wouldn't mind if she stayed longer. That's just the way they were.

"When the admissions clerk asked her for the name of someone to notify in case of emergency, Megan said there wasn't anyone." He'd stopped by the desk on the way out and told the woman to put down his name. "I overheard her tell Cindy that she hadn't seen her doctor for a couple of months because she's been low on money. She had to give up her job because she had morning sickness around the clock until about a month ago."

"It's bound to be hard finding another job now," his dad said thoughtfully.

"Exactly. And she only put down a post office box in Austin for her address."

"So you're thinking she may not have any place to go."

"If someone was expecting her, either to stay with them or to go to work anytime soon, seems to me she'd want to let them know." Will had a strong suspicion that Megan Smith was homeless, pregnant, and down to her last dime.

"No mention of a husband or boyfriend?"

"Nope."

"If this little gal is in as tough a spot as you and I suspect, Sue will invite her to move in."

"Are you okay with that?"

"For now." It was his father's turn to pause while he sorted out his thoughts. "I'll call Peters and have him see what he can find out about her."

"I'll try to get more info after she's settled in a room. Talk to you later." Will hung up, thinking about the time years earlier when a cousin brought her new boyfriend for a visit. They'd all liked him until Dub caught him stealing. Ever since then, if the family didn't know their houseguests well, his dad quietly had them investigated.

The whole thing irked Will, even though he knew it was wise. They didn't keep any real valuables at the house now, but thieves didn't know that. The Callahans were wealthy and that made them potential targets for all sorts of crimes. They trusted the Lord to take care of them but did their part by being prudent.

Will relied more on his instinct than his father's private investigator. His gut told him that they didn't need to worry about Megan.

Pressing the speed dial on his cell phone, he tapped his toe on the sidewalk.

"Hey, bro." Chance sounded a little out of breath. "How's Megan?"

"All right, I think." He told him what he knew so far. "What about her van?"

"It'll probably still run, but it's a mess. It looks like a deranged monkey took a ball-peen hammer to the body. All the glass needs to be replaced, and everything inside is soaked. Joe is here and setting up the wrecker to pull it upright. I'll have him haul it to the house for now. It may not be worth repairing. I'll be surprised if the claims adjuster doesn't total it."

"I doubt she has insurance," Will said. "Tell Joe that I'll pay the towing charge."

"All right. Nate and I have been wandering around the pasture gathering up her things. One suitcase was still intact, but two others were ripped apart, and clothes and other stuff are scattered all over. There's a sweater up in a mesquite tree that I can't quite reach, and the branches aren't thick enough to climb. I'll have to drive the pickup around. I think I can reach it from the truck bed.

"I don't know if we got everything. We found a few canned goods, a big mixer, some baking stuff, and a photo album — with pictures of cakes and other fancy desserts."

"Cakes?" Will flipped his hand at a fly that was pestering him. So the lady was a baker. No wonder she had to give up her job when she was sick.

"Fancy wedding cakes and some of the prettiest desserts I've ever seen. The album was still in a plastic bag, so the pictures are fine. Nate just walked up with a small, ratty-lookin' teddy bear and what's left of an ice chest. Best I can tell, she's been camping in her van. I don't know how much she had with her, but we didn't find a whole lot."

"I'm sure she'll appreciate you recovering what you could."

"I can tell you one thing," Chance said. "A miracle happened out here this afternoon. That tornado blasted a strip about three blocks wide right through here. I checked alongside the road to see if I could tell where she lay down."

"I've been curious about that myself." The bar ditch was wide and shallow for miles south of the ranch.

"I found it. She'd wiggled down as far as she could, but there's no way she was out of harm's way. There were trees, limbs, all kinds of debris covering the area of the highway where the tornado came through — except for right where she was. I took a picture with my cell phone before we dragged the big stuff off the road. The only clear spot anywhere along here was roughly a thirty-foot circle around her."

Will whistled softly. "No wonder she said she believed in God after today." His stomach growled, and he checked his watch. "I'll go grab something to eat in the hospital cafeteria. They should have Megan in a room by the time I'm finished. I'll give her the good news that you've recovered some of her things and visit with her a while. She hasn't exactly been forthcomin' about her situation, but maybe I can pry something out of her."

"Gently, brother."

"I know that." Will still smarted a little from Cindy's comment about him not being as tactful as the rest of the family — even if it was true. "Just because you've been married a whole year doesn't mean you're the only one who knows how to sweet-talk a lady."

"Well . . ." Chance drew out the word. "I am the one who got the girl."

"Just 'cause you staked your claim faster than a gold prospector." Will had liked Emily Rose from the get-go too, but he'd stepped aside when his brother boldly announced within a few days of meeting her that he wanted to marry her. "I'm gonna go eat before my stomach gnaws a hole in itself. Talk to you later."

After his brother's adios, he ended the call and sauntered into the lobby to check on Megan.

"They haven't moved her up to her room yet, Mr. Callahan. It'll probably be another half hour."

"Good enough." He nodded to the cute blonde at the admissions desk. He figured she was ten to twelve years younger than him, if not fresh out of high school. He was tempted to tell her that Mr. Callahan was his father, but he supposed he had reached the age where *Mr.* was appropriate in those circumstances.

And that irked him. Lately he'd been feeling kind of old and left out. It didn't help any that both Chance and Nate were married and happy as pigs in slop. Even their friend Dalton was about to get hitched.

Have I been too picky, Lord? he asked silently as he wandered down to the hospital cafeteria. He'd dated plenty during high school and college and after he settled back in at the ranch. He'd never found anyone he wanted to spend his life with, though many of the women he'd gone out with hinted they were willing to marry despite the absence of love. That wasn't good enough. If he couldn't have the kind of marriage his parents and siblings had, he'd stay a bachelor.

But it was a lonely existence. He hadn't taken anybody out in two years because he'd already dated all the single Christian women near his age in Callahan Crossing. And a fair share from surrounding towns.

He couldn't very well start visiting churches in other towns to see who might

66

be available. The Callahans were well known throughout the area, and word would spread like wildfire that he was on the prowl. If he stuck with Callahan Crossing and lowered his self-imposed age restriction — say to the level of that cute clerk — folks would gossip about him robbing the cradle.

Megan wasn't much older, twenty-four, according to the date of birth she'd given the clerk. Certainly old enough to be married, especially with a baby on the way.

Will skimmed the menu items and opted for meatloaf and scalloped potatoes with a side order of fried okra. When he thanked the middle-aged woman behind the counter, he nodded toward the refrigerator case with the desserts. "Did you make those cakes and pies, Alva?"

"Just the cakes. Nadine made the pies. Take one of each, Will. You need a little fattening up."

"I don't know about that, but you know I'm a sucker for dessert."

"That I do." She laughed and rearranged the grilled chicken in the warming pan with some tongs, separating the various pieces into appropriate piles. "You know all the ladies at church get a kick out of how you heap up your plate with the casseroles at a potluck, then come back and polish off a whole plate of desserts."

"I'm a hard-workin' man. I need a lot of food to keep me goin'. I have to load up at the potlucks."

"What you need is a wife."

Will grinned and winked at her. "But you're already taken."

She laughed and shook the chicken tongs at him. Her smile faded, replaced by genuine concern as she leaned closer and lowered her voice. "How's that little gal you brought into the ER?"

"She's okay." Will knew all about the privacy rules, but he also figured most folks who worked there pretty much knew what was going on with everybody. It was a small hospital in a small town. Nothing much flew under the radar. "Dr. Cindy is going to keep her overnight for observation, but she'll probably cut her loose in the morning."

"Good. I'm prayin' for her. And for that fella in the truck too. I hear they're planning to fly him to Angelo soon as they can."

"That's what I figured. Thanks for the food." He angled over to the dessert case and settled on a big piece of chocolate cake. Alva was the only woman he knew who could make chocolate cake better than his parents' housekeeper, Ramona.

Will stopped to speak to some folks he

recognized and asked about their mama. When he learned that she wasn't doing well, he promised to pray for her, then moved on to let them continue their hushed discussion.

He found a table in the corner with a good view of the small courtyard. The yard man kept that little area nice and green even during the summer. No easy feat when the temperature often topped one hundred. Colorful flowers and shrubs surrounded the grass, and a few tall oak trees provided shade at the right time of the day.

The food was excellent, but his thoughts were on Megan. Why wasn't she married? Who was her baby's father? Was she really so alone that she had no one to contact in an emergency? Or was there just no one she wanted to turn to?

He knew he was more fortunate than many people because his family was close and loving. They didn't always agree on everything, especially he and his dad when it came to managing the ranch. But they worked it out most of the time. To keep peace in the family, more often than not, Will backed down. He and his siblings might be partners in the ranch, but Dub still had the final say.

Even though he would do all right on his

own, he hoped he never had to be without his family's love and support. He couldn't imagine what that would be like. *Lord, guide us in this. Show us how you want us to help her.*

He polished off his supper, taking a little longer with the cake. Some things deserved extra appreciation.

After putting the tray and dirty dishes on the designated counter, Will moseyed back to the emergency room waiting area. The clerk motioned for him to come over.

"They've moved Miss Smith to room 135. Dr. Cindy said you could drop by there whenever you want to."

"Thanks." Will flashed her a friendly smile and headed down the corridor. When he reached Megan's room, the door was open, so he walked on in. As he'd requested, she had the room to herself. He hoped nobody blabbed and let her in on his secret. Since the hospital was only half full, she probably would have gotten a room to herself anyway, but he'd made sure of it.

She held a thick wad of cotton over the vein in her elbow as the very pregnant lab technician stuck a piece of tape over it.

"There you go, Miss Smith. No more torture tonight." She made certain everything was secure on her cart and turned, pushing it toward the doorway. "Evenin', Will."

"Evenin', Ana. You just gonna keep working until that baby makes a grand entrance?"

"Might as well. That way I'll be close to the delivery room." She smiled and rocked side to side. "I have about three weeks to go till Junior arrives, so I'm working only a couple of afternoon shifts a week. It's usually pretty slow. Today is the exception. Say hello to Jenna for me."

"Yes, ma'am." He stepped aside so she could easily roll the cart out the door and turned toward Megan. Her hair was damp, and the skin on her arms a bit red. "You must feel better without all that dirt and glass."

"I do." Her brow knit in a slight frown. "But I could have gotten rid of it myself. Peg brushed most of it off and then let me shower."

"So your idea to brush off what you could and hose off the rest would have worked."

"Yes. And saved the expense of being in here."

"I told you. Don't worry about the expense." He moved to the side of the bed. "I won't mind if it takes you ten years to pay me back, or if you never repay me. But it would trouble me somethin' awful if you

71

hadn't come in here and you or the baby had a problem."

"You'd feel responsible," she said quietly. "Even though it was my decision."

"Yes, I would." He pulled the lone chair closer to the bed and sat down.

She studied him for a moment. "You have nice wide shoulders, Will Callahan, but you can't carry the world on them."

He smiled and shook his head slightly. "Not interested in carrying the whole world — just my little corner of it."

"So you're a fixer."

"I do what I can. We all do."

"All, as in your family?"

He nodded. "It's a long-held tradition. 'Course, sometimes folks consider it meddlin' more than helping."

A hint of a smile hovered around her mouth. "Are you here to meddle?"

"Maybe. But first let me tell you about my helpful brother and brother-in-law. They've been stomping around the pasture gathering up your belongings. Found one suitcase intact, but the others were smashed and the contents scattered."

"Probably from here to Amarillo."

He chuckled, glad to see she was more relaxed than she'd been in the emergency room. "That's possible. But Chance said they found some clothes and other odds and ends. Including some baking stuff and your photo album of the cakes. It was still in the plastic bag, so the pictures weren't damaged." Her face lit up in a beautiful smile, and Will caught his breath. "So I assume you're a baker?"

"Just an amateur."

"He said those were some of the prettiest cakes and desserts he'd ever seen."

Her smile changed to one of shy pride. "They are pretty, and they tasted good too. My neighbor, Mrs. Hoffmann, got me interested in baking. She made the most wonderful German cakes, and she taught me how to make some of them. She passed away four years ago, but I'd caught the baking bug. So I took some cake decorating classes." She winced and shifted her position on the bed. "I enjoy cooking in general, but I love to make desserts the most. I'm kind of a cooking show junkie."

So she hadn't always been in dire straits.

"Did your brother mention finding a plastic storage tub of recipes and cookbooks?" Sadness slipped across her face. "I had five years' worth of recipes in that container."

"No, but if they haven't run across it, we'll keep searching." Will stretched his legs out in front of him. "Should we look for a computer too?"

"No, I finally sold it two months ago to help pay the rent. It was a great laptop, but old enough that I didn't get a whole lot for it. Still, it kept me in the apartment for another month."

"In Austin?" When she raised an eyebrow, he shrugged one shoulder. "You gave the clerk an Austin post office box for your address, so I'm assuming you lived there."

"I did."

When she didn't volunteer any more info, Will asked gently, "Have I gone to meddlin'?"

She hesitated, looked away, and shook her head. "Not really. You deserve to know something about the person you've so generously helped. I've lived in Austin since I was sixteen. For the past four years, I worked in a real estate office. First as an assistant, then as an agent. I was doing okay before I got pregnant. I hadn't sold anything in three months, but that's not all that unusual. Sometimes you'll have several months with sales, then a lull.

"I had four listings, so I was spending money on advertising as well as the normal monthly expenses, including desk space, with nothing coming in. I'd started dipping into my savings last fall, even before I got pregnant and couldn't work." She smoothed the edge of the sheet over the top of the blanket.

"After I got so sick, I had to turn my listings over to another agent, which cut down on the money going out. None of them sold, so I didn't get any referral payments either. The listings expired, and the owners didn't renew for various reasons. Two months ago, the office sold to another company that had its own group of agents. By the time I felt well enough to go back to work, there was no place to go."

"Couldn't you move to another office?"

"Yes, technically. I don't have to renew my license until October. But I didn't have the money to cover the expenses. Even without listings, you have to pay for a cell phone, internet at home, multiple listing services, and general office supplies. There is also the desk cost, your share of what it takes to run the company. Most places take a portion from each sale, but some require the money each month whether or not you have any sales. All my clients have moved to other agents, so I'd be starting pretty much at square one.

"So now I'm looking for something that requires some computer skills — or a waitress position. Those are the two things I'm qualified to do."

"Waiting tables would be too hard on you." He meant it in a concerned way, but somehow it sounded dismissive. She glanced at him sharply. "Sorry. I wasn't being critical. It just seems like carrying heavy food trays and being on your feet all day would be tough. Where were you headed?"

Again, she paused before meeting his gaze. "Originally I was thinking Lubbock, then decided Abilene might be better. If I don't find any work there, I'll go on to Dallas or Fort Worth."

"My mom is in Abilene for the day, but she wants you to stay at the ranch for a while."

"That's very kind of her, but I don't want to impose."

A nice polite phrase if he'd ever heard one. Where was she going to go? Did she plan to hitchhike and see where she wound up? He could tell her where she'd wind up — in trouble.

Gently, brother. Remembering Chance's admonition, Will drew in a deep, steadying breath. *Stubborn woman.* Did he have to be the bad guy and remind her that she couldn't camp in her van anymore?

"Do you have someplace else to go?" He

76

was proud that he'd kept his tone casual.

"Not really. Is there a homeless shelter in Callahan Crossing?"

"No. We had one set up at the church for a while last year after the fire, but it's been closed for a long time." Not that he'd let her stay there even if it was open. That gave him pause. Why was he being so possessive of this woman? "My mom likes to have guests at the ranch."

"I don't want to be a bother to anyone."

"You won't be. Mom will enjoy it. And her housekeeper, Ramona, will be glad to have someone else to cook for. She always prepares more than we need and then gripes because she winds up with too many leftovers. Years ago, she made the meals for the bachelor cowboys as well as our family. Now we have only two hired hands, and they're both married. All of us kids live near the ranch house, so we eat there often, but whenever Jenna or my sister-in-law Emily decide to do their own cooking, it throws Ramona off her game."

Megan smiled wistfully. "I like leftovers." Which told him she hadn't had any for a while. "Okay. Just for a few days. Until I decide what to do with the van."

"Chance says it's a mess."

"It is."

"Do you have insurance?"

"Just liability. I had to drop everything else. I guess I'll have to junk it."

"I don't know if you'd get much for it. But if you aren't in a hurry to leave, I have an idea for getting it fixed without costing much. A couple of high school kids I know want to open a body shop after they graduate next year. I think they'd love to work on it for the experience. If it's all right with you, I'll ask them to take a look at it." They'd provide the labor, and he'd provide the parts. He expected she'd figure that out later when she didn't have so much on her mind.

"That would be great if it wouldn't take too long to repair it."

"Won't know until we ask them. It may not come out perfect, but usually they do good work." Movement in the hallway drew his attention. Suppertime for the patients. "Can I get you anything before I head home?"

"I'm fine for tonight, but I'll need some of my clothes tomorrow. I don't want to waltz out of here in this silly hospital gown."

"Might start a new fashion." Will stood and set the chair back by the wall.

"Thank you, Will. For everything." Tears misted her eyes. She shook her head and wiped her eyes with her fingers. "Don't mind me. I'm just pregnant."

"No kiddin'?" He gave her a wink and was rewarded with a chuckle. He walked around to the bedside table and rummaged through the drawer until he found a little notepad and pen. "Here's my phone number." He met her gaze. "I get up at five, but if you need something before then, call. I don't care what time it is."

"Five?"

"Yes, ma'am. We get up early. During the week, the folks have breakfast at six, even on Saturday. But they don't rouse their guests that early. When Emily — that's Chance's wife — was staying with them, she rarely got up before seven. Even then it didn't do any good to talk to her for a while until after she had her coffee. You'll be able to get up whenever you want, but if you're too late, you might have to settle for do-it-yourself cereal or throw a frozen waffle in the toaster."

"I can certainly do that. I don't want to make any extra work for anyone."

"Y'all will get along fine." He moved the tray table across the bed. "Eat plenty of supper and get some rest. Let the folks here pamper you a little bit."

And when she got to the ranch, he'd take over that chore — if she'd let him.

Megan had never heard anyone mention
pampering along with a hospital stay, but
after her supper was delivered a few minutes
later, she decided they must be doing more
than normal. With a large bowl of water-
melon and cantaloupe chunks, a huge piece
of chocolate cake, and the covered plate,
there was barely room on the tray for the
silverware.

"I'll get your milk," said the young woman
as she set the tray on the rolling table. "Be
right back."

Megan removed the metal cover from her
plate. The refreshing fragrance of lemon
asparagus teased her nose, and the heaping
mound of beef stroganoff, with what surely
was extra beef, made her mouth water.

The attendant returned with two cartons
of milk instead of the one she'd checked off
on the menu sheet.

"Are these your normal portions?"

"Dr. Cindy mentioned that you and the baby were a little underweight and said to give you a little extra. Alva — she's the head cook — thought a lot extra was better." Her eyes sparkled with humor.

"I don't think I can eat all of this, though it looks wonderful."

"Fill up on the main dish and veggie and save the fruit and cake for later. If you're like I was when I was pregnant, you'll be hungry again in a few hours."

"That's true."

"They have a refrigerator near the nurses' station. If you want them to keep the fruit cold, just ask. They also have juice, milk, and Jell-O." The young woman reached into first one pocket, then the other of her pink uniform, taking out two packages of cheese and crackers, two of peanut butter and crackers, and three small bags of trail mix. "Alva sent these along in case you get hungry during the night. She thought they'd hold you better than Jell-O."

"Thank you. At this rate, I'll gain five pounds before I leave in the morning."

After the woman left the room, Megan stared at the feast spread out before her. Even if she'd been able to afford any of this during the past month, she would have been compelled to make it last a couple of days.

As a young child, she had learned to hoard food when she had some because too often there wasn't any. She might have a package of crackers during the night for her baby's sake, but the rest would go into her emergency stash.

She took a bite of the stroganoff and sighed. Delicious. "I wonder if the cook will share her recipe?" she murmured, scooping up another forkful. Though it tasted rich and creamy, she doubted they'd use real cream in a hospital. To her amazement, she polished off all the main dish and the asparagus. She wasn't even stuffed, just sleepy. She rolled the table out of the way and settled in for a nap.

The nurse woke her up to check the baby. She held the fetal monitor disc in place for a couple of minutes, then the roar of a helicopter drew their attention. The nurse helped her out of bed, and they went to the window to watch it land.

"Are they picking up the truck driver?" Megan asked.

"Yes. They're flying him to San Angelo."

"Is he going to be all right?"

"The doctor thinks so, but things were touchy for a little while. Peg called a few minutes ago with a message from Mr. Bentley. He wanted us to let you know how he was and to thank you for helping him."

"I didn't do much. Will would have found him anyway."

"What you did really helped. If his head wound had kept bleeding until Will reached him, he might not have made it. You were supposed to be there."

The nurse helped her get back into bed, though she didn't really need the assistance. She paid little attention as the woman checked her vital signs then left the room.

You were supposed to be there.

If she'd been injured or killed in the tornado, Ted Bentley might be a lot worse off. Maybe not even alive. Had God saved her only because he wanted to save the trucker? Maybe God didn't really care about her and Sweet Baby at all. She looked around the room, her gaze resting on the giant piece of chocolate cake. It had been months since she'd had dessert. The cake in itself was a gift, something she didn't deserve.

If he didn't care about her — or at least the baby — why would Will Callahan have been the one to pick her up? Anybody could have brought her to the hospital, and the hospital would have had to treat her. It was the law. But if Will hadn't insisted on helping her and hadn't physically put her in his truck, she wouldn't have come.

"That doesn't matter," she whispered, lowering the head of the bed, turning off the light, and settling down to try to get another half hour of sleep. "None of that matters. I made a promise to learn about you, God. To find a way to thank you for saving me and Sweet Baby. Even if you did it to rescue Mr. Bentley, I'm so very grateful. Maybe someday, somehow I can be good enough to deserve what you've done for us."

At 7:30 the next morning, Megan heard familiar footsteps coming down the hall. Will hadn't been lying when he said he was an early riser. He tapped lightly on her open door, then walked into the room.

She tried not to stare, but it was next to impossible. Western summer straw hat, burgundy shirt, crisply ironed blue jeans with a sharp crease, a big ol' I-won-this-at-the-rodeo belt buckle, and him all freshly shaven and smelling um-um good — it all added up to one drool-worthy cowboy with a capital *C*.

Here she was in a pale-blue checked hospital gown — totally the wrong color for her — no makeup, smashed frizzy bed-hair, dark circles from lack of sleep, and her mouth full of scrambled eggs and toast.

His dark, serious eyes lit up when he saw her, even before he smiled. The concern in his expression melted into tenderness and joy. Her heart rate shifted into overdrive, and her mouth went dry.

"Good mornin'." Removing the hat, he laid it upside down on the end of the bed, well beyond the reach of her feet, and finger-combed his hair.

Megan swallowed her food and croaked, "Good morning." She cleared her throat and took a sip of orange juice. "You're out and about early."

"I have a bank board meeting this morning, so I thought I'd drop by and visit with you a spell. With all the excitement yesterday, I forgot all about the meeting. But we won't leave you stranded. Mom and the girls will be by later to pick you up."

"Oh, okay." Great. That sounded brilliant. She'd been able to talk to him fine yesterday. Why was she being a dunce this morning? Because no man had ever looked at her the way Will just did. "I hope I'm not being a bother."

"Not a bit. Mom said they were coming to town this morning anyway." He angled the chair toward her and sat down, stretching out his long legs. "How are you feeling?

86

Did you get any sleep?"

"Not much. They checked me every thirty minutes. I'd just doze off, and the nurse would be in here again."

"Is everything okay? Are you having any contractions?" A frown creased his forehead.

"Just a few more of the Braxton Hicks ones."

"Those are kind of like practice contractions, right?"

"That's what I've read, and that's what the night nurse called them." That didn't seem like common subject matter for a bachelor. "How did you know about them?"

"I heard you and Dr. Cindy talking yesterday, so I looked it up on the internet when I got home. Is Sweet Baby's heartbeat still good?"

"Yes. The nurses said it's been in the right range the whole time."

"Good. How are they treating you?"

"Everyone has been very nice. The meals were certainly better than I'd expected. I think they brought me a double serving of everything plus snacks."

"I thought Cindy might try to fatten you up. Alva, Nadine, and their helpers are great cooks. They prepare the food in the cafeteria too. I eat there occasionally when I'm visiting someone, like last night.

"I was also in here for a few days my junior year with a broken leg. Ran into an overzealous tackle. The food was the only good thing about it. Seemed like I'd just get to sleep, and somebody would come wake me up to check this or that or some visitor would come stompin' down the hall." His grin was a little sheepish. "Of course, half the time, my football buddies were the ones doing the stomping. I was real happy to go home. Mom would just peek in the door and leave me alone if I was asleep."

Her mother had checked to see if she was asleep only when she wanted her to do something or to steal money from her purse. Sometimes she'd barged in when she was drunk and angry.

Megan was nervous about staying with the Callahans. Would she be able to sleep without a chair shoved against the door? Logically, she knew such a thing wasn't needed in a normal family. Having grown up with an alcoholic mother, she found that logic didn't always override fear.

Worrying about it wouldn't do any good. She just had to adapt. Time to get the subject off of mothers before he asked about hers. "They airlifted Mr. Bentley to San Angelo last night."

"That's what I heard. Dalton Renfro, the

deputy sheriff who covers this part of the county, is a good friend. He's been living at the ranch since his house burned in the fire. He stopped by the folks' on his way home last night and told us. He'll be checking on Ted periodically and will keep us posted. The doctors think he'll be all right, though his recovery might take a while."

She nodded and pushed the table out of her way. "That's what the nurse told me last night. He asked Peg to let me know, which was really sweet of him."

"He thought you were sweet too. He called you an angel and a purty little gal."

"The poor man hit his head awfully hard. He was delusional."

"Not by a long shot." Will grinned and eyed the last half slice of toast. "Are you going to eat that?"

"No. I'm stuffed. Help yourself."

"Thanks. Do you know when you'll have the sonogram?" He stood, picked up the toast, and took a big bite.

Megan noticed the nurse park a wheelchair outside the door before she went back toward the nurses' station. She motioned toward the waiting wheelchair and took a deep, shaky breath. "Soon I think."

Will laid the remaining bit of toast back on the plate and wrapped his fingers around hers. "Are you okay?"

"Nervous." She gripped his hand, feeling like a ninny. "What if something is wrong with Sweet Baby?"

"If Cindy had been real concerned, she would have had the technician come in last night. I'd offer to go with you, but that would be a little awkward considerin' we just met and all."

That made her giggle. "You got that right."

"I'll hang around if it will make you feel better."

"You have a meeting to go to." She couldn't let him see how much she wanted him to stay.

"It's not until 10:00, and it will take all of five minutes to get there. I'll visit with some other patients while you're gone."

"I'm being silly."

"No, you aren't. I'll ask the nurse to come get me when you're back." He gave her hand a light squeeze and released it. "Besides, I'm curious to find out if your baby is Sweetie Pie or Sweetie Guy."

She laughed. "Baby isn't going to get stuck with either of those nicknames. But I do appreciate you staying so I can share the news with someone."

"I'll see you after a while." He strolled out of the room, leaving his hat on the end of

90

the bed.

Fifteen minutes later, Megan lay on a bed in the radiology department. The ultrasound technician smeared some cold gel around on her stomach, and Megan sucked in a sharp breath.

"Sorry. I warmed it up a little, but it's still a shock." She flipped some switches, and the monitor lit up. "Are you ready, Doctor?"

"Yes, go ahead." Dr. Cindy grinned at Megan. "I don't know about you, but I'm excited to see this little person. This is a 3-D ultrasound, so it gives us great pictures. Will's sister, Jenna, bought it for the hospital and sent the whole radiology staff to Dallas for special training to run it."

Megan lay still, trying to stay calm as the technician placed the wand on her stomach. She couldn't see the monitor and assumed the doctor wanted to make sure everything was all right before showing her anything. Of course that made her more nervous.

"Ah, we're looking good. Your baby is a little small but not enough to worry about." Dr. Cindy studied the monitor as the technician moved the wand around. "I don't see any abnormalities or anything that raises a red flag. But we have some other areas to check." She patted Megan's hand. "So far, so good. But it takes a while to cover every area thoroughly. We also take measurements to make sure the baby is growing properly. Hang in there just a little longer, then we'll swing the screen around so you can see too. I like to have it turned this way so I can see it more clearly. I don't want to miss anything important."

After what seemed like forever, but the clock on the wall said was only fifteen minutes, the doctor stepped around to the other side of the bed and nodded to the technician. She turned the monitor around to where Megan could see it. "It appears that you're going to have a little girl," Dr. Cindy said, resting her hand on her patient's shoulder. "A healthy little girl."

Megan stared at the screen in awe. Unlike the fuzzy black and white picture a co-worker had shown her when she was pregnant, this was almost like watching a movie. Her little baby looked like a real person!

"Oh, my goodness! She's sucking her thumb!" She watched Sweet Baby blink her eyes and even turn her head slightly, as if she heard Megan's voice. "Her eyes are open," she added in hushed amazement.

"Yes. She can sense light changes now. And she can hear pretty well too, so be sure and talk to her."

"I already do." Mainly because Sweet Baby had been about the only person around to talk to.

"Good. Keep doing it often. Read to her. Sing to her, play music. She's very aware of sounds now and recognizes your voice."

All the more reason to always speak lovingly to her child. "The tornado was so loud. Do you think it scared her?"

Dr. Cindy tipped her head thoughtfully. "Maybe not. I'm guessing the increase in noise was gradual?" When Megan nodded, she continued. "When I was about this far along in my pregnancy, Misty would kick at a sudden noise." She chuckled quietly. "Although she might have moved because I jumped. But I never detected any agitation when I was in a generally noisy situation. Do you see her heart beating?"

"It's supposed to be fast like that, isn't it?"

"Yes. Theirs goes faster than ours."

Megan studied the picture. Sweet Baby had popped her thumb out of her mouth and opened and closed her hand. It was amazing.

The doctor laughed. "She's practicing grasping things so she can grab hold of your finger after she's born."

The thought of the baby holding her hand sent even more joy spiraling through her.

The top of her baby's head was dark. "Does she already have hair?"

"Yes. Looks like she's going to start off as a brunette, but that could change after she's born."

Megan hoped she stayed a brunette. She'd worried that her little one might be blonde like her father, which for some weird reason would be a constant reminder of her foolishness. Most people would consider the baby the reminder, but she didn't think of it that way. Sweet Baby might have been conceived by mistake, but she was a precious gift.

Thank you, God, she thought. Her heart was full of love for this tiny child. "Can I keep a picture?"

"Of course. We'll print one out for you. I need to check on another patient, but I'll drop by your room in a few minutes. We can go over your lab results."

The technician put the wand away, cleaned the gel off Megan's stomach, helped her off the bed, and directed her to the bathroom in the hallway. When Megan came out, she was waiting with the wheelchair. Once Megan was seated, she handed her two pictures of Sweet Baby. "I did an extra one for fun."

"Thank you." Megan smiled all the way back to her room.

A few minutes after she was settled back into bed, she heard Will's footsteps in the hallway. Odd how she could pick out his from everyone who went up and down the hall.

He tapped lightly on the door and peeked around it. "Safe to come in?"

"Sure."

He walked into the room, met her gaze, and grinned. "Well?"

"Sweetie Pie." Laughing, she motioned him closer to the bed. "Come see my beautiful baby."

When she handed him the first picture, his jaw literally dropped. "Wow. I didn't know they could take pictures like this."

"Dr. Cindy said your sister bought the new 3-D machine."

He scratched the back of his neck and wrinkled his face. "I heard about that, but I guess I didn't pay too much attention when she was prattling on and on about it. Now, I'm impressed." He stared at the picture. "Her eyes are open." Wonder filled his quiet voice. "What's she reaching for?"

Megan shrugged and laughed. "Only she knows. The doctor said she's practicing grasping things so she can hold my finger when she's born."

Will's face softened into a sweet smile. "What a cool thought."

"They made me two pictures." Barely holding back a grin, she handed him the other one.

Will took one look at it and burst out laughing. "Your kid is already sucking her thumb. That's amazing." He studied the picture, glanced at her, then back at the picture. "Does she already have hair?"

"Uh-huh. Brown like mine, according to the doctor."

He handed her the photos with a satisfied smile. "Now, aren't you glad you had the ultrasound done?"

"Yes. But even happier and relieved that the doctor said she looks fine. A little small but not enough to worry about."

"She'll be petite, like her mama."

Megan laughed again. She was so happy she thought she would float down the hall when she got out of bed. "I didn't think cowboys knew words like petite."

"Hey, I'm not just a cowboy. I'm a college grad-u-ate. So I know stuff."

"Like petite."

"Yes, ma'am. It's the itty-bitty steak on the menu, so when it applies to a woman, it means a small one. And if I hadn't figured that out, strolling through the petites department in a clothing store trying to find something for Jenna explained it."

Dr. Cindy walked in.

"Very astute," Megan said.

"I thought so. 'Course, it was easy considering my sister is only five-three." He glanced at the papers in the doctor's hand. "Do you need to speak to Megan in private?"

"Only if she wants me to. I have your lab results." She sent her patient a questioning look.

"I don't mind if he stays. He'd probably hunker down outside the door and eavesdrop anyway."

"Probably." The doctor winked at Will and turned her attention back to Megan. "Your blood sugar is fine. So no concern there. You are anemic, however. Not badly, but we need to get more iron in you. Here is the brand I want you to take because it's easier on your stomach. It's over the counter. They have it at the pharmacy in Miller's Grocery. Continue taking your regular prenatal vitamins. You've picked a good brand of those." She handed her a sheet of paper. "Here is some other info about iron, what foods contain it, what to avoid. Get Will to buy you a big steak."

Megan couldn't remember the last time she'd had a steak. Since she'd been able to keep food down, she'd tried to eat hamburger at least a couple of times a week because she knew she needed some red meat. But that was all she could afford.

"No need to buy one. I've got some in the freezer. So do the folks. We'll feed her good."

Dr. Cindy raised an eyebrow. "You're going out to the ranch?"

"Just for a few days, until we figure out what to do with my van."

The doctor paused, tapping her finger on the bed rail. "Megan, I don't really know what your situation is, and if I'm sticking my nose where I shouldn't, I apologize ahead of time. If you don't have anywhere to go and the Callahans offer you a place to stay, I strongly recommend you take them up on it. You're going to have a baby in about three months, and you really shouldn't try to go it all on your own. You need a support group, so to speak, now and after your baby arrives, and the Callahans are one of the best around. But I'll let y'all work that out.

"Personally, I hope you stay around Callahan Crossing. It's a good town, and I'd enjoy being your doctor and bringing that little girl into the world."

"Thank you. I appreciate all you've done for me." Megan let it go at that. She had some serious thinking to do. Maybe even praying, if she could figure out how. During the night, she'd convinced herself that it would be all right to go to a shelter in Abilene or Dallas and try to find work.

But if the Callahans were willing to give her a place to stay, not just for a few days but until the baby came, wouldn't it be irresponsible to turn them down?

7

A short time later, three ladies trooped into her room, bringing bright smiles and laughter. Even without an introduction, she knew the Callahan ladies had arrived. The two redheads bore a slight resemblance to Will, but the clincher was the familiar blue suitcase pulled by the blonde.

Will's mom appeared to be in her late fifties, with strawberry blonde hair and bright turquoise eyes. The petite woman standing next to her was obviously her daughter, Jenna, with the same eyes and brighter red hair. Megan estimated her age at close to thirty.

The blue-eyed blonde, whom she assumed was Chance's wife Emily, was a little younger and a few inches taller. They all wore jeans, but where the older woman had opted for a short-sleeved western shirt and boots, the others had chosen colorful tank tops and running shoes. Jenna and her mother were slim and pretty. Emily was beautiful enough to grace a fashion magazine.

Megan felt fat and frumpy.

"Good morning. I'm Sue Callahan. This is my daughter, Jenna, and my daughter-in-law, Emily Rose. We heard it was time to spring you."

Megan laughed and greeted them. "I'm ready. Dr. Cindy said I was free to go. That does sound like I'm getting out of jail, doesn't it?"

"Hopefully it's been more comfortable than that," said Jenna. "The guys rescued the suitcase with maternity clothes. I checked to make sure that was what was there. If it hadn't been, I would have stopped by the Mission and picked up some things for you. They found a bunch of other clothes too, but they need washing. They're just muddy and not filled with glass."

"That's a relief. I was afraid I might not see any of them again. Well, except for a sweater I spotted in a tree and a pair of jeans caught in a cactus."

"They got those too. Chance could just reach the sweater by standing in the back of the pickup. I think he made Nate — that's Jenna's husband — pull the jeans out of the cactus." Emily heaved the big suitcase up

101

on the foot of the bed.

"Thank you for bringing it."

"Will said you didn't want to waltz out of here in that spiffy hospital gown." Jenna grinned. "I can't imagine why."

"Real clothes will be much more comfortable."

"Do you need any help?" asked Emily.

"No, thanks. I can manage. I've been climbing in and out of bed and walking around without any mishaps."

"Then we'll tell the nurse that you're getting dressed," said Sue. "Just wander out into the hall when you're ready. We'll keep an eye out for you."

"It shouldn't take long." Megan waited until they walked out, shutting the door behind them, then climbed out of bed. Opening the suitcase, she breathed a sigh of relief. Thank goodness she'd packed almost everything she needed these days in one bag. Clothes, toiletries, even some extra makeup she'd bought on a two-for-one sale before she got pregnant. Her sandals were there too, so she wouldn't have to wear muddy tennis shoes.

She chose a soft knit sleeveless print top with a creamy background and tiny peach flowers. It went well with a pair of cotton beige shorts and would minimize the fabric rubbing against myriad cuts and bruises.

Slathering her face with moisturizer was much better than merely using the lotion the hospital provided. Mascara, blusher, and a bit of lipstick came next. It was amazing what a little color did to make a girl look and feel better.

She added the bag of toiletries provided by the hospital to her suitcase. The extra toothpaste, lotion, and hand sanitizer would come in handy. Using the comb that came with them, she combed the back of her hair, then ran her fingers lightly through the curls on top. Now that she had her suitcase, next time she could use setting gel and it would look better. Donning a pair of gold loop earrings cheered her up even more. She couldn't compete with the Callahan ladies, but at least now she didn't look quite so dumpy.

Zipping up the suitcase, she carefully slid it off the bed so it didn't make a loud clunk when it hit the floor. She took the plastic bag containing her clothes and shoes from the previous day out of the closet and set it on the bed.

Opening the door, she stepped out into the hall. The Callahans were in the room across from hers, visiting with an elderly lady. The nurse spotted her and came around the desk with a clipboard in her hand.

"You can't escape yet," she said with a smile. "I need to go over your dismissal paperwork."

Megan remembered that procedure from when her mom had been in the hospital for a few days. She walked back into the room.

"There's not a lot. Just remember to pick up your iron pills and to consult the sheet the doctor gave you on what foods to eat to increase your iron intake. Get plenty of rest for the next few days and keep an eye on those cuts. If any of them start looking inflamed, Dr. Cindy wants to see you right away. She also wants to see you in two weeks for a follow-up. Of course if you have any problems or anything about the pregnancy that is bothering you, she wants you to make an appointment right away at the clinic.

"Mrs. Callahan gave us her phone number." The nurse checked the sheet. "Will's is on here too. So the doctor's office will be calling the ranch to set up your appointment."

"I'm not sure how long I'll be there." A chill ran down Megan's back. She didn't like other people controlling her life, and it appeared they had it all mapped out for her.

"If you leave, just let Dr. Cindy's office know." She flipped over the sheet and quickly read through the one underneath it. "That's basically it. I need you to sign here and here."

Megan signed the papers, and the nurse gave her copies.

"All done. I have a volunteer bringing over a wheelchair to take you out."

"I can walk."

"Sorry. Hospital rules. We'll wheel you out to the sidewalk. Then you're on your own."

Hardly. For the first time in years, she was dependent on someone else for food and shelter. It didn't sit well, but she had to accept the reality of her situation. For now. She was grateful for the Callahans' help, but that gave them power over her. If they tried to abuse it . . . *Stop it. They're good people. Everybody says so. God didn't save you from the tornado to plunk you down in a bad situation. Trust him.* She hoped God understood how hard it was for her to trust anyone, even him. *I'm working on it, God.*

When the volunteer came in with the wheelchair, the Callahan ladies said goodbye to their friend and stepped out into the hall. Jenna hurried into Megan's room. "I'll pull your suitcase."

Emily was right behind her. "I'll get the

plastic bag."

Sue gave her a big smile after she sat down in the wheelchair. "That's a definite improvement over the gown." Her smile faded as she inspected the bruises on Megan's arms and legs. "Are those big ones from the hailstones?"

"Yes, ma'am. I can't imagine what it would have been like if I'd been out in the open. At least I had some shelter, but what about the cattle or other animals?"

The aide pushed the wheelchair out into the hallway. Sue walked on one side of her and Emily on the other. Jenna trailed along behind with the suitcase. Will's mom said hello to someone they met but kept walking. "Buster and Ollie — they're the ranch hands — found five cows and five calves that had been injured. Thankfully, none of them were badly hurt. They'd gathered in a grove of oak trees, which blocked some of the hail. I think the cows instinctively protected the calves as much as they could."

"Should Chance and Nate have been out looking for injured animals instead of gathering up my stuff?" Megan had worried about that half the night.

"We had only a small herd in the section that was hit with hail, so Buster and Ollie could handle it. Most of the livestock are in other areas of the ranch. I don't know how the wild animals fared, but I expect most of them did all right. Animals have a sixth sense about storms and often take shelter before humans realize what's coming. More than once Dub has hightailed it home before a storm hits because of how the birds or cattle are acting. They know the difference between a little rain and something bad."

"Was this area under a tornado watch yesterday? The radio in the van went out yesterday morning, so I never heard a forecast."

"It was a severe thunderstorm watch until about an hour before the storm actually hit. Then they changed it to a tornado watch. They issued a tornado warning about two seconds before Dub spotted it. I had just enough time to unplug the television before he ordered us to go to the storm cellar."

Emily shuddered lightly. "I still think we should wait until we know the tornado is headed right for us before going down there." She gave Sue a sheepish smile, then met Megan's curious gaze. "I love my father-in-law dearly, but he has as big a phobia about tornados as I do being in cellars."

"I'm not particularly fond of cellars,"

Megan said. "But after my close encounter yesterday, I'll gladly go underground the next time a tornado is anywhere in the area."

The automatic doors opened as they moved toward the entrance. "You and Dub both," Sue said. "He's mellowed some over the years. When the kids were little, any night there was a tornado watch posted, we slept in the cellar."

"Correction, tried to sleep." Jenna pulled the suitcase to the back of the Lincoln, and Sue unlocked the trunk. "Will and Chance always thought it was a big adventure. If they didn't come up with some game or weren't playing with toys all night, they'd make up stories."

"Ghost stories, no doubt." Emily opened the front door for Megan then walked around to the back of the car.

"Usually." Jenna hoisted the heavy suitcase into the trunk without any problem. She might be petite, as Will said, but Megan suspected she did her fair share of work around the ranch. Emily laid the plastic bag in the trunk and returned to the side of the car.

Megan stood up from the wheelchair and thanked the woman who'd pushed it outside.

"You're welcome, dear. I hope I'm here

the day you have that baby." With a smile, she turned and pushed the wheelchair back inside, leaving it near the entrance.

Megan got in the car, smiling to herself when Emily waited and shut the door. People around here sure believed in taking care of pregnant women. Or at least one who'd spent the night in the hospital. She fastened her seat belt and looked up to find Sue watching her. "Will told me to let the folks in the hospital pamper me, which they did. But I think his expectations were influenced by the way his family treats people."

Sue laughed and started the car as Emily and Jenna slid into the backseat. "Just passing on God's blessings."

"That's what he said."

His mother's smile widened. "Good. I must have raised that boy right after all."

"Well, other than being a little bossy, he seems like a very nice man."

"Boy, do you have him pegged," Jenna said with a chuckle. "He even volunteered to be the director at our fledgling community theater just because he's good at ordering people around."

"We nixed the idea at the first meeting," Emily added. "Actually, to be fair, he unvolunteered, admitting he didn't know the

109

first thing about drama. So we put him to work as the head stagehand and helping Chance build the sets for the play we did on Valentine's Day."

"It's probably a good thing we won't be doing another one until Christmas. Taking orders from his little brother drives him crazy." Jenna grinned at Megan when she glanced back at her.

"Now, girls, it's not as bad as that," Sue gently chided. "His grumbling is all in fun."

"Most of the time," murmured Jenna. "The old sibling rivalry rears up on occasion. If you have any brothers, Megan, you probably know what I mean."

"No experience there. I'm an only child." Which she'd always considered a blessing. She'd taken care of herself, and often her mother, for as long as she could remember. It would have been much harder — and impossible to leave — if there had been another kid involved.

Pushing those thoughts aside, she took a moment to admire Sue's car. It must have every bell, whistle, and luxurious extra available. If their home was anything comparable, she was going to be a fish out of water.

She shifted her attention to the town as they drove down the street. Yesterday, she'd dozed on the way to the hospital and hadn't noticed any of the scenery. Interspersed between mostly wooden homes thirty to fifty years old were newer brick ones. Most were nice but not fancy, mainly one story. All were well cared for.

Several had lush green lawns, but in just as many yards, there was more red dirt than sparse, struggling grass. Almost all of them had a shade tree or two, a few shrubs, and a handful of flower-filled pots to brighten up the landscape. Rain was normally scarce in West Texas, and summers were hot. Plenty of people couldn't afford to buy the water needed for a nice green lawn.

If you don't water, you don't have to mow. As a kid, Megan had gladly accepted her mother's philosophy.

Sue turned a corner, and Megan spotted a beautiful old three-story Victorian on the next block. "Oh, my goodness, what a beautiful house."

"That's the Bradley-Tucker House, home of one of our pioneer ranching families." There was a note of pride in Sue's voice. "It belongs to the Historical Society and is an annex of our local museum. Emily is the curator of both sites."

"That's how we lured her to Callahan Crossing," said Jenna. "She came to set up

111

the museum, and Chance convinced her to stay."

"And I'm very glad I did. I don't miss the city one bit."

Sue drove slowly past the lovely old home. "I'm so thankful this part of town wasn't hit by the fire."

"I saw that on the news," said Megan. "It looked terrible."

"It was. But we're coming back. Sixty homes have been rebuilt, and more are under construction. Chance's company has done about half of them. Out-of-town companies have built some, and church groups from all over Texas have provided material and labor for others. If you aren't too tired after we stop at the grocery store, we'll make a loop through the part of town that was hit." She made another turn and immediately pulled into the Miller's Grocery parking lot. "Do you feel like going in? Or do you want us to just pick up your iron pills?"

"I'd like to go in. It will be nice to move around. I got a little bored walking up and down the hall." Megan wasn't about to let them buy the pills. Unless they cost more than she had.

8

Inside the store, Jenna grabbed a cart and went with Megan to the pharmacy section. Sue and Emily also took carts and split up to do their shopping. Megan found that comforting. Will had mentioned a housekeeper, so she'd expected his mother to leave that chore to the hired help.

"Is there anything else you need?" asked Jenna. "Maybe something that was blown away? I'd be glad to pick it up for you."

"No, thanks. I'm good. I just need the iron pills and a hair pick. Mine was sucked out of my purse."

"I have one at home you can have. I tried a curly perm last summer, but I didn't like it all that well. Nate didn't either, though he was kind enough not to tell me until after it had grown out." Jenna made a face. "But Zach thought it looked funny, like a clown's hair, and he let me know right away."

"Who's Zach?" Megan put the bottle of

supplements the doctor had recommended in the small top basket of the cart.

"Our little boy. He's three and a half, but even last year he talked a lot and didn't hold back his opinions."

"I don't know any toddlers who do." Not that she was well acquainted with many little kids. There had been a couple in her apartment building and one of her clients had a two-year-old. "I don't think tact is an inborn trait."

"There are a few in my three- and four-year-old Sunday school class that make me wonder on occasion, but I think mostly they're just shy. They don't blurt out what they're thinking like some of the other children, but if it's one-on-one, they say whatever comes to mind."

They moved around to the next aisle past the shampoo and stopped in front of the display of brushes, combs, and other hair accessories. There were two styles of hair picks. Either would cost almost four dollars with tax, making it a luxury she really couldn't afford.

I hate this! Megan glanced at Jenna's smooth, layered hairstyle. "If you're sure you don't need the one you have at home, I'll go with it."

"It's yours. I need to get some Goldfish

for Zach and taco chips and salsa for Nate." Jenna nodded to her left. "They're over a few aisles. I have to get a big box of crackers and a couple of bags of chips because they'll wind up sharing both. I've never seen two guys have as much fun eating a snack together."

There were several people in the snack aisle, including one of Jenna's friends, a young woman about the same age. "Lindsey, this is our friend Megan Smith from Austin."

Lindsey glanced at the bruises on Megan's arms, shifted slightly, putting her back to the others in the aisle, and mouthed "tornado?"

Jenna nodded. "Megan, this is Lindsey Moore, one of my best friends. You'll see a lot of her. Her fiancé, Dalton Renfro, has been living on the ranch while he rebuilt the home he lost in the fire."

Megan and Lindsey exchanged greetings, even as Megan considered the way Jenna had introduced her. She hadn't missed the fact that a couple of other women had moved nearer as soon as Lindsey stopped to talk to Jenna. Under the guise of deciding between potato chips and cheese puffs, they were obviously eavesdropping. She wondered if, like Lindsey, they'd heard about what had happened to her. Or maybe people in this small town wanted to know everything about the Callahans.

Megan appreciated Jenna's discretion in simply calling her a friend, though she used it in the loosest sense of the word. Mentioning Austin gave the busybodies a snippet of info so they would conclude that she was visiting the Callahans without really saying so.

"Is Dalton still moving tomorrow?" asked Jenna.

"Yes. He and Chance are doing the final walk-through this afternoon, but Dalton has already checked everything." Lindsey smiled proudly. "Since he basically built the first house himself, he knows what problems to look for."

"Chance and his crew don't make many mistakes."

"The only things he's found were a few nicks in the paint and one missing outlet cover."

"I know he'll be glad to get back to his own place, but we've enjoyed having him at the ranch." Jenna looked at Megan. "He was in the same class as Chance and Nate. They've been good friends forever."

Megan wondered if he was Peg Renfro's son but decided to wait and ask Jenna later.

No sense bringing up the hospital in front of the other women. One of them was already leaning around Lindsey, trying to get a better look at her. "When is your wedding?"

"June eighteenth. Less than a month away."

Jenna laughed. "Barely."

"Okay, only two days less, but now I can start saying weeks instead of months. So far everything has fallen into place, except Dalton won't tell me where we're going on the honeymoon. He wants it to be a surprise." She giggled and leaned a little closer to Jenna and Megan, lowering her voice. "He just said to bring my swimsuit, suntan lotion, and a light jacket."

"Maybe a cruise?"

"I hope not. He knows that doesn't appeal to me. Every week he drops another hint, mainly what I should take. I might have it figured out by the wedding. I'd better run so I can take my groceries home and get back to the bank. It's nice to meet you, Megan."

"You too." Megan scooted the cart over so another lady could move past. There really was enough room, but the woman was looking for something on the shelves and not paying a lot of attention to where she was going.

They picked up the chips and salsa then went down the cracker aisle for the biggest box of Goldfish in the store. "Is Dalton Peg Renfro's son?"

"Yes. Was she your nurse?"

"In the ER. I really like her."

"We do too. I don't have any experience with her as a nurse, but I hear she's good."

"She was with me. Kind but no nonsense. I like that."

Next came a bag of Dove chocolates, a package of oatmeal cookies, and one of chocolate chip cookies from the bakery. "I'd better pick up some healthy food too, or this will be totally classified as a junk food run. Nate and I both have a sweet tooth. I do a lot of my own baking, so I can cut down on the fat and sugar a bit, but I don't always have the time."

"I'm guessing you both work hard enough that you burn up the calories."

"We do. I may have to be more careful when Zach gets bigger, but he keeps me hopping now. Is there anything special you want while we're here in the bakery? I'm being sorely tempted by one of those doughnuts with chocolate icing."

Megan's mouth watered as she surveyed the display case. "They do look good."

"Then let's indulge. I'll get some for Mom and Emily too."

Megan nodded. She really should offer to buy them or at least her own, but that would be foolishness. She figured Jenna knew it. Besides, the doctor said she needed to gain some weight.

Jenna bagged up the treats and grinned at Megan when she set them in the cart. "We'll pick up some of those little cartons of milk to go with them."

They found Sue and Emily in line at the checkout. When Jenna told them about the doughnuts, Emily ran back to the bakery for an assortment so they could take them to Chance and his construction crew.

Soon they were driving through the part of town ravaged by the wildfire eighteen months earlier. Most blocks contained at least one or two new homes. A few blocks were almost filled with new houses.

There were dozens of empty lots with bare dirt and weeds. On some, concrete or paved driveways indicated that a house had once been there. It was hard to tell on others if they had ever been occupied. The handful that held FEMA trailers often had a house in some stage of construction beside them, sometimes with a crew working. There were still some large trees scattered about, their trunks blackened but the limbs full of summer leaves.

Sue explained that they'd lost ninety-eight homes in town and two in the country, including their friend Dalton's. Several businesses and other buildings, along with the cotton gin, also burned or were so badly damaged they had to be torn down.

"It started southwest of town. The firefighters couldn't establish a fire line until that night. Dub and the boys are members of our volunteer fire department and were right in the thick of it. Until the wind died down, all they could do was make sure everyone was evacuated. It was heartbreaking for them to have to let so many homes and businesses burn."

"That must have been frightening for you." Megan had followed the news reports on TV. She couldn't imagine having someone she cared about fighting the monster blaze, much less practically your whole family.

"It was. I prayed constantly and tried not to look scared because of Zach. Jenna was in town when it first hit, and Zach was home with me, so it was even more important to try to make things seem normal until she got home." She slowed the car as they approached a busy construction site.

As Sue parked across the street out of the way, Megan watched two men put up sheeting on the sides of the roofed and framed house. She'd worked with a builder in Austin, a small contractor who built one thing at a time. This crew worked well together, no effort wasted. Unlike most of the other new homes, this was a two-story.

She shifted her attention to the tall, muscular, dark-haired man standing in front of a pickup, a set of plans spread out on the hood. When he spotted Sue's car, a wide grin lit his face, and he rolled up the drawings. Even if she hadn't seen him at the wreck the day before, he resembled Will enough that she would have known they were brothers.

They got out of the car, and a pickup pulled up behind them. Megan was surprised to see Nate. She turned to Jenna with a bemused smile. "Does your husband have a built-in radar for sweets?"

Jenna laughed. "Not quite. He was in town, so I sent him a text that we had goodies and were stopping by the job site." Will came zipping around the corner, parked behind Nate, and hopped out of his truck. "Looks like he passed on the message."

Chance walked up, gave Emily a quick kiss, and greeted everyone. "Party time."

"The word got out," Nate said with a grin as he and Will joined them. He slipped his arm around Jenna's waist and gave her a squeeze. "You know we never turn down an opportunity for food and the company of pretty ladies."

Chance turned to Megan. "I'm Chance. Nice to finally meet you."

"Nice to meet you too. Thank you for searching high and low for my belongings yesterday. Thank you too, Nate. It's wonderful to have clean clothes."

Will took a step closer, drawing her gaze. "They suit you better than mud. You clean up good, Miz Smith," he drawled, a glint of admiration in his eyes.

"Thanks. I agree, mud isn't my style." She was glad she'd taken the time to put on makeup.

When Jenna handed Chance the big box of doughnuts, he hollered at his crew to take a break. Then she gathered up the smaller bag of chocolate ones and the milk for the ladies. "Sorry, guys, we didn't buy drinks for everyone."

"There's a case of water in the back of my truck if anybody wants some," said Chance. He set the doughnut box on a stack of lumber.

Will fell in step beside Megan as they

moved toward the house. "How are you feeling?"

"Pretty good. I have some sore spots but nothing too bad. They'll be gone in a day or two."

"Did you find the pills Cindy wanted you to get?"

"Yes. They had them at the grocery store like she said." As they maneuvered around a pile of scrap lumber, Will cupped her elbow. She enjoyed his gentle touch, but at the same time she was a little annoyed that Mr. Macho thought she wasn't capable of dodging broken boards. "I'm okay. I worked with a builder so I'm used to walking around job sites."

"Were you pregnant then?" They were on clear ground, and he dropped his hand.

"No, but what does that have to do with it?"

His smile held a trace of mischief. "Center of gravity? Seeing where you put your feet?"

Megan stopped, rested her hands on her hips, and attempted to glare at him. Not easy to do when she was about to laugh. "I'm not that big!"

"No, you aren't. But can you see your feet?"

She looked down. No feet. Just a round stomach in a loose top. She burst out laughing and held out one foot. "I can still see when I take a step."

"Yeah, but I made you laugh." He lowered his voice and leaned slightly toward her. "And that's a sweet sound."

Oh, he was a charmer, but in an endearing way. "There you go, being Mr. Nice Guy again."

He just grinned. "We'd better grab a doughnut before the guys eat them all."

"Not a problem for me. Jenna bought us ladies some of our own. I'm going to enjoy every bite."

A little later, as she was licking the last bit of chocolate off her fingers, she looked up and caught Will watching her. His tender expression took her breath away. He nodded toward the big box of sweets. "There are still some left. Help yourself."

"Thanks, but I'm good. Don't want a sugar overload." She glanced around to see if anyone was watching them. Thankfully, they were busy chatting with the carpenters.

Maybe she was just paranoid, but she didn't think a wealthy mama would be too keen on her son looking at her that way. Even nice rich people had expectations for their children, and they didn't include getting involved with poor white trash.

She'd worked hard to rise above that

stigma, but it clung to her like stink on a skunk. No matter what she did, she still came from a long line of crooks and drunks. People who looked for what they deemed an easy buck and who seldom did an honest day's work. If the Callahans learned of her background, they'd think she was just like her mother's family and out to get whatever she could.

The crew headed back to work while the Callahan clan discussed their plans for the day. Curious to see the inside of the house, Megan started toward the building. Will tagged along. Not exactly what she'd planned, but she couldn't deny that she liked his company.

"Checking to see if my brother does good work?"

"I'm sure he does. I like to look at houses under construction, see if I can figure out what goes where."

"He'll show you the plans."

"That takes away the challenge." Smiling, she stepped up onto the block that served as a temporary porch. Will instantly rested his hand against her back to steady her even though there was no need. The block was on flat, solid ground. His concern was touching, even if she didn't want it to be. She'd never had anybody treat her with such gentle care, not even the man she'd hoped was going to marry her.

"This is the entry." She made a sweeping motion with her hand and met Will's twinkling gaze. "And a guest closet."

"I never would have guessed."

"This part is easy. A great room, dining area, and kitchen combination." She studied the framed-in walls and pointed to a smaller room. "Den or office. Maybe a TV room." She led him down a hallway. "Master bedroom and bath. Nice size too."

When she looked up toward the second floor, Will laid his fingers on her arm. "Don't even think about going up that ladder."

Frowning, she drew her arm away. "I'm not stupid."

"Sorry. I know you aren't, but if you weren't pregnant, I bet you'd be zipping up that ladder faster than a kid climbing up a waterslide."

"How'd you know?"

He smiled that lazy, enticing smile of his. "You have a very expressive face. For a second you were tempted to go up there for a better look, then you decided against it."

"Wrong. I wanted to go up there but knew better from the get-go. Wanting to do something and actually being tempted to do it are two different things." She was talking about more than going up a ladder, and he knew it.

"I stand corrected." He tipped his head slightly to the side. "You're good at this."

"I was a good agent, and I enjoyed it. But I don't think I'll go back to it until Sweet Baby is in school. Maybe not even then. It's not easy to sell real estate when you have a baby or small children. One of our best agents tried it, but she soon gave up. You have to be flexible and fit your schedule around your clients' needs. If someone you've been working with comes to town to look at houses, you can't leave them hanging because you have a sick baby. Sometimes another agent might fill in for you, but they aren't always able to do it."

"I have a friend from college who went into real estate after we graduated. He works long hours, as many as I do on the ranch. He's done well, but he doesn't have nearly as much fun as I do."

"How do you know that?"

"He doesn't get to ride a horse."

They went back outside. "Not everyone thinks that's fun."

"Have you ever ridden a horse?"

"No, and I don't intend to start now."

He chuckled as they walked back to rejoin

the family. "I'm not recommending it. But you should give it a try sometime."

"I'll put it on my someday-adventures list." Near the bottom since she'd never been around a horse and wasn't sure she wanted to be.

"What do you think of the house?" asked Chance.

"It's a great floor plan. How many bedrooms upstairs?"

"Three and two bathrooms. I'll show you the drawings tonight if you want. Can't do it now because I have to get back to the office for a meeting."

"I'd like that. Thanks." Megan turned to Sue. "I hope I didn't keep you waiting."

"Not at all. Though we should head on home and put the groceries away." She looked at Chance. "Will we see you at dinner?"

"Sorry, not today. Too busy. But we'll come over tonight." He glanced at Emily, who nodded.

As they strolled back to their vehicles, Will once again walked beside Megan. They didn't talk, but as he opened the car door for her, she noticed Sue watching them with a tiny frown.

Busted.

9

After dinner, Will was about to stretch out on one of his folks' big red leather sofas for a short afternoon snooze when his mother asked him to join her and Dub in their office. Megan was lying down in her room. The rest of the family had scattered after they ate, heading back to their respective houses.

He followed his mom into the office. His dad looked up from the computer and motioned for Will to shut the door. After he sat down, Dub said, "I heard from Peters. He confirmed what Megan told you about being in real estate. He didn't find any marriage or divorce records. Got the scoop on the boyfriend from a former co-worker. He's married and already has four kids."

Will's heart sank. She'd had an affair with a married man? It happened all the time, but somehow he hadn't expected her to do something that sleazy.

"The woman didn't think Megan knew he was married, but she wasn't positive. Megan was friendly enough at work but didn't do anything with the people from the office any other time. So her associate didn't know too many details of her life outside of work.

"The manager of her apartment building said she kept to herself. Though he saw her talking to a few other tenants occasionally. Never had anybody over except for one guy several months ago. He was there four times for dinner and stayed the night once."

"Good grief, was the manager spying on her?"

"That was my reaction too, but Peters thought he was equally nosy about all of the tenants. It's a small building."

"Life in the big city." Will grimaced. "No thanks." It didn't sound to him like she'd had a long-term affair. Which meant she might not have known he was married. Some guys were experts at that kind of deception. "Anything else?"

"He also confirmed that she'd worked at a restaurant before going to the real estate office. She'd been there about eighteen months. But he didn't get any leads on where she worked before that, if she did. You said she'd lived in Austin since she was sixteen?"

"That's what she told me."

"He hasn't been able to find any school records."

"Does that mean she didn't finish high school?"

"Not necessarily. He's still working on it. Though he did say that a high school diploma or GED isn't required for a real estate license. All you need is to be eighteen, take all the required real estate classes, and pass the exam."

"Does he know where she's from originally?"

"No. In fact, so far he hasn't been able to find any earlier info on her. The trail goes cold at the restaurant. Evidently they've had a big turnover from management on down. There was only one waitress that remembered her, but she started working there right before Megan left and didn't know her well."

"So no obvious family to turn to for help."

Dub nodded. "Things are going to be mighty tough for her to keep going on her own."

"She won't have to," Will's mother said. "God put her in our care, and here she'll stay."

"I don't know if she'll go along with your plan, Mom. She has an independent streak a mile long and doesn't like being indebted to anyone. It took the promise of Ramona's leftovers just to persuade her to come out here for a few days."

Sue stared at him. "Leftovers?"

"I told her that Ramona still cooks like she's feedin' a bunch of single cowboys. So unless all the family is here, she winds up with a lot of leftovers." He shook his head. "You should have seen Megan's face. She looked like a little kid longing for a special treat."

"Bless her heart. That settles it. She's staying. We'll convince her." Sue's eyes narrowed. "You'll have to help, but it's going to be tricky. You don't want to give her the wrong impression."

Her tone made Will uneasy. His mother didn't miss much where her kids were concerned. Sometimes she saw things they didn't know they were revealing. Or maybe hadn't realized yet. Occasionally she also read them wrong. "About what?" he asked cautiously.

"Your feelings for her."

He caught his dad's quick frown and lowered his gaze, buying a few seconds to think. His brother had fallen in love with Emily the first day they met, and his mother had thought it was wonderful. Did she think he'd done the same thing? If so, she didn't look at all happy about it.

"Like you, I'm concerned about her and know that God led me there to find her." He met his father's concerned gaze. At one time Dub hadn't thought Nate was good enough for Jenna. Did he or Sue have the same idea about Megan? That wouldn't sit well with their oldest son. He didn't believe they were any better than anyone else, even if they had a lot of money.

"I like her and admire her spunk. I want good things for her. But I'm not in love with her." He focused on his mother, expecting to see relief in her expression. Instead, she appeared even more concerned. "Could I fall in love with her? Maybe." He sat up a little straighter. When he spoke, he kept his voice calm but firm. "Does that bother you?"

His dad twirled a pen around on the desk. He glanced at his wife. "I learned my lesson about judging people with Nate, but there are different things to consider with Megan."

"Like the baby." Will had spent a lot of time thinking about that during the night. "Care for the woman, care for her kid. It's a package deal."

"I don't have anything against Megan,"

his mother said quietly. "Of course, none of us really know her, so our opinions may change. You have a tender heart, son. I'm worried that you may mistake compassion for love. Or that she might. For someone in her situation, you're the knight in shining armor who can make all her dreams come true. I don't want to see either of you hurt."

"We need to help her. To take care of her until after the baby is born, and she gets back on her feet financially," Will said. "Show her she's not alone in the world, that she has friends. With the whole family involved, she won't focus on me."

His mother laughed softly. "That'll be the day. You're the last eligible Callahan. Why should she be any different than every other single female in the county?"

"I'm no expert on women" — that drew an unladylike snort from his mother — "but given how her boyfriend apparently abused her trust, I doubt she's all that interested in finding another man."

"You have a point there."

"I've never met any woman who is so blasted determined to take care of herself. I'm sure she appreciates having a place to stay until she gets her bearings, but it wouldn't surprise me if she takes off as soon as she can."

"We'll have to show her that there are good people in the world." His mother's eyes twinkled with a hint of mischief. "I have a couple of ideas that may make staying here more palatable to her."

Will relaxed back against the chair. "What do you have in mind?"

"With Dalton moving out of the camp house, we can offer her a choice of places to stay, either there or here with us."

"That's a good start. But I'm not sure she has enough money to buy food if she has a place of her own."

"She can take most of her meals here, especially if she's working for us. Jenna, Emily, and I have decided we need a personal assistant."

Will didn't laugh, but he couldn't hold back a grin. The women in his family were busy, but they always managed to get everything done on time.

"I'd also love to have someone prepare nice desserts for the luncheons at the museum. If she's willing, that would be part of her job. We don't plan on having her work full time. She needs to get plenty of rest too."

"I should have known you'd come up with something." Will stood and leaned down to drop a kiss on his mom's forehead. "Thank you." He looked back at his father. "Anything else?"

"That's all Peters had. If he finds anything else, I'll let you know." Dub stood too. "Are you goin' over to Red Ridge this afternoon?"

"That's the plan. I need to check the cut on that heifer's leg. It looked pretty good day before yesterday, but nobody's made it over there since then. Nate's going with me. For some reason that silly cow refuses to stand there peacefully and let me doctor her leg."

Dub laughed and walked around the desk toward the door. "Wouldn't it be nice if they were that cooperative."

Megan slept all afternoon. She and Will shared a quiet supper with his parents, then he invited her to walk out to see her van and to show her what Chance and Nate had recovered from the pasture. He had helped them set up several tables in the old bunkhouse the night before and spread her things out to dry.

It was a pleasant stroll from the ranch house, past flower beds vibrant with roses of all colors and numerous other flowers, as well as the large vegetable garden.

"Who takes care of the grounds and the garden?"

"Ace." Ace was Ramona's husband. She'd met them at dinner, but his dad had simply introduced him as their jack-of-all-trades. "He grows the vegetables and fruit in the orchard, and Ramona and Mom freeze or can what we don't eat fresh. He takes care of a lot of things around here, which frees up Dad and me to run the ranch."

She looked across the garden to the three other houses in the family compound, each an acre apart to give them some breathing room. "Who lives where?"

"Jenna, Nate, and Zach live in the older house. It was built in 1910 and served as the ranch house until Dad built the current one. After my grandparents passed on, Mom converted it into a guest house. When Chance and I moved out, she wound up having visitors stay in the ranch house, and the old place sat empty for a while. She kept it furnished and clean in case it was needed for overflow if we had a crowd. Jenna and Zach moved into it a few months before she and Nate got married." He glanced at her, noting a tiny frown. "Jenna was married before. Nate isn't Zach's daddy by birth, but he is in every other way."

"They sure seem to love each other. That's what counts." She motioned toward the other two houses. "Which house is yours?"

"The one with the wraparound porch. I've always enjoyed the one on the ranch house, so it was at the top of my want list. Second was an open floor plan with the kitchen, dining area, and living room all combined. Chance's house was the first he ever built. Mine was second. He was learnin', so they aren't perfect. But it's still a good family-sized house."

"So you aren't set on being the town's most eligible bachelor forever?"

"Reckon you picked up on the eligible bachelor part at the hospital."

"Hard to miss when the handsome bachelor alert went off and every single woman on the premises happened to wander by."

Will laughed and leaned down to pull a weed from the edge of the otherwise meticulous garden. "I've always suspected there was such a thing."

"Guys have a girl alert too."

"Yes, ma'am. We go through a special initiation in the seventh grade and promise to never, ever reveal the secret to a female."

She laughed and started walking along the path again. "Oh yeah, the old elbow nudge and 'check her out, dude' is such a big secret."

"Oh, man! Who betrayed us?"

"Half the guys in any group."

All of whom would notice her when she walked into a room. She wasn't a stunning beauty like his sister-in-law, but she was more than pretty enough to catch any man's eye.

No one had talked to her yet about working for them. Emily spent the afternoon at the museum, and Jenna had been at the Mission, receiving a shipment of goods for the food bank. His mom had gone to a planning meeting for an upcoming luncheon at the museum. His mother quietly told him that she and the girls wanted to talk to Megan together, hoping if one couldn't persuade her to stay, then the three of them could.

When they reached her van, she sighed heavily. "There are more dents than I remembered."

"About a gazillion. And the right side got pretty banged up when it flipped over."

"Can they hammer out the fender so the front tire will turn?"

"Should be able to. But the only way to get rid of the mold and musty smell will be to completely gut the interior."

"It already stinks, and it will only get worse." She tugged on the front passenger door but couldn't get it open. "Did y'all get everything out of the glove box and console?"

"Yep. Even checked under the seats. Found one ballpoint pen and two rock hard French fries."

"An indulgence from a couple of weeks ago. I was so hungry for fries that I just couldn't help myself."

"Aren't pregnant ladies supposed to crave ice cream and pickles?"

"For me it's French fries and ice cream, though not together. Sometimes I'd give anything for a bowl of Blue Bell orange swirl."

"But you haven't had any," he said quietly.

"I gave in last week and bought a pint. Since I was living in the van, I had to eat the whole thing at once." She smiled up at him. "I enjoyed every bite, but I need to eat healthy."

And she couldn't afford frivolous things. Will made a mental note to pick up a good supply of orange swirl ice cream.

"Do you know of a junkyard that will buy the van?"

"There are some in Abilene that should. I'll give them a call tomorrow if you want. After I saw it, I didn't check with the high school kids about fixing the body. The inside is ruined too. It needs more work than they

140

can handle."

"It would be a waste of money to try to repair it." With a resigned expression, she looked away from the destroyed vehicle. "Is that the bunkhouse?"

When he nodded, she turned and walked through the tall, natural grass toward the one-story, rectangular building. He caught up with her in two steps.

"Selling it for scrap would give me a little cushion while I look for work in Abilene. I could also make my first payment toward what I owe you."

"You don't need to worry about that." When she started to protest, he held up his hand. "Not until after you have the baby and are settled in somewhere with some money coming in."

They walked onto the long bunkhouse porch, and he opened the door, stepping back so she could enter first. "We spread things out so they'd dry. Most of the clothes are just dirty, no glass slivers. Probably because the suitcases were sucked out of the car before they burst open."

"That's something to be thankful for. I don't know how to get glass out of cloth." She smiled when she saw the blue sweater. "Emily said Chance retrieved it from the tree. That must have taken a bit of ingenuity."

"Not much. He just stood in the pickup bed and stretched real tall."

"My cookbooks and recipes!" She hurried over to a plastic tub and opened the lid. "And they didn't get wet. I could live without them, but I'm so glad I don't have to. You rescued the mixer and most of my baking equipment. I couldn't bring everything with me, especially all the pans. There just wasn't room."

"I didn't find any of it. Chance and Nate had already collected everything by the time I got home from town. Is this most of your things?"

They'd left the photo album of the cakes and desserts at the ranch house so his mom could see them. She'd given it to Megan when they brought her home from the hospital.

"There are some clothes missing, but not a lot." She walked slowly around the room, touching a blouse here, a pair of dressy pants there. "There were a few towels and washcloths, two pillows, and a light blanket."

"I tossed those because they were full of glass."

Nodding, she picked up a slinky black

142

shoe with a two-inch heel. "Just one?"

"Sorry, they didn't come across the other one." He figured she'd worn those shoes with the little black dress lying on the other end of the table. When she wasn't pregnant and could fit in it again, she'd be a knockout in that simple little number.

She stopped beside another covered plastic tub, resting her hand on it. "My business and tax records. That's a relief. I doubt if I'll ever need them, but I could just imagine what the IRS auditor would say if I told him a tornado ate them."

Will laughed with her, then picked up the tattered teddy bear and held it out to her. "So they found most of the important stuff?"

She took the bear and held it close, a tear slipping from one eye. "Yes, they did. There's nothing missing that can't be replaced." Looking down at the stuffed toy, a tiny frown creased her forehead. "How did Bear get picked up by a tornado and not come out a dirty mess?"

Will rubbed the back of his neck and smiled. "He took a bath."

Amusement replaced her frown. "He took a bath? Will Callahan, did you wash this thing?"

"Yes, ma'am. He was soaking wet and

muddy, so I figured a little more water couldn't do any more damage. He still looks pretty scruffy, but he's clean."

"Mom bought him at a garage sale. He's always been ratty-lookin'."

"But loved," he said quietly.

"Yeah. He's good at keeping secrets."

He wondered what Megan had shared with her fuzzy little friend. "When I was little, my secret-keeper was a stuffed horse. I switched to a real one when I got older. He talked back sometimes, but he never spouted off to anybody else."

"That's good. If he'd been gabby, Chance could have blackmailed you."

"He did that occasionally anyway, as I did him."

As they started to leave, she paused and glanced around the room. "It's a tremendous relief not to have lost everything."

"We already had too many people here in that situation after the fire. I'm very glad you aren't another."

"Your mom told me some about it this morning. It must have been horrible." Still clutching the bear, she headed toward the door.

He opened it for her and followed her out. "It was the most frightening day and night of my life. I pray I never have another one like it."

When they returned to the ranch house, he rested his hand lightly at the small of her back and guided her toward a group of big wicker chairs and a couple of wicker rockers on the wraparound porch. "Is it too hot for you to sit out here for a bit?"

"I'm fine." She sat down in one of the rockers and laid the bear on a small table. "It's so quiet and peaceful here."

He took the chair nearest her. "A big change from the city."

"Yes, but I'm used to the city. I've always lived in town."

"Where besides Austin?"

"We moved around a lot but settled in San Angelo when I was eight."

Another lead for the investigator. Will was tempted not to share the info with his dad, but he knew he would.

"Dalton is moving out of the camp house tomorrow."

She nodded. "Jenna and Lindsey were talking about it this morning."

"Since it will be vacant, you're welcome to live there. It's furnished because Nate left just about everything when he married Jenna. Dalton isn't taking much because he and Lindsey picked out new things for their house. Or if you'd prefer, you can stay here with the folks. Either way is okay with us, but we'd like you to remain at the ranch, at least until after the baby comes."

"Why would y'all do that for me?"

He shrugged. "Because we can, and God put you here. Because we like you." He reached over and flicked a soft brown curl with his fingertip. "And we're suckers for little kids."

10

That evening, Chance and Emily arrived first, but Jenna and her family were only five minutes behind them. Their little boy, Zach, made a beeline for Megan. They'd hit it off at dinner, but she had a feeling the cute little guy made friends with everyone he met. She hadn't been around kids a lot and was surprised at how well — and how much — he talked.

Giving her a big grin, he handed her a small G.I. Joe action figure and climbed up on the couch beside her, sitting on his knees facing her. "That's Duke. He's a sergeant like my daddy."

Megan didn't quite know what to make of that statement. No one had mentioned that Nate was in the military. The toy was a bit worn. "He looks like he's been in some battles."

Zach nodded, his short, pale blond hair gleaming in the lamplight. "He was Daddy's when he was little. He played with him a lot."

He looked up at her, his expression serious. He had amazing dark blue eyes with light gray starbursts radiating outward from the center. He was a beautiful child.

When the little boy held out his hand, she laid the toy in his palm. "Maybe you should turn around and sit down. I'm afraid you'll fall off."

He frowned slightly but did as she asked, plopping down beside her. "Daddy was in the army. In I-wrak."

"And Afghanistan," said Will, sitting down on the other side of his nephew.

Zach walked Duke across the couch cushion and up onto Megan's arm, then he pretended the G.I. Joe character jumped off, landing on his feet on the couch. "But he won't ever go back. He's gonna stay right here with me and Mommy."

"That's right." Will gave the little boy a hug. "We all like that, don't we."

"Uh-huh. I want to play Legos." Zach scooted forward and slid off the couch with a little help from Will. "You play with me?" he asked, looking up at him.

"Sure. We'll use the coffee table. Do you need some help?"

"I can get 'em." Zach walked around the

massive dark brown leather and oak coffee table that sat between the two red leather couches. A matching red leather chair occupied the space at one end, a mission style rocker with red and gold southwestern print cushions at the other.

Jenna joined them on the couch, making Will scoot a little closer to Megan. She noted that he was careful to leave a little space between them, which was fine with her. Nate took the rocker next to Jenna. Chance, Emily, and Sue occupied the other couch, and Dub settled into the big chair.

"Amazing," Dub drawled. "All the adults are sitting on the furniture." He met Megan's gaze and smiled. "Usually at least one or two of them are sprawled on the floor playing with my grandson." When the child walked past him, lugging a box that was almost too big for him to carry, the pride and love on Dub's face tugged at her heart.

Sweet Baby would never have a grand-parent to love her like that. *I'll love you enough to make up for it,* she silently promised.

"I've got a gripe," continued the rancher. "I wasn't invited to Megan's gettin'-out-of-the-hospital party this morning."

"It wasn't a party." Sue gave him an indulgent smile.

"Well, sure sounded like a party to me, with doughnuts and everything. And y'all didn't even bring me one."

Will laughed and looked at Jenna. "Don't let him razz you, sis. You saw how he made up for it at dinner by eating half the plain cake."

"There was enough for everybody."

"I don't know, Dad, I had to eat crumbs." Will winked at Megan.

She chuckled at the family's banter. Will had scraped the crumbs from the bottom of the pan and sprinkled them on top of the four scoops of ice cream that covered a big piece of cake. The women, including her, had passed on dessert since they'd had a treat earlier. But these hardworking men didn't have to worry about watching their weight.

The family chatted about their day while Will and Zach built a couple of Lego cars and a garage to put them in. Zach practically built one car on his own while Will made the other. The little boy needed more help with the garage, but Will took his time and showed him how to put it together.

She was surprised by Will's patience and gentleness with Zach. She'd never known her father, but her two stepfathers, most of her mother's boyfriends, and her grandfather hadn't been patient or gentle. They'd had no use for her. She'd learned very early in life to stay out of their way. The only relatives who had shown her a smidgeon of kindness had been her Uncle Riley and her cousin Josh.

She'd had a variety of male bosses over the years. Some gruff, some kind, all demanding. On a personal level, out of the handful of guys she'd dated, only one had truly been a kind person. But he'd moved to California and found himself a blonde surfer girl. The rest, like her baby's father, Ken, had seemed nice enough at first but turned out to be jerks.

The interaction between the Callahans was fascinating. Were they being nice to each other because they had company? Or did they really get along so well? Not all rich families were this happy. She'd worked with people who had tons of money but a lousy family life.

Will had said that he didn't always agree with his father, but that he loved and respected him. Jenna had talked about how Will and Chance used to fight over things when they were younger. Did they still argue? Or sometimes get in knockdown drag-outs like her uncle and grandfather? Surely not. It would be impossible to do that and have the kind of relationship they seemed to have.

After half an hour of chitchat, the men decided to move into the TV room and watch the baseball game. When Zach tagged along, Megan felt a twinge of disappointment.

"We have a proposal for you." Jenna's face broke into an excited smile. "I expect Will has already told you that we'd like for you to stay here at the ranch. Mom, Emily, and I were talking this morning — complaining a little, actually," she said with a laugh. "We're all pretty busy, and sometimes we can't keep up with things without getting a little frazzled."

From what she'd seen of these women, Megan didn't think anything stressed them out.

"So we were wondering if you'd be our assistant." Emily's expression mirrored Jenna's enthusiasm. "It wouldn't be anything hard, ten to fifteen hours a week. If you could take care of some of our computer work and organize some things, it would be a tremendous help."

"For the most part, you could set your own hours and pace, so you can rest when you need to." Sue paused for a sip of iced tea. "Emily would like some help at the museum with newsletters, inputting things on the computer, and only she knows what else."

"Trust me, I can find plenty of things for you to do." Emily kicked off her sandals and curled her legs up on the couch.

"Dusting the displays?" Megan grinned at her.

"Nope. Thankfully, volunteers do that. Our primary museum on Main Street is in a wonderful old building that Chance restored and donated to the Historical Society. As Sue mentioned this morning, the Bradley-Tucker House is also part of the museum. It was built by Dr. Bradley, a physician and rancher who came here in 1895."

"Did he arrive here before or after the Callahans?" Megan shifted her position and put her feet up on the leather portion of the coffee table, which she'd noticed also served as an ottoman.

"After," said Sue. "Dub's great-grandfather, Aidan, and his brother Jack brought a herd of longhorns out here in 1880. They established the ranch and the town.

"Dr. Bradley built his home in 1904. His daughter, Sally Tucker, died a little over a year ago at 102. She had a keen interest in history and saved practically everything that had belonged to her parents and her own family."

"Sue convinced Sally's daughter to donate the whole place, including all the contents, to us." Emily smiled at her mother-in-law. "Besides wonderful antique furnishings in the main part of the house, Sally had enough treasures in two garages and the attic to practically fill the downtown museum." She rested her head against the back of the couch with a happy sigh. "It's the kind of donation museum curators dream of."

"I imagine so." Until Megan got into real estate and saw homes decorated with beautiful antique furniture or in a casual country style, she hadn't placed much value on old things. When she was growing up, everything in their home — when they had one — came from garage sales or junk stores.

Not that she had anything against either one. For years, she'd filled her tiny apartment with Goodwill or garage sale finds. But she'd tried to pick quality items, not pans with peeling Teflon or tables with broken legs. Or a ratty-looking teddy bear that had already spent its best years with some other kid.

"I can use your help at the Mission occasionally too," Jenna said. "It's our local food bank, but we also have clothing and some furniture and household items. Everything is free. But we need to keep track of who visits as well as the donations and orders from the larger area food bank in Abilene. Sometimes I get behind on the paperwork."

Sue glanced at Emily and smiled. "But our main need is for someone to be in charge of luncheons and teas at the museum. We rent half of the building for meetings, and sometimes they involve food of some kind. One of the older ladies in the Historical Society had the idea, and Emily ran with it.

"Most of the time the food is prepared by our members, so we earn money for the museum. We're averaging two meetings a month. We need someone to coordinate it all. Make sure we have people lined up to prepare the food, serve it, and clean up. We need someone to keep everything running smoothly."

"We'd been trying to handle it by committee," added Emily, "but that didn't always work out. We came close to having a couple of disasters. Sue and I have been doing it the last couple of months, but we both have plenty of other things to keep us busy."

Sue nodded. "It would be better to have one person in charge so nothing slips through the cracks, especially now while Emily is working on a grant proposal and developing some new displays. We're guessing that your background working in restaurants would be helpful, as well as your real-estate experience. I have a friend who was a Realtor for a while, and she juggled a dozen things at once."

"That describes it pretty well." Megan tried not to get too excited. She wanted to trust God and the Callahans in this, but nothing in her life had ever come easily. "I think I could do the things you've mentioned. It all sounds interesting, especially coordinating the luncheons and teas. That would be right up my alley and a lot of fun."

"What about making fancy desserts or decorating cakes for the luncheons?" asked Sue. "I apologize for snooping in your things, but Chance was so impressed by the photos of your wonderful creations that he showed them to us." She grinned at her. "We were just as impressed."

"Thank you." Megan returned her smile. "Of course, I only took pictures of the things that turned out well." They laughed with her. "I would love to make the desserts. And for the family too, if Ramona won't mind sharing the kitchen."

"I don't think she'd mind a bit, other than fussing about you overdoing it. However, it might be best if you use the kitchen in the camp house when you're cooking for the museum. That would give you plenty of room, and you wouldn't have to compete with Ramona for the stove."

"Supervising the luncheons and doing the baking would be your primary job," said Emily. "That may turn out to be all you do. If there isn't much going on in the off weeks, then Jenna or I will have you help with the other things. But we don't want you working too hard. If keeping the luncheons organized and doing the baking is too much, you can choose which one you'd prefer. We don't do any actual cooking at the museum, so all the meals are made up of salads or sandwiches and dessert."

"You're welcome to stay here with Dub and me and use the other house only for the desserts." Sue met her gaze. "Or you can live there so you have a place of your own if you'd prefer that. You can check it out after Dalton leaves and decide then.

"Even if you move, we'd like for you to join us for meals as often as you want. You'll discover that all the family is here more times than not. And it will make it easier for the three of us to coordinate with you on your work schedule."

Jenna spoke up. "Since Will found you a car —"

"What car?" Megan frowned. Why hadn't Will said anything about it when they were looking at the van?

"Oops." Will's sister made a face. "Guess I ruined his surprise. Some friends at church just bought a new SUV to haul their kids to all their sporting activities. Their other car is small and still in pretty good shape, but it wasn't worth enough to bother with a trade-in. They were going to post a giveaway note on the bulletin board at church on Sunday. Will saw them in town this morning in their new ride and asked about the old one. When he learned they were going to give it away, he suggested they give it to you."

"The car is yours if you want it," Sue said quietly. "Whether you stay here or leave. But I hope you'll consider our offer before you make up your mind."

"We need to finish the details on the offer." Jenna shifted on the couch so that she faced her more fully. "Two hundred dollars a week, with a maximum of fifteen hours work a week."

Megan blinked. That was a good wage for

a part-time job, even in the city. For a rural area like Callahan Crossing, she suspected it was way over scale.

"And medical insurance," Emily added.

Megan's mouth fell open, but she quickly closed it. "Insurance too?"

Sue's eyes held a gleam of triumph. "We have a group policy for all of us and everyone who works for us. I talked to the insurance company this morning and confirmed that we can cover you and the baby, including the pregnancy."

"You must have some fantastic insurance."

"We do, and everyone who works for us has the same coverage."

She couldn't believe everything they were offering her. Her choice of a place to live, a car, more money than the position was worth, and medical coverage.

This time the tears that burned her eyes had nothing to do with hormones and everything to do with gratitude. "I don't know how to thank you."

"You're welcome. You'll return the favor in two weeks when you wow the Rainy Day Quilters with one of your desserts." Emily uncurled her legs and propped her feet up on the coffee table. "That alone will bring us more bookings."

"Guess I'd better make sure it's extra

special." Megan envied Emily's bright pink toenails. She'd tried to paint hers last week, but she was no longer that flexible.

The guys came wandering in with Zach leading the way. "The Rangers are losing." He waved his arms dramatically. "Really bad."

"Ten to two in the ninth," Will added, reclaiming his spot on the couch between his sister and Megan.

"I'm ready for some of that peach cobbler you wouldn't let us eat at supper." Dub looked at Sue. "You want me to dish it up?"

"I'll do it." Sue hopped up from the couch. "If I let you in there first, nobody else will get any."

"Now, sugar, you know I always leave enough for everybody else."

"Only if they use the itty-bitty bowls."

Jenna and Emily followed Sue into the kitchen. Megan started to join them, but Will stopped her by lightly resting his hand on her arm.

"What do you think of their job offer?"

"It's too good to pass up and far too generous. But I'm thankful for it."

"Just don't let them work you too hard."

"Do you honestly think they would?"

"Not really. I have a feeling you might do it anyway."

"A year ago, but not now." Sweet Baby gave her a good kick in agreement. Megan flinched, then tipped her head, looking up at him. "Why didn't you tell me about the car earlier?"

"I was afraid you'd pack up and leave before you knew what Mom and the girls had in mind." He held her gaze. "This is a safe place for you, Megan."

Staring into those intense dark brown eyes, her mouth went dry. She wasn't so sure about that.

11

On Sunday morning, Megan attended church for the first time. The family took up a whole row, with Megan right in the middle. As often happened when they were all together, she wound up with Will beside her.

And people noticed. It didn't seem to matter that she also sat next to Sue. Or maybe that made it worse. Some of the women were openly curious, their gazes flitting between the handsome cowboy and obviously pregnant her. Several of the younger ones watched them with a frown. She hoped a couple of them weren't carrying guns.

Within seconds, the whispers began. She'd spent her life being the object of gossip, and she supposed Will had too, for different reasons. Over the years, she'd learned to ignore it. But she couldn't this time. The speculation was obvious, and it made her heart ache to know that they were imagining the worst about him.

Women weren't the only ones who stared. Several men did the old elbow nudge, but they weren't looking at her with admiration. They were wondering if Will Callahan had gotten himself into trouble.

Just as she was about to ask him to take her home, he calmly reached over and curled his hand around hers. "Don't worry about them."

"I shouldn't have come," she murmured as a group walked up onto the wide platform at the front of the room. "Can't you see what they're thinking?"

"Sure. Some are putting two and two together and coming up with five. Their human nature is showing, which is a real shame. But there will be more who will welcome you with no questions asked and no assumptions made." He leaned a little closer, and she got a pleasant whiff of subtle aftershave. "I don't care what people say about me, good or bad." When she looked up at him in disbelief, he gave her an encouraging smile. "I do care what they might say about you. So Pastor Brad is going to set the record straight in a few minutes."

Megan fought down a wave of panic. What

could the preacher know about her? How much would he reveal to the congregation? "What's he going to say?"

"That God saved you from the tornado, and that you're going to be staying at the ranch for a while. Now relax and let God take care of you."

She took a deep breath. "Okay."

He gave her hand a light squeeze and released it. "Time to make a joyful noise." The night before, they'd sat outside on the porch for a while, enjoying the cool of the evening. She'd confessed that she'd never gone to church before, so he gave her an idea of what to expect.

When she looked back at the front, the musicians had taken their places. There were four men, three with guitars and one on the drums. One young woman was seated at the keyboard. Two other women, plus one of the guitar players, were the vocalists.

The song leader strummed his guitar and called out, "Good morning!"

At least fifty people shouted a greeting in return.

"Everybody stand up and worship the Lord."

As everyone got to their feet, the band struck up a lively tune, and Megan blinked in surprise. She had assumed that the music and the congregation would be somber, like she'd seen in a few movies. But these people clapped their hands or tapped a foot, their faces alight with joy. She didn't know the song, but the words were up on a big screen behind the musicians so she followed along. By the time they repeated the chorus for the third time, she had the music figured out and joined in.

They sang another peppy song, but the rest were slower, more worshipful. On the last one, she closed her eyes and let the beautiful music and thankful praise to a holy God seep into her soul. When it was finished, she felt Will's hand rest gently at the small of her back.

"Are you all right?" he whispered.

She nodded as they took their seats. "Better than all right," she whispered back.

His smile warmed her heart even more.

A man stepped up in front of the podium, and Will leaned close again. "That's Pastor Brad."

The minister had a relaxed, easy manner. He read a passage of Scripture, said a short prayer, mentioned a few announcements in the church bulletin, and welcomed the visitors in a general way.

Then he looked at Megan and smiled. Her

heart jumped to her throat, and heat flooded her face. "We'd like especially to welcome Megan Smith, who is sitting back there with the Callahans." Even more heads turned this time as people stared at her. She hoped her smile didn't appear as weak as it felt.

"I expect most of you heard about the tornado that ripped through the ranch country south of here on Thursday and turned over a semi, injuring the driver. Megan was caught in that storm too, and rode out the tornado by lying in the bar ditch."

Hushed murmurs went around the room.

"Her van was demolished by the hail and tornado. She was soaking wet and pretty beat up, but she took off up the road walking. I expect she was hoping there was a house nearby and somebody to help her." His voice gentled even more. "You see, Megan is pregnant, so she not only had her own welfare to consider, but her baby's too.

"Instead of finding a house, she found the injured and trapped truck driver. She did what she could for him, then took off again to look for help. According to Will, she was really hoofin' it up the road when he spotted her. She told him about the trucker, and they went back and stayed with him until the EMTs arrived. Only then did she let

Will take her to the hospital to see about her own injuries and health."

Though she was embarrassed to be the center of attention and undeserving of his kind praise, she was relieved to see approval on the faces of many who twenty minutes earlier had been ready to condemn her because they jumped to conclusions.

"But that's not all of the story. You see, God worked a miracle to bring Megan to us." He nodded, and someone dimmed the lights to more clearly reveal the picture up on the big screen — a clear spot on the highway surrounded by debris.

Megan gasped softly.

"Chance took these pictures when he and Nate checked on her van. The indentation beside the road is where she was when the tornado passed right over her. That's where Chance stood when he took the rest of the pictures, one in each direction." The pastor slowly clicked through the remaining photos to show the destruction all around her.

She was awed all over again.

When he clicked back to a blank screen, the lights came up, and the minister bowed his head. Megan lowered her head since everyone else did too. "Father God, thank you for your mercy in saving both Megan and the truck driver. We ask that you bring complete healing to Mr. Bentley and allow him to go home to his family soon. Please continue to guide and bless Megan. Thank you for the opportunity to show her your love. In Jesus' name, amen."

Will leaned close to her ear and murmured, "Feel better now?"

She nodded, whispering back, "Thank you."

During the sermon, she jotted down Scripture verses and what seemed to be important points on the blank space in the bulletin designated for notes. When she ran out of room and started writing in the margins on the inside, Will handed her his bulletin. She filled up the notes section on that one too.

After the service, a crowd formed around them, with folks wanting to meet and welcome her. Even the two younger women who had been so obvious in their instant dislike changed their tune and joined in. They acted all sweet and concerned for a few minutes, until the tall, platinum blonde slyly asked the question on everyone's mind. "Your husband must be so relieved that you and the baby are all right."

Megan felt Will tense beside her. *Might as well get it out in the open.* "I'm not married." She glanced around the group, noting blinks of surprise, brows wrinkling in disapproval, and an unexpected number of concerned expressions.

The bottle-blonde's heavily made-up brown eyes narrowed. "That's what I thought."

"Zip it, Kim." Will shifted slightly closer to Megan, a move she figured just about everybody noticed.

"My, my, aren't you being protective of your new little friend. Or maybe your relationship isn't all that new?"

Megan automatically curled her hand into a fist, a plan of defense — or attack — racing through her mind. *Punch in the stomach. Purse to the head. Run like mad.*

"You're way out of line," growled Will.

"And making a fool of yourself." Peg Renfro wiggled her way through to Kim's side. "Put your claws away and go have a dish of milk."

"Huh?"

Peg rolled her eyes. "Please tell me you aren't that dense. Quit being catty and go home. Everybody knows you've been chasin' after Will forever. They also know he's not interested. No man will be if you keep acting like this." She shook her head. "You know I love you, but sometimes you make me ashamed to be your aunt."

Peg's gaze skimmed those around them, finally settling on her niece. Her voice was clear, calm, and just loud enough for all of them to hear. "When Will brought Megan into the hospital on Thursday, it was evident that they had just met. Subject closed."

"Not hardly," muttered Kim, bumping Will's arm as she pushed past him, her red-faced friend trailing along behind her.

"I'm sorry." Peg sighed heavily.

Sue gave her a hug. "It's not your fault."

"No, but it's still awfully embarrassing. For me and for y'all."

"Better here than at the Boot Stop." A tiny elderly woman with white hair and twinkling eyes smiled kindly at Megan. "We're glad you came this morning, dear."

"Yes, we are."

"You're always welcome."

"Hope you visit with us again."

"I will. Thank you." Megan was relieved when folks moved away.

She and Will waited a few minutes before following them. Will stopped at the door and shook Pastor Brad's hand.

The minister focused on Megan, his eyes filled with concern. "I hear I missed a little fireworks. Are you all right?"

"I'm fine. Thank you for telling them what happened with the tornado. I hadn't seen

170

those pictures."

"Yours is an amazing story of God's love."

"Yes, sir, it is."

"I hope you won't let Kim and her theatrics keep you away. Like most any church, we have some who are strong in their faith and wise in their walk, some who are just starting out and stumble a lot, and a few troublemakers." He smiled kindly. "If you ever want to chat, give me a call."

"Thank you. I'll keep that in mind."

As she and Will walked toward the car, he rested his hand lightly against her back. She glanced up at his troubled expression. "What's up?"

"Kim. I always figured she filed her nails on a whetstone, but I can't believe she made a scene like that in church."

"Hey, at least I didn't punch her."

He looked down, a hint of amusement crinkling the corners of his eyes. "She's bigger than you."

"Doesn't matter. I could've taken her."

"You think so?"

"I know so. Words are her weapons."

"And what are yours?"

She held up her purse and her fist.

He burst out laughing. "The purse I can understand. But that little hand? Naw, don't think so."

"I'll have you know I have a good right hook. But I figured with her, a punch in the stomach would do it. If not, whop her with my purse. She'd be down in thirty seconds or less."

They had reached the car ahead of his parents. He opened the back door, and she slid onto the seat. He walked around to the other side and got in beside her. His troubled frown was back. "How many times have you had to defend yourself?"

Uh-oh. She should have kept her big mouth shut. "A few." She shrugged lightly, hoping he'd think it was no big deal. But it had been. And it had happened more than a few times. "I've been on my own since I was sixteen, so I had to learn to take care of myself. I would have used words with Kim, honest. No fisticuffs in church, right?" *Drop it, please.*

He studied her face, then nodded. "Right. Pastor Brad is pretty easygoing, but that would be a bit much."

His parents got in the car and buckled up. "The other kids are going to the Boot Stop for dinner," Sue said. "Shall we join them?"

"Fine by me." Will turned toward Megan. "Are you too tired to go out to eat?"

"Not at all. I'm starving."

Dub chuckled and started the car. "Then

Irene's is the place to go. Best food in town."

"Irene wanted to build a truck stop," explained Will. "But she couldn't afford enough land out by the highway, so she opened a restaurant downtown. The way she tells it, she wanted a place big enough for the cowboys and cowgirls to park their boots and stay a while. So she called it the Boot Stop."

"Clever idea. I expect they get a lot of the church crowd." When she'd worked in restaurants, Sunday around noon had been one of their busiest times.

"They do." Sue flipped down the sun visor. "Chance and Emily scooted out right after the service to save us seats. You'll see some folks from Grace Community." She pulled a tube of lipstick from her purse. "And meet some other folks too. Overall, Callahan Crossing is a friendly place."

Megan tried to stifle a twinge of anxiety. She hoped all the Will-rejects stayed at home.

12

Late that afternoon, Will drove her down a
dusty ranch road to the camp house Dalton
had vacated. It was a modest white wooden
single story with a tin roof and a large chinaberry tree to shade it in the late afternoon.
There were covered porches across the
length of the front and back. The yard was
mostly dirt. Trying to keep the sparse
patches of grass watered and green probably hadn't been a priority for a long time.

Will parked in the shade near the back
porch and hustled around to help her out
of the pickup. He'd done the same thing at
the hospital. That time, having a hand to
steady her had been appreciated, but she
didn't need it now. She had the door open
by the time he reached it. "I'm not so far
along that I can't get out of a truck."

"I know." He held out his hand. "But my
mama taught me to be polite." He gave her
a boyish grin. "Besides, holding a pretty

woman's hand is fun."

Megan swung her legs around, took hold of his hand, and slid her feet down to the running board before stepping to the ground. "Smooth, Callahan. Did your mama teach you that too?"

"Pure natural ability." He tucked her hand around his arm, pushed the door closed, and laughed. "I'm real modest too."

She let the comment pass. "It looks like a nice house."

"It's been around a while. We remodeled it several years ago, but it's still not fancy."

"I don't need fancy."

He unlocked the back door and opened it, letting her go inside first. She was surprised to find the kitchen cool, with an air conditioner or two humming in the background.

"I asked Dalton to leave the air conditioning on so it wouldn't be sweltering in here."

"Thanks. This is a great kitchen. Lots of cabinets and counter space." She shot him a smile. "I'm going to have fun cooking in here."

Dalton had left an electric can opener, a coffeemaker, which she wouldn't use until after the baby was born, and a toaster on the counter. She figured she'd put it to good use.

Opening a cabinet door, she found a set of dishes for four, twice that many glasses, and two casserole dishes. Another cabinet held a fry pan and a couple of saucepans. Silverware was in one drawer, and another held a spatula, one big spoon, long-handled tongs for barbecuing, a carving knife, and a paring knife. She smiled to herself. Was this a typical bachelor pad?

"What's that little smile all about?"

"Does your kitchen look like this? Do any of you guys ever actually cook?"

"Hey, grilling is cooking. My kitchen is well stocked with equipment, though a little light on food. I also make a mean breakfast. Eggs, bacon, pancakes, cereal, toaster waffles — all the normal stuff, as well as the occasional cold or warmed-up pizza."

She grinned and peeked in the pantry. Empty as expected. "I love pizza for breakfast, but not sausage or pepperoni. Can't handle something that spicy, even when I'm not pregnant."

"I'll keep that in mind when I order us a pizza."

Just the two of them sharing a meal was way too inviting. "So you don't eat with your parents all the time?"

"Nope. Though I hang out with some or all of the family a lot, I try to give them some space." He shrugged lightly. "Jenna and Chance have their own families now. Mom and Dad would never tell me to get lost, but I think they're enjoying having more time as a couple."

Which was another reason for her to live here instead of at the ranch house.

Was it hard for him to be the odd man out? He was older than she was, probably in his early thirties. A lot of men were married by that age. Did he want a wife and family? Or was he happy being single?

She had been in the happy-single category for a long time, slipped out when she met Ken, then crashed back into it when he turned out to be such a creep. But she had a feeling Will Callahan could make her yearn for companionship and love if she wasn't careful.

She wandered into the living room, stopped, and smiled again. The blue flowered sofa, loveseat, and chair looked comfy, and the blue leather recliner would be a great place to put up her feet and relax. There were also end tables, a coffee table, and two lamps. None of it was new, but nothing was damaged or badly worn.

"I like the furniture, but other than the recliner, it doesn't strike me as something a cowboy would pick out." Unless he bought it secondhand.

"It belonged to the family who lived here before Nate. They had been here for forty years. Virgil finally retired when he turned eighty. He and his wife moved near San Antonio to be close to their kids and grandkids. New house, new furniture, so they left several things, including the washer and dryer. Nate left his bedroom set and the kitchen table and chairs. If there's anything you need, let me know, and I'll pick it up for you."

She walked down the hallway, checking the rest of the house. Three bedrooms, a bathroom off the hall, and another off the master bedroom. There were towels in the bathrooms and linens and pillows in the hall closet. "When you said it came furnished, you weren't kidding. I can't see anything right off that I need to get."

"I have a spare TV. I'll bring it over tomorrow and set it up."

Who had a spare TV? "Are you sure you don't need it?"

"It's just sitting in the closet. I bought a bigger one about a year ago." He followed her back to the living room. "I'm assuming you'd like to live here, but if you'd rather stay with my parents, they're cool with that too."

"I appreciate their offer to stay with them, but it would be better if I had a place of my own. I get up a lot at night these days. I don't want to disturb them." She plopped down on the sofa. "I've been alone for eight years, Will. I don't know how well I'd do living with someone else for more than a few days. I need some space too."

"I understand. The folks will too, as long as you come by and see them real often." He sat down on the other end of the couch. "So what did you think of church this morning? Besides Kim's shenanigans." Frowning, he stared across the room and shook his head. "That was so weird. That stuff happens at the honky-tonk, not at church."

"You spend a lot of time at the honky-tonk?" She shifted around to face him and curled her legs up on the cushion.

He laughed and shifted too so he could see her easier. "No. Went in one in Abilene once just to see what it was like. Walked out five minutes later."

"With a girl on each arm."

He rested his elbow on the couch arm. "Reckon I could have, but those aren't the kind of women who interest me."

Megan practically bit her tongue to keep from asking what kind of woman did. Better go back to his question about church. "Some of the music this morning was livelier than I'd expected."

"You expected dirges or chants?" he asked with a lazy smile.

"Maybe. Things I've seen in movies. I liked your music better. I like Pastor Brad. He seems like a very nice man."

"He is. And very wise."

She traced her fingertip around one of the blue flowers on the sofa. "Can I ask you something?"

At her hesitant request, his brow knit in a tiny frown of concern. "Sure."

She almost chickened out, afraid he'd think she was stupid. "I know God protected me from the tornado."

Will nodded. "That's a fact."

"Does God only do big things like that? Or does he help with everyday life too?"

"If you trust in Jesus, I believe God helps you constantly. I pray every day and ask him to guide me, to help me make the right decisions, to do the right things. I mess up sometimes, so either I don't get the message or maybe I ignore it, but that's not God's fault."

"How do you pray?" Her face grew warm under his scrutiny, but she plowed on. "Sorry, but this is all new to me. After the tornado, I promised God that I'd learn about him, learn what he wants from me. But I don't know how to do it. Is there something special you say when you pray? Or some particular way you say it?"

"Don't be sorry. This is a good thing." His voice was gentle and reassuring. "I just talk to God or Jesus like I was talking to my dad."

Well, that doesn't help much, she thought. *I don't know how to talk to a dad.*

"It's like everyday conversation, but with the greatest respect, honor, and love thrown in. Even more than I'd show my own father. I don't always agree with my dad, and sometimes I get ticked off at him. But I still love and respect him. It's the same with God. I don't always understand what he's doing, or always like it, but I still love and respect him."

He rubbed a spot in front of his ear, his expression thoughtful. "I don't know if I'm explaining it well or answering your question. Just talk to him like he's your best friend, because he is."

She could relate to that. Mrs. Hoffmann had been her best friend — her only real friend — and they had talked a lot. Even some about God and Jesus because the elderly lady had believed in them. She'd invited Megan to go to church with her a few times, but Megan had weaseled out of it.

He met her gaze. "However you prayed last Thursday, God heard, so I'd say he approved of your method, whatever it was."

"If you ask him things, does he answer?"

"Yes."

"How?"

"Various ways. Though, I admit for me, sometimes his answers are clearer than at other times. They don't always come right away. I might be pondering something and come across a passage in the Bible that gives me guidance or understanding about that very thing. He might even tell you where to read if you ask him."

That was a little too weird for her. Megan frowned and shifted her position.

"I don't mean he speaks to me out loud, though he could. I figure God can do anything he wants to. The way it works for me, a verse will come to mind, and almost always when I look it up, it's pertinent to what I'm dealing with."

"Not always?"

"Occasionally I don't see a connection, though I expect he does." He chuckled. "Every so often I think he's given me a verse, and when I look it up, it isn't there.

The other day it was Zephaniah 3:25, and the book ends with verse 20. I don't let it bother me. I'm not a scientist where everything has to be proven. I live by faith."

"I need to get a Bible. Will they have one in town somewhere?"

"I don't think so. But I'll loan you one. I have several versions."

"Versions?"

"There have been quite a few translations over the years. Some are easier to understand than others."

"I'd better have an easy one."

"Can do."

That evening, he brought her three different Bibles, so she had a choice. After she retired to her bedroom for the night, she propped a stack of pillows against the headboard, crawled into bed, and picked up the first one from the nightstand.

She rested it carefully on her stomach, not sure where to begin. Mrs. Hoffmann had sometimes read things to her, but she'd jumped around all over the book.

Feeling uncomfortable and a little silly, she decided to take Will's advice. "God," she asked softly, "what do you want me to learn tonight? Where should I read?"

Psalm 18.

As the words ran through her mind, she

swallowed hard. Was that God? Or just her? Like Will, Mrs. Hoffmann liked to read from the psalms. But Megan didn't remember any one in particular.

Her fingers trembled slightly as she looked up the page number for Psalms in the table of contents, turned to it, and began to read.

I love you, O LORD, my strength.

The LORD is my rock, my fortress and my
  deliverer;
  my God is my rock, in whom I take
  refuge.
  He is my shield and the horn of my
  salvation, my
  stronghold.

I call to the LORD, who is worthy of
  praise,
  and I am saved from my enemies.

The cords of death entangled me;
  the torrents of destruction overwhelmed
  me.

The cords of the grave coiled around me;
  the snares of death confronted me.

In my distress I called to the LORD;

I cried to my God for help.
From his temple he heard my voice;
　my cry came before him, into his ears.

Megan reread the passage, amazed at the instructions God was giving her and how appropriately it fit what had happened to her as well. Love him. Trust him. Let him be her strength, her shield, her stronghold. He was worthy of praise, so she would praise him.

She didn't understand it all. What did "horn of my salvation" mean? Checking the footnote, she saw that horn symbolized strength. So he was her shield, the strength of her salvation, her stronghold. He would protect her from her other enemies — poverty, homelessness, fear.

The torrents of destruction had certainly overwhelmed her, and she had definitely been confronted with the snares of death.

But he had heard her cry and saved her.

The psalm went on to describe how the earth shook and trembled because God was angry. It told how he came down from heaven and flew on the wings of the wind. She loved that phrase. She kept reading, admiring the beauty of the words and the images they evoked. No wonder Mrs. Hoffmann had enjoyed the psalms.

The last part of verse 19 stopped her. Tears of gratitude silently slid down her cheeks as God revealed his truth to her.

"He rescued me because he delighted in me."

13

Will understood Megan's decision to move into the camp house. But he would have preferred having her an acre away from his house instead of half a mile down the road.

She'd been in her own place for two weeks. He'd seen her almost every day at noon when they ate at the ranch house, and she'd visited with the family in the evenings several times. But she'd eaten in town that day because she had a doctor's appointment and some errands to run.

He was bitin' at the bit to spend some time alone with her, and to find out what Dr. Cindy had to say. He parked the pickup behind her house and walked up onto the back porch, intending to knock softly in case she was asleep.

Before he reached the screen door, she called, "Come on in."

He walked into the kitchen and stopped, watching as she removed a small saucepan from the stove and set it on a trivet on the counter. She quickly added some chopped-up chocolate and whisked it around in the pan, stirring until the concoction was smooth. A funny-looking pan with what he thought was a single-layer chocolate cake sat on a wire rack nearby. "Is that the icing?"

She nodded. "Ganache. It's just cream and semi-sweet chocolate." She poured the mixture on top of the cake and set the saucepan aside. Gently shaking the cake pan, she spread the icing evenly. "There." She smiled in satisfaction. "Would you open the refrigerator?"

"Sure." He hurried to do as she asked. "Does it set as it cools?"

"Hardens, actually. It's like a layer of chocolate candy on top. With a slight adjustment of proportions, you can make truffles."

After she carefully set it on the refrigerator shelf, he closed the door and grinned at her. "Do I get a piece?"

"At supper. I want your mom and the girls to try it too, and make sure it will work for the Littleton baby shower on Thursday. Sue mentioned that one of the ladies is allergic to wheat, so I suggested making a flourless cake."

"I didn't know there was such a thing."

"I'm sure there are lots of recipes, but this is the only one I've tried. It also happens to be some serious chocolate."

Will laughed. "That should please just about every woman I know. Do we get to sample everything you make for the luncheons?"

"Unless I do a repeat. Then I probably won't make one ahead of time."

"No sense doing the extra work." He noticed a book on the table and walked over to see what she'd been reading. "Quilting. Is this where you got the patterns for the quilt cake?" She'd baked it for the Rainy Day Quilters the week before, and people were still talking about it.

She'd made a smaller one for the family, minus the fancy decorations. He'd been to fancy restaurants and dinners, but he'd never eaten anything like it. It had two layers of white cake with strawberry mousse in between, then a layer of custard and two layers of chocolate cake with some kind of dark filling separating them.

On the family cake, she'd used plain buttercream frosting, but the one for the luncheon had been decorated like an old-fashioned sampler quilt with six different patterns. It was a big cake. He'd put it into his mom's Suburban and carried it into the museum for her.

Smiling, she joined him. "I found the patterns I wanted there, but I used the computer at the ranch house to get some online so I could print them out. Then I made a pattern, traced it onto the cake, and decorated it. I do a lot of designs that way."

Which would be easier if she had a computer of her own. He had a laptop that he didn't use much. Problem solved.

"Are you all tuckered out?"

"No. I took a nap earlier. Don't tell anybody, but this cake isn't too hard to make."

"Won't tell a soul. I'm going to drive over to one of the pastures and check on the cattle. Would you like to ride along?"

"Sure." She filled up a water bottle, grabbed a banana, and turned to him. "Want one?"

"I'm good. Had an apple a little while ago."

"Apple instead of an energy bar. You must not be working hard today."

"Mostly pickup work — checking fences and the cattle." He opened the door and let her walk out ahead of him. When they reached the pickup, he opened that door too, ready to give her a boost if she needed help getting into the truck. Unfortunately, she didn't.

He climbed into the truck and drove around the house. Pulling out onto the dirt road, he headed in the opposite direction from the ranch house. "What did Cindy have to say?"

"Everything looks fine. Both Sweet Baby and I have gained some weight. She was happy about that. My blood test was a little better than when I was at the hospital, so the extra iron and all those steaks y'all have been feeding me are helping. She said things are improving."

"Are you resting enough? Or are you working too hard?"

"I'm fine." She smiled at him. "Thanks for your concern, but I'm being careful and resting when I need to."

"Good. Make sure you keep doing that." He flinched inwardly at his commanding tone. "Please."

When she chuckled, he relaxed. "We'll go to Aidan's Spring first. If we were horseback, we'd cut straight across the pasture, but it's too rough to go that way in a vehicle."

"It would be too rough on a horse too."

"Under current conditions. But if you weren't pregnant, you'd probably enjoy it. Jenna loves riding. 'Course, she grew up on the back of a horse. She started helping round up cattle when she was just a kid. Emily rides too, though she'd never done any real ranch work before she got married. She's pitched in several times and does fine. We just finished the spring roundup a few days before you arrived. Too bad you weren't here to see the big production, but you'll get an idea of what we do at the Ranch Rodeo on July 4th."

"Is your roundup like in western movies, with a chuck wagon and everything?"

"Not anymore. We've used the chuck wagon in the past, but Dad decided to donate it to the museum last year. It had been a working part of the ranch since 1885, so Emily and Mom were both thrilled to put it on display. What do you think of the museum?"

"It's amazing." Her face lit up with enthusiasm. "I'm no expert on museums, but this one is fascinating. And going into the Bradley-Tucker House is like going back in time a hundred years."

"Emily's done great with both of them. She came here just to set up the museum, with no intention of staying in Callahan Crossing."

"Chance changed her mind."

"That he did. But it wasn't easy. She was

bound and determined to become an assistant curator at a big city museum. Until she fell in love with my brother and decided she preferred the slower pace of Callahan Crossing to a hectic life in the city." He slowed the truck to watch a roadrunner race down the road ahead of them before dashing into some brush.

"It does take some getting used to, but I think I'm going to like it. Except for everybody knowing everybody's business."

"That is a drawback. About the only one I can think of. I lived in Lubbock while I went to college. That was as much big city as I care to experience."

"You went to Texas Tech?" She took a sip of water.

"Yep. Got myself a bachelor's degree. The official title is long, but it's basically ranch management and animal science. Not sure it was worth it."

"Why not? Isn't it important to keep up with all the latest science and trends? Surely things change in ranching just like they do everywhere else."

"They do, but that doesn't mean old ranchers change with the times." Will drove carefully around a pothole, making a mental note to have Buster bring the grader over and smooth out the road.

He used to gripe to his brother, but since Chance got married there hadn't been as many opportunities to use him as a sounding board — or a complaint department. Though Chance and Jenna were partners in the ranch too, they weren't as involved in the everyday running of the place as he was.

Ever since the fire hit Callahan Crossing, his brother had been busy as a windmill in a whirlwind. Between his new wife and all those houses he was building, Chance didn't have a lot of time for his older brother. Will understood, but that didn't make life any less lonely.

These days he kept his disagreements with the ol' man to himself. So why had he said anything to Megan? He considered the question for a moment and concluded that he really wanted — needed — someone to talk to. His horse just didn't give good advice.

"Your dad isn't open to new ideas?"

Will pulled off his cap and tossed it in the backseat. Running his fingers through his hair, he sighed. "Sometimes. It just seems like lately he's shot down most everything I've mentioned."

Megan grabbed the armrest when they hit a bump.

"Sorry. I didn't see that one in time."

"It's okay. Your ranch is successful, isn't it?"

"Yes. Dad manages it well. But there's room for improvement. I'd like to experiment with a couple of pastures by planting some different varieties of perennial native grass. I'd also like to give a TV cattle auction a try and bring in some competition from several buyers. A company in Ft. Worth does that. They broadcast the auction live via satellite on RFD-TV. They've been doing it for years."

"That sounds like a good idea. Why is your father against it?"

"He's been dealing with the same cattle buyer for a long time. When I was a kid, we used to haul the cattle to the local auction house. It closed while I was in high school, and Dad arranged for a buyer to come out here to the ranch. It's worked better than hauling the cattle somewhere to an auction. Easier on both the animals and the cowboys. I understand being loyal to folks you do business with, but a little competition wouldn't hurt either.

"Then there's the wind power potential. He's adamantly against leasing out land to put up wind turbines. I think it's the future. I'm still studying the pros and cons, but there are an awful lot of wind turbines going up around the area. It would provide additional income and help supply some of the country's energy at the same time."

"Would it affect the cattle? Or the value of the land?"

"That's what I'm looking into." He smiled at her, appreciating her interest. "It's a new idea in my noggin so I don't have the particulars worked out."

He drove down a slight slope and stopped in the grove of large pecan trees near the spring and along the creek it fed. "This is Aidan's Spring."

Megan studied the area with a smile. "It's beautiful." She pointed to a bench nestled between two large rocks. "Who built that?"

"My grandfather made that one. We're not sure if it's number ten or eleven. There's been one here for generations. Family lore has it that Great-great-grandpa Aidan built the first one for his wife, Clara. It's been the tradition to replace them before they start falling apart."

"Did your great-great-grandpa live here at the spring?"

"He and his brother Jack camped here the first year. Maybe the second. Family history is a little fuzzy on that point. Then they built a one-room shack. When they first came here, it was still pretty much open range, but they wanted to have secure water. So they bought this section and another that had a creek running through it."

"If this is Aidan's Spring, is the creek named after Jack?"

Will chuckled and turned off the ignition. "Yes, it's appropriately named Jack's Creek. After the second winter of living together in the shack, they were about ready to shoot each other."

"They must not have gotten along as well as you and Chance."

"If I had to live in a one-room shack with my brother, I'd be ready to wring his neck after the first winter," he said with a laugh. "We both get ornery if we're cooped up for too long."

"Not the office type."

Will shuddered. "No, ma'am. I'd be crazy as a lizard with sunstroke if I had to stay indoors all the time.

"Back then there wasn't a lot of work in the winter, other than to keep track of the cattle and herd them back to the home range if they wandered too far or drifted in a storm. At least these days we haul feed for them, but the early ranchers depended on natural grass. I reckon they got mighty tired of playing checkers or toothpick poker.

"Aidan and Jack were complete opposites.

Jack had a propensity to go to town and blow money. Aidan was tight as a tick. So they grated on each other's nerves somethin' fierce." He leaned his elbow on the armrest.

"They'd made some money, and thanks to Aidan's frugal ways, still had some of it. So they each built themselves a house, situated so they couldn't see each other. Jack's was over near his creek. It's pretty dilapidated now. Aidan's is the dogtrot near our big barn."

"Why didn't he build here at the spring?"

"It was too secluded for him. The county was building a road where the highway runs now, and he wanted to be closer to it. The ranch headquarters is higher in elevation than here, so back then before the trees were planted around the ranch house, he had a pretty good view of the property.

"This is pure speculation on my part, but I think part of his motivation had to do with the wildlife that comes here to the spring and creek. Deer, wild turkeys, coyotes, bobcats, and an occasional mountain lion come here to drink. If the headquarters had been built here, the critters would have been scared away. One house might not have bothered them too much, but adding a bunkhouse, the big barn, corrals, and people coming and going all the time would have been too much." Will's grandpa always told them to be respectful of the wildlife because God put them there first, and he agreed.

"Aidan hauled water from the spring at first, but he put in a windmill before too long. He married Grandma Clara in 1888. They lived in the dogtrot until 1895. They had two kids and plenty of money by then, so he built her a new home in town."

"What happened to Jack?"

"He was tired of ranching and wanted to move on. Aidan bought his share of the ranch, and Jack went to England in search of a wife."

"England? You're kidding."

"Nope. He found himself an aristocrat, a lady with an impoverished viscount father who was more than happy to take Jack's money in exchange for his daughter's hand. He brought his lady wife back to America and settled in Boston. City life and marriage suited him. Once he settled down, he became a good businessman and investor and parlayed his ranching fortune into an even bigger one. His family continued his success, so it worked out well for them. And for us. I wouldn't want to have to share the ranch with another family."

He started the pickup. "That's your history lesson for today, ma'am. I'd better go count cows."

She watched the scenery as he slowly drove across the creek. "Okay, this is going to sound dumb, but why are you going to count the cows? Don't you know how many you have?"

Will glanced at her and smiled. She sure was cute with a touch of pink in her cheeks, a little embarrassed to ask the question but curious enough to lay it out there anyway. He liked that.

"We do, and we know where they're supposed to be. But they don't always go along with our rules. Sometimes they meander off to another place on the ranch or visit the neighbor's land." He drove across the pasture on what was only a semblance of a road. In consideration of his passenger, he drove slower than he normally would. "Occasionally rustlers help them disappear."

"Rustlers?" She stared at him with wide eyes.

Was she thinking about the movies again? He almost smiled, but losing livestock wasn't a smiling matter. "They come in a pickup and trailer in the middle of the night. Sneak in and load up three or four head, more if they're after the calves. We lost four heifers a couple of months ago. We considered putting a locked gate at the ranch entrance, but that would be a real pain. They'd probably just cut the wire next to it and drive on in."

He slowly drove by six cows that were grazing and their calves napping. They stopped eating and lifted their heads, watching Will and Megan curiously. A couple of the calves raised their heads, and one hopped up and moved next to his mama.

"Will, stop. There's an armadillo." Her excitement tickled him.

He shifted into park. Resting his hand on the back of her seat, he leaned over to look out her window and silently thanked the small, weird-looking armored critter that gave him an excuse to move closer to her. "Yep, that's an armadillo all right."

"I've never seen a real one before."

"City girl."

She laughed softly. "I suppose that's it."

"Actually, we don't see them too often, either. They usually forage at night due to the heat, but he's probably out early this afternoon because it's cooler."

"He's sticking to the shade too. What do they eat?"

"Insects and grubs. They help us out that way, so we leave them alone, except when we brand them." He leaned toward the window a little more. "Can't tell if that's one we've caught or not."

That prompted her to look at him, with her face nice and close just like he'd hoped. "You can't possibly be serious."

"We don't use an iron. Just paint the brand on the shell at the shoulder."

"Will Callahan, I'm not that gullible."

"I had you there for a minute."

"Did not."

"Come on, admit it."

"Can't, 'cause it's not true." She turned back toward the window and sighed softly. "We scared him away."

"He was probably ready to move on anyway." He shifted back to his seat and put the truck in drive, hoping she'd enjoyed that little bit of fun as much as he had.

Five minutes later, Will stopped on a small rise where he had a good view of that section of the pasture. Glancing at Megan, he noted she was counting the cows too, and using her index finger as a pointer.

As if feeling his gaze, she looked at him. "That makes twenty-six cows and twenty-six calves." She lowered her hand as a faint blush tinted her cheeks. "Guess it's impolite to point."

Will laughed. "The cows won't notice, and I don't mind. I've done it myself when they're bunched up." He pulled a little spiral notebook from his shirt pocket and jotted down the number.

Grinning, she pointed to a cow and six calves, all about the same size, a good distance away by themselves. The cow grazed while the calves scampered around chasing each other. "Are those all hers? Do cows have sextuplets?"

"I've never heard of any. Even triplets are rare. We've had some twin calves, but it doesn't happen real often. That mama cow has babysitting duty today."

Megan stared at him, her expression dubious. "She's baby-sitting?"

"They take turns watching over the calves when it's playtime. I don't know how they figure out the schedule, but it works. We may see two or three others doing the same thing. We have a hundred cows plus their calves in this pasture." He tried to keep a straight face but didn't quite succeed. "They're typical females. They form cliques." Her eyes narrowed, and he fought a grin. "Each little bunch sticks fairly close together, with the different groups staking claims to various sections of the pasture."

"So if a woman — or a cow — has a group of friends, that's a clique."

Her serious expression made him uncomfortable. Had he touched a nerve when he'd only meant to tease a little and get a good-natured rise out of her?

"Well, I guess I could call it a hen party. But bein' cows, they might object to that." He put the truck into gear and drove down the slope.

"And women don't?"

"Naw. That's just teasin'."

"What do you call a group of male friends?"

He gave her his aw-shucks grin, the one guaranteed to soften the hardest feminine heart, and thought he saw the corner of her lips twitch. "A bunch of good ol' boys."

Smiling, she shook her head. "And you get away with it too."

"Yes, ma'am." He turned his attention back to the job, scanning the pasture for more cattle.

Neither of them said anything for a while, but the silence was comfortable. She was relaxed, enjoying the outing, and taking in the scenery.

He liked the scenery too, but he'd observed it all his life. Today, he was more interested in looking at her. He couldn't remember any woman who fascinated him as much as Megan. Unlike Chance, he hadn't limited all of them to one or two dates. There had been a few relationships that he'd thought might actually go somewhere, but over time he'd realized that true love wasn't part of the equation.

It wasn't part of this one either. Yet. But her combination of inner strength and vulnerability intrigued him. Maybe part of his interest was because he had a lot left to learn about her.

Peters still hadn't turned up anything new. There were around eight hundred Smiths in the San Angelo phone book. He and Dub agreed that it would be a waste of time to try to sort through them all. It might not even be her mother's name.

The detective had checked school records, though Will didn't know how he got access to them. Peters knew all the tricks and had a lot of contacts, but he didn't discover any information on a Megan Marie Smith. There wasn't one in the system for any of the years she would have attended.

Will stopped and added a dozen more cows and calves in the little notebook. When he started up again, he noticed a tiny frown knitting her brow. "You okay?"

She nodded and looked at him. "These little bunches of cows are sure spread out. How big is this pasture?"

"Five thousand acres. The east portion is

hilly and has some steep ravines so it's not as big as some of the others."

"Five thousand acres sounds big to me."

He drove around a large prickly pear cactus. "It isn't when the ranch has sixty thousand. Where the terrain is flat and doesn't have a lot of brush, we have a couple of pastures that are ten thousand acres. This is arid country, so it takes a lot of land to support one cow and calf. When we've had good winter and spring rains and the grass is plentiful, we'll put cattle in every pasture. In normal years, like this one, when the grass gets low in one pasture, we move them to another one that hasn't been grazed."

"Does the grass grow back in the first one?"

"If we get enough rain. But having lived in San Angelo, you know that's unusual in West Texas."

"Most of the time I didn't care one way or the other, but if we lived where there was grass I was happy if it didn't rain. Then I didn't have to run the lawn mower."

"So you got stuck with that."

A fleeting grimace passed over her face. "And everything else. My mother isn't exactly the domestic type."

Isn't, as in present tense. So her mother was still around. "Does she have a career?"

"No." The word was a quarter-inch shy of curt.

"So what type is she?" he asked, keeping his voice casual.

Her jaw clenched for a second, and when she turned to him, the hardness in her eyes told him he was treading on dangerous ground. "A drunk and a freeloader who likes to party. And she's not real particular who provides the booze." She took a deep breath and added softly, "Or what she has to do to get it."

"Was she always that way?"

"Yes."

He stopped the truck under the shade of a mesquite and shut off the engine. When she shot him a worried glance, he lightly rested his hand on her shoulder. "So you left home at sixteen, when you could work full time?"

She nodded. "On my sixteenth birthday, I got up like always but went to the bus station instead of school. I'd worked as a dishwasher and bussed tables at a local cafe since I was fourteen, but the hours were limited by law. I saved as much as I could, so I would have a little when I left."

"You headed to Austin?"

"Yes. I lived in a homeless shelter until I found a job."

"That must have been tough."

She shrugged and shifted position. "My mom and I had lived in them some when I was a kid, so I knew the ropes. It didn't take too long to find work. The owner of the cafe gave me a letter of recommendation."

Will frowned and moved his hand down to the console. "He knew you were leaving?"

A faint glimmer of amusement touched her face. "She knew I was leaving. I didn't tell her I was going by myself, but I think she had it figured out."

"What did your mom do?"

"I expect she had a big party. She'd blown through what she got from her third divorce, but her new boyfriend would foot the bill." She took a deep breath and released it slowly, a cleansing sound instead of a regretful one. "I haven't talked to her since I left. I'm sure she never missed me, except maybe when she was broke."

"She took your money?" He was appalled. Again.

"As long as she had a husband or boyfriend to take care of her, she left me alone. If she didn't, she figured whatever I made belonged to her. I got good at stashing it in places where she'd never think to look." She smiled and rested her hand on her stomach.

"Like the bag of the lawn mower."

Will chuckled because it was the appropriate response, but his heart ached for Megan. He couldn't imagine growing up with a mother who didn't dote on him. Or one who would have been happy to see him leave anytime, much less when he was too young to be on his own.

He thought of her comment after the tornado. *Mostly I just feel like I've been beaten up.* Had her mother beaten her? Or one of her stepfathers or mother's boyfriends? Or had something happened when she was on her own?

He'd felt protective of her from the very beginning, a feeling that had grown in intensity the more he'd gotten to know her. Glancing at her as he started up the pickup, he silently promised that no one would ever hurt her again.

14

That evening, Megan chalked up another success as the Callahans devoured the chocolate cake with fresh raspberries sprinkled over the top. She smiled as Will attempted to sneak a berry off her plate. She let him have it, though he wasn't very stealthy. "For the party, I thought I'd use strawberries for the garnish on one and raspberries on the other. Good idea?"

"Perfect," said Emily. "Is this hard to make?"

"Not really. The only tricky part is wrapping heavy foil tightly enough around the springform pan to keep out the water." Seeing Jenna's questioning frown, she added, "The cake pan sits in a pan of water to bake. Getting the water the right height is a challenge too, so you don't slosh water into the batter. But the rest of it is easy."

"More trouble than I have time for." Ramona licked a bit of ganache off her fork.

"But it sure makes a good cake."

A knock sounded on the front door, then it opened, and Lindsey and Dalton came inside. Megan had seen both of them at the ranch several times since her arrival. He was as excited as his bride-to-be about their upcoming wedding, which was less than two weeks away.

Tonight, Lindsey's eyes were puffy and red, and the normally calm deputy sheriff looked as if he wanted to punch somebody.

"What's wrong?" Chance asked as Emily scooted closer to him, making room on the couch for their friends to sit down.

"There was a fire at the bakery that was supposed to make our wedding cake." Dalton reached over and took Lindsey's hand. "So they can't do it."

Tears welled up in Lindsey's eyes. "I've called every bakery in Sweetwater, Big Spring, and Abilene, but nobody will take an order on such short notice. June is just too busy. I don't know what we're going to do."

Megan hesitated. Unless they wanted something huge and terribly intricate, she could do it. At least she thought she could. Doubt pricked her. Who was she to think she could make something so beautiful for a real wedding? Botching a class project, which she had done, only disappointed her. If the cake for the wedding didn't turn out, she would hurt Lindsey, Dalton, and everyone else involved. She decided to keep her mouth shut.

"Megan could make it." Jenna smiled at her. "You've made some before."

She sensed Will tense beside her. Did he doubt her ability? "Just in class. I've never made one for a wedding."

Lindsey's face lit up. "Would you? I've heard about the quilt cake. Everyone who was there said it looked and tasted amazing. I hope you took a picture before they cut into it."

"Jenna took one." Megan's camera was one more thing that had been lost in the tornado. "I don't know, Lindsey. A wedding cake is a lot different than a single-layer one. I would feel terrible if you were depending on me, and I couldn't pull it off."

"Of course you can do it." Emily glanced at Lindsey before focusing on Megan. "If you want to make Lindsey's cake, go for it."

"I don't know if that's a good idea." Will propped one boot on the leather edge of the coffee table.

Who asked him? Megan looked up at him with a frown. "Why not?"

"You're liable to get awfully tired.

Wouldn't you be on your feet a lot?"

"Yes, but I can pace myself."

"But will you?" he mumbled. He turned his attention to Lindsey. "Did you try any bakeries in San Angelo?"

"Yes. I found one that would take the order, but their delivery fee was terrible."

"I'll pay for the delivery if you want to use them," said Mr. Bossy. "Part of my wedding gift."

Megan scooted forward on the couch — no easy feat — and turned to glare at him. "I'd like to speak with you."

"Go ahead."

"Alone."

"Uh-oh, you're in trouble now." Chance winked at her and grinned at him. "Give him what-for, Megan."

Will picked up a pillow from the floor beside the couch and tossed it at his brother. "Mind your own business."

Chance caught the pillow and laughed. "Man, talk about the pot calling the kettle black."

Will rose easily to his feet and held out his hand. It annoyed her to accept his help, but it made her exit swifter. She heartily disliked people who made a scene, and here she was doing it. It would have been simpler and less disruptive to just quietly tell him that what she did wasn't up to him.

She noticed Sue's tiny smile as she moved around the coffee table. Was she smiling because she thought Megan would put Will in his place? Or that he would set her straight? Remind her that she was the hired help and couldn't just work or not work as it suited her.

Megan led him down the hall into the TV room. Will closed the door behind them. Hands on her hips, she glared at him. "What do you think you're doing?"

"Trying to keep you from doing something stupid."

"Do you think I'll mess up the cake? Ruin the day for Lindsey and Dalton? Embarrass you in front of your friends?"

"Why would that embarrass me?"

"I'm here because of you."

"That doesn't make much sense, Megan."

"Key word being *much*. You obviously think it makes some sense."

"I don't think you'll mess up the cake. At least not intentionally." When she started to speak, he held up his hand. "I'm concerned that you're taking on more than you can handle right now. That you might get too tired, or even sick, and won't be able to do it."

"I finish what I start. Always." Well, not

quite always. She'd been on her way to Lubbock, or Abilene, or Dallas when she got caught by the tornado. She hadn't reached that goal. Yet. Packing up and leaving were sounding better by the minute. She lowered her hands and walked away from him, returning a few seconds later. "I want to do that cake."

He rubbed the back of his neck. "You're giving me a headache. Five minutes ago you were worried that you couldn't do it."

"I didn't exactly say that. I just said it's a lot different."

"And harder."

"Not really. Using a lot of colors of icing and making six different quilt patterns was very tedious and time consuming." She paced back and forth across the room. "I'll admit the idea of making Lindsey's cake scared me for a minute. It is a challenge, but unless she wants something crazy, I can pull it off with the techniques I know." She stopped in front of him. "I suppose you mean well . . ."

"I do."

"I need to do this, Will. If it's good enough, there might be orders for more."

"To supplement your income."

"Yes. Your mother is very generous, but extra money is always a good thing. I won't take pay from your mom if she gives me time off to go to Abilene for supplies or to work on a wedding cake," she added quickly. "And I won't commit to one later if there is something going on at the museum."

He laid his hands gently on her shoulders. "Then how will that supplement your income? You're just trading one job for another."

"Not necessarily. Wedding cakes are expensive. A basic cake is usually four dollars a slice minimum. Certain types of icing and decorations run more. I wouldn't charge that much to start with, but it will have to be enough to cover supplies and my time."

"So if you charge three dollars a slice and serve one hundred people, you might net out two hundred dollars, or what you make working for Mom."

"I think so. If they want fondant or expensive decorations, I'd have to charge more." She'd been wanting to rest her hands against his chest since the moment he touched her. She finally worked up the courage to do it. "Even small weddings would be beneficial, because people would hear about me. Larger weddings would actually bring me more money than what I earn from your mom. More importantly, when I leave Callahan Crossing, it would give me another option or at least something to fall back on."

"Still determined to leave?"

"Not really." When she felt one hand slide around her back, she swallowed hard. "But it's always wise to have contingency plans."

"Pays to be prepared." He gently nudged her face upward with his knuckle. "For the record, I don't have any doubts about your ability to create an amazing cake. But I think you have a tendency to try to do too much. Promise me you won't overdo it. Any of it. Working at the museum, baking wedding cakes, or whatever idea you get in that pretty head of yours. Don't push yourself too hard. I care about you, Megan. I don't want anything to happen to you or Sweet Baby." He dropped a light kiss on her forehead, and she thought she just might swoon like the ladies of old. "So promise me you'll take good care of yourself."

"I will." She hoped he couldn't hear her heart pounding. "I'm not going to do anything to harm my baby. I'd appreciate it, though, if you'd quit trying to run my life."

He released her and gave her one of those buckle-your-knees smiles. "Sorry, can't do that, sugar. Ridin' herd on people is what I do best."

How could he annoy her and charm her at the same time? "You are an exasperating man, Will Callahan."

"Yeah, but I'm loveable."

Smiling, she shook her head and opened the door. *Yes, you are.* But she wasn't about to tell him that.

Five minutes later when Megan learned that Lindsey expected three hundred people at her wedding, she almost backed out. The wedding cakes she'd done in class were sized to serve less than one hundred, and Lindsey had her heart set on one big, glorious cake. She also needed a groom's cake.

After Megan went online and she and Lindsey looked through the Wilton cake decorating site, she felt better. They found a cake similar to what Lindsey had originally ordered, and she liked this one even better. It wasn't beyond Megan's abilities, just bigger than what she'd done before. If she did it well, it would make a great impression on future customers.

Lindsey and Dalton left much happier than they'd been when they arrived. Everyone else left about the same time, but Megan stayed for a few minutes. "Sue, could I use the computer a little more? I need to get directions to the Michaels store in Abilene." She and Sue had gone there the week after they hired her to pick up more baking equipment, but she wasn't positive she remembered the way.

"Sure. Use it as long as you need. We're going to watch TV for a while."

Megan settled in, printing the directions to Michaels as well as another craft store. Earlier, she'd printed the list of needed supplies and instructions for making and decorating the cake. As she considered printing out some other instructional information, Will walked into the office carrying a large briefcase.

He set it on one of the chairs in front of the desk. "Would all this be easier if you had a computer at your house?"

"Yes. I know as I go along I'll think of things I need to research, like how to transport the cake to the church."

He plopped down in the other chair. "Mom will let us use the Suburban."

"That's not the part that concerns me. I can't imagine trying to carry the cake with it all put together. But assembling it there is a little scary too." She yawned and covered her mouth with her hand. "Guess that's something to check out tomorrow. It's past my bedtime."

Will glanced at his watch. "Five after ten. Past mine too." He stood and picked up the briefcase as she gathered the things she had printed. "You can use my laptop as long as you need it. There's a portable printer in here too. The camp house is set up with broadband internet along with the TV cable. Which reminds me, is the television working all right?"

"It's great." Megan turned off the lamp and walked around the desk. The day she moved in, as promised, he showed up with an HD TV. He'd also brought her a prepaid cell phone. Now he was providing her with a computer. His generosity still amazed her, though it seemed to be ingrained in the Callahan family. "You don't need your laptop?"

"No." He followed her into the living room. "I thought having it in the pickup would come in handy to keep the cattle tally, but it was too much of a bother. Scribbling numbers in a pocket notebook is easier. I haven't used it for much else, either."

She bid his parents good night and walked out back to her car with Will beside her. He opened the back door and set the briefcase on the floor. "The house is set up for wireless, so you should be able to use this anywhere, even on the porch. If you have any trouble, holler and I'll see if I can sort out the problem."

"So you're a computer whiz, as well as a rancher, firefighter, and rescuer of damsels in distress?"

"Nope. Can't claim that title. But I know how it's supposed to work because my house is set up the same way."

"I'll give it a try in the morning. Thank you for being so thoughtful."

He brushed a tiny bug off his arm. "Just trying to make up for being a jerk earlier."

"You already did."

"Good." He closed the car door and caught her hand before she could open the driver's door. The porch light softly illuminated the driveway, and the moon played hide-and-seek behind a puffy cloud. "Will you be my date for the wedding?"

15

Her heart skipped a beat as she searched his face in the filtered moonlight. "I'll be going, but as a worker bee. In case the cake needs a touch-up." He lightly caressed the back of her hand with his thumb, and she suddenly felt a little light-headed.

"You can do whatever you need to with the cake, but I'd like for you to go with me." The bright three-quarter moon popped out from behind the cloud the same instant Will smiled. "Ride in together — just us. Sit together. Eat supper and cake together." His expression grew serious. "I want to spend the evening in your company, Megan, and I want everyone there to know that you're with me. Not with my family, but with me."

Oh, how she wanted to! She'd be like Cinderella going to the ball, only escorted by the handsome prince instead of meeting him there. But when the evening was over, her handsome prince wouldn't come searching for her with a glass slipper. He'd see how foolish he'd been. Merely sitting next to him in church every Sunday caused enough gossip to start a whirlwind.

Though not wanting to stir up more talk was only an excuse. It would be so easy for Will to make her long for things that could never happen. Falling for him and then being spurned by him would be the worst pain she'd ever known. Better to nip it in the bud.

"Thank you, but I can't." She eased her hand from his.

"Why not?"

"You aren't supposed to ask that. You're supposed to be a gentleman and let it go."

"Sometimes being a gentleman is overrated. Why won't you go with me? I want the real reason, not some lame excuse."

"You're a heartbreaker, Will. I don't want to go down that road again."

Frowning, he muttered, "I'm not a heartbreaker." He was silent for a few seconds. "Okay, maybe once. But I started out with good intentions. After a while I realized that I didn't love her. There were a couple of other times when I had high hopes, but the feelings didn't go deep enough for either one of us."

He studied her face in the moonlight.

"Tell me about the man who deserted you when you needed him most."

She leaned against the car, considering his words. Though she had shared some of her history with him and had told him she wasn't married, he'd never asked if a boyfriend might show up at any time. It was odd that none of the Callahans had ever brought it up themselves. Politeness went only so far.

Nor did she believe that they would simply accept what she told the hospital clerk about having no one to contact in an emergency. She knew Will overheard it because he was sitting right beside her. The Callahans were kind, generous, and inherently good people, but they weren't naive. Why should they take her word about anything?

Maybe her family and her upbringing had made her cynical, but she didn't believe someone with their kind of money would welcome a stranger into their lives without trying to learn something about her. But by doing so, they put themselves in a pickle. They couldn't simply announce that they'd run a background check or had her investigated.

"Why don't you tell me?" she asked quietly, crossing her arms.

Will's eyes widened. "What?"

"Come on, Will. Surely y'all had some-body check up on me. What did your private investigator find out?" She was taking a stab in the dark, but his sudden unease told her she'd hit the mark.

Stuffing his hands in his jean pockets, he turned, leaned against the car, and stared at the ground. "How did you find out about that?"

"Just a wild guess."

His head jerked up, and he stared at her. "No wonder you've made it on your own since you were a kid." He hesitated, prob-ably sorting out what he should tell her. "The investigator, Peters, talked to a woman you worked with at the real estate office. I've never met him, but he must be a friendly, charming guy. He's good at getting people to reveal things."

Sweet Baby wiggled and kicked. Megan uncrossed her arms, resting her hands on her stomach, rubbing the little foot that poked her palm. "Most people are more than willing to share gossip."

He nodded. "True. She said that you'd never been married, which he confirmed by checking the marriage records. She also said that your boyfriend was a married man, but that she didn't think you knew it when you were seeing him."

"I didn't. He told me he was divorced. Ken was sweet and a lot of fun." Megan's sigh was filled with regret. "I thought he really cared about me."

"Since he has kids, I assume he was older?" Will pulled his hands from his pockets and rested them on the car.

Megan flinched. She'd hoped he hadn't learned about the kids. "Yes. Thirty-four. I haven't dated a lot, but all my other boyfriends were about my age. He had me completely fooled. I knew he had kids. He showed me their pictures and talked about them, but I never suspected that he was only separated from his wife. So much for my street smarts."

"Some men lie well."

"He was a pro. I learned later that his wife had kicked him out four months earlier because he was cheating on her with someone else. Once I gave in and slept with him, he wasn't interested in me anymore. Evidently all the time he was seeing me, he'd been trying to get her to take him back. He spent the night at my apartment and moved back home to his wife the next day. He sent me a text message letting me know our affair, as he called it, was over." She noticed Will's hand curl into a fist and eased a little farther away. It was an instinctive reaction, though when her brain shifted gears, she knew she had nothing to fear from him.

"He wasn't man enough to talk to you face-to-face?"

"No. I called him when I found out I was pregnant, but he didn't want anything to do with me or the baby. I was relieved. He already has four kids and is a lousy husband and father. I didn't want to break up his marriage or get support or anything. But I thought he should know."

"You did the right thing." He relaxed his hand. She wondered if it was a conscious effort or a subconscious one.

"That was the only thing I did right where he was concerned." She tried to lighten her tone. They obviously didn't know everything about her family or she wouldn't still be there. "So what else did Peters find out?"

"He only got as far back as your last restaurant job in Austin. There had been a lot of turnover, and only one person remembered you. Nobody knew where you worked before that. After you mentioned living in San Angelo, he did an initial check there, but he didn't find anything on you."

Thank goodness.

When he looked at her, she glanced away. "Oddly, there weren't any school records on a Megan Marie Smith."

"After I left, I heard they had a fire in the building that housed the records." It was true, but there wouldn't have been anything on Megan Marie. That wasn't her name back then. By not telling him, was she only protecting herself? Or lying?

There had been a time in her life when lying didn't bother her a bit. Mrs. Hoffmann had taught her about integrity. She had a feeling her old friend wouldn't be happy with her right now. Which meant God probably wasn't either. *Please forgive me if this is wrong. But I don't want him to find out about my family.*

"That could be it. There are too many Smiths in San Angelo for him to try to question them all. Or any for that matter."

"There are a lot of them." And she wasn't kin to any of them.

He waited a moment, no doubt hoping she'd enlighten him. When she didn't say anything else, he said quietly, "Megan, I didn't like Dad having you investigated. I don't think he liked doing it, either." A tiny smile touched his face. "And Mom was ticked. But we had some trouble several years back when my cousin and her new boyfriend came for a weekend visit. We all liked the guy until Dad caught him with a handful of Mom's jewelry that he'd taken out of the safe. It was always locked, but he opened it."

"Combination?"

"Yep."

"So he was a pro." She tried to keep a straight face when he slanted a quick, questioning glance in her direction. Her cousin Josh had tried his hand at safecracking, but he wasn't any good at it. He gave up after his second attempt, complaining that he needed a pro to give him some tips, but he couldn't find anyone who'd do it. "I assume he'd fooled your cousin as well."

"Yes. He was an auto mechanic by day and a thief by night. So to keep from being robbed — or avoid shooting somebody — Dad hired Peters to investigate houseguests that he didn't know well. The only thing valuable that my folks keep in the house now is the silver."

"It would be a little hard for a guest to sneak the teapot out of the house."

"Might be a little obvious. Still, Dad doesn't want to risk having a criminal around. I understand his reasoning, but it still doesn't sit well."

"But it's wise."

He turned to her with a frown. "You aren't offended?"

"Not really." Should she come clean? Was

it better to tell them that she came from bad blood than have Peters discover the truth? "I learned early not to trust people. If I were in your father's shoes, I'd want to know the background of anyone staying under my roof or living on the ranch. To be honest, it's been bugging me because you haven't asked me more questions, especially about Sweet Baby's father. So when you asked me to go on a real date, I figured you already knew for certain that I wasn't married. But how could you tell me?"

"It's been a dilemma. Now that we have all that out in the open, will you go to the wedding with me?"

"You're persistent, aren't you?"

"Yes, ma'am." He caught her hand in his. "Megan, I understand your fears."

Not by a long shot.

"The last thing in the world I want to do is hurt you. I don't want to get hurt, either, though that's a distinct possibility. But there's something between us. I think more than friendship. I'd like to see if God has something good waiting for us."

"It won't work, Will. We come from two different worlds."

"That doesn't matter."

"I'm going to have another man's baby."

"That doesn't matter, either. Honestly,

sugar, it doesn't. Nate loves Zach like his own son, and if God puts us together, I could love Sweet Baby like my own too."

He gently cupped her face with his work-worn hand. "We may find that friendship is the only relationship for us. We may even get hurt in the process. But we'll never know what might be unless we hitch up the wagon and ride down the road a spell. I'm willing to try it. Are you?"

Her heart longed to say yes. Her head screamed for her to run the other way. There could never be anything serious between them. He was a Callahan. She was a nobody. Worse than that, she was the only person in her family that hadn't spent time in jail.

"Will you go to the wedding with me?"

"Yes."

Please, God, don't let this be a mistake.

231

16

The Friday before the wedding, Will pulled up in back of Megan's house at twelve o'clock on the dot. She wasn't expecting him, but he didn't think she'd turn him away. At least not until after they ate.

She met him at the back door. "Do I smell French fries?"

He grinned as she opened the screen door. "Yes, ma'am. Supersized. I thought about getting pizza, but since you mentioned craving fries again yesterday, I opted for the burger. Along with cherry 7UP and two gallons of orange swirl ice cream."

"You do know the way to a girl's heart." She took the beverage holder he was juggling.

"I'm tryin'." If all it took to win her heart were fries and ice cream, he'd have it made. "How are you doin'?"

"Hungry and ready for a break. Perfect timing." She glanced around the kitchen.

"But we'd better eat in the living room."

He surveyed the room. Dirty mixing bowls, cake pans, and utensils filled the sink. There were pages of instructions scattered on the table, along with a roll of white satin ribbon, a long box labeled Silver Fanci-Foil Wrap, three packages of twisted, crystal stick-like things, a roll of masking tape, and several flat boxes of varying sizes.

The counter also contained tools of the trade. The big mixer, pastry bags, numerous tips, a small ruler, two different-sized bowls, a can of meringue powder, a bag of powdered sugar, and a can of vegetable shortening.

Next to all that was a wide empty space with a few dollops of white icing on the counter. On the other side of her work space was a sheet of wax paper with seven rows of white icing roses. He paused to make a quick count. Ten flowers to a row.

"That's a lot of roses."

She set the beverage carrier beside the sink and removed the drinks. "It's not as many as I started with. The recipe calls for eighty-five rosettes, but I made a bunch extra in case some got messed up. Some are already on the cake. After we eat, I'll show you what I've accomplished so far."

He set the white paper bag of burgers and

fries on the counter and put the ice cream away in the full-sized freezer while she removed a couple of plates from the cabinet.

"Are the burgers the same?"

"Yes." He closed the freezer door and walked over to join her. "Tomato, extra pickles, and no onion."

"Just the way I like it." She smiled and scooted a plate over to him as he opened the bag.

"Me too. Sometimes I add onion, but not when I'm eating with a pretty lady." He winked at her and handed her a burger and the supersize box of French fries. "If I'm with Chance and Nate, they can just put up with it."

"They probably do the same."

"Not since they got married. Dalton got just as bad after he started dating Lindsey. Before that, he didn't care if he knocked over the bad guys with onion breath."

She dumped the potatoes out on her plate, laughing when they almost took up the whole thing. "You could have skipped the sandwich."

"Nope. Can't live on fries alone. Gotta have that red meat."

"Yes, Dr. Callahan." With a wink and a smile that went straight to his heart, she picked up her plate and drink and headed toward the living room. "Do you want the recliner?"

"Nope. You go ahead and put your feet up." A few days earlier, she'd mentioned her feet swelling, and that worried him. Jenna and his mom told him it was pretty normal. But they thought it was sweet of him to be concerned.

"Talked me into it." She popped a fry into her mouth before she even reached the chair and sighed contentedly. "You're spoiling me."

"Doin' my best." The best he figured she'd let him do at that point. He wanted to shower her with gifts, have her relax in a recliner all day long, and not do a lick of work. Sleep, read, knit baby booties, or anything her heart desired except work so hard that she had dark circles under her eyes.

He took a seat on the couch as she settled in the chair. After they'd both eaten for a few minutes, he asked, "When is your next appointment with Cindy?"

"In a couple of weeks. Why?"

"You look tired."

"Of course I'm tired. I'm pregnant." She made a face and stuck three fries in her mouth.

"You're working too hard." He half-expected her to hit him with a pickle.

She glared at him and took another bite. Chewed it, swallowed, and leaned her head against the backrest. Suddenly, tears rolled down her cheeks.

He practically tossed his plate on the coffee table and hurried over to her, kneeling beside the recliner. "Sugar, what's wrong?"

"I'm worn out, my back hurts, and the wedding is tomorrow. I have to finish the cake, and I just want to sleep." She met his gaze, her eyes filled with tears. "You were right, Will. I shouldn't have taken this on. It's too much. I'm not good enough. I'm too slow, and I won't get it finished on time."

He took her plate, carefully leaned across her, and set it on the end table. Sliding his arms around her, he held her close. "Don't cry, sweetheart. You'll get the cake done, and it will be beautiful."

"How do you know? You haven't even seen it."

"I've seen the roses —"

"Rosettes. They're different." She sniffed loudly.

"If you say so." What she'd made looked like roses to him.

She pulled back a little and frowned up at him. "Roses have petals. They're a lot harder to make. At least for me they are. You have to make the petals one at a time, building up the flower."

"Then it's good you're doing a cake with rosettes."

She nodded, fresh tears welling up in her eyes. "I can't do it."

He drew her close again, gently rubbing his hand up and down her arm. "Yes, you can. You just need to take a nap. What time did you get up this morning?"

"Five," she mumbled against his chest, snuggling a little closer. Her tears dampened his shirt, the spot cool on his skin. He wished he could hold her forever and never let anything make her cry.

"When did you start working?"

"Five-thirty."

"Did you take any breaks?" He brushed a light kiss on the top of her head.

"A couple. Short ones." She sniffed and swiped her nose with a napkin.

So much for pacing herself.

"Okay, Master Cake Lady, here's the plan. You finish your dinner, then you take a nap. Here in the chair, in bed, wherever you want to stretch out."

"I can't. I'll sleep too long."

"I'll make sure you don't." He slowly released her, and she straightened, easing away from him. Resting his hands on the chair arm, he asked, "Is an hour good enough? Or two hours?"

"An hour will do it. But don't you need to go to work?"

He grinned unrepentantly. "I'm the boss, remember? I can set my own schedule." He stood and pointed to her plate. "Now eat up."

"I'll never finish all these fries." She picked up her plate and ate a few of them. "Even if they do taste wonderful."

"It won't bother me. The burger is healthier anyway since it's broiled."

"I'll probably have to change my eating habits soon. The doctor said I may start getting indigestion a lot when Sweet Baby is a little bigger."

"Then you should enjoy it while you can." He sat back down across from her and took a sip of soda before picking up his plate. "I talked to a friend of Dalton's this morning about your van. He might be interested in it for a parts car. He'll be out Monday to take a look at it."

"Will he pay more than the salvage company?"

"Maybe. Gotta get you the best deal I can."

"I appreciate it."

238

They finished the meal, chatting occasionally, and Megan went to nap in her bedroom, after making Will promise again to wake her in an hour. He rested in the recliner for about fifteen minutes, not wanting to make any noise that would keep her from going to sleep.

Then he quietly went into the kitchen and peeked into the refrigerator to see how her project was coming along. Practically the whole fridge was full of cakes.

The groom's cake was a large sheet cake with chocolate icing and chocolate shavings covering all the sides. A replica of Dalton's deputy sheriff badge, a five-pointed silver star with bands of red and blue and "State of Texas" decorated the top.

Will had never studied Dalton's badge closely, but he figured the emblem on the cake was right on the money. From what he'd seen, Megan strove for perfection in everything she did.

There were four graduating tiers of the wedding cake, all covered in smooth white icing. She had already decorated the two largest ones. Rosettes were placed in a row around the side at the top of each layer, extending slightly above the edge. Alternating rows of beaded icing draped from one flower to the next like pearl necklaces of two and three strands. A compact row of slightly larger beadlike balls circled the bottom of each layer.

It was one of the prettiest wedding cakes he'd ever seen, and he had seen plenty. He'd heard the girls discussing the flavors. Megan was doing something different with each tier. He couldn't remember all the combinations, but they included chocolate and white cakes, and strawberry, pineapple, and chocolate mousse for the fillings. His pretty little baker already had people talking about her creations, but she was definitely going to make a name for herself with this one.

She wouldn't be able to do anything else so grand until after she had the baby and recovered, but he expected she'd be able to keep as busy as she wanted after that. The bakers at Miller's Grocery did fine with doughnuts, cookies, and everyday cakes, but neither of them had the time or inclination to do more than write a few lines on one of the regular cakes if someone wanted something for a special occasion.

He closed the refrigerator door, staring at the orderly rows of rosettes on the counter. Megan claimed that she was utilizing only things she'd learned in the classes, but she was as much an artist as someone who painted on a canvas or created a sculpture.

Will washed and dried all the dishes that were in the sink. He could have put some of them in the dishwasher, but this way they'd be clean if she needed to use any of them again right away.

When he heard a distant rumble of thunder, he walked out onto the back porch to check the sky. A line of thunder-bumpers were forming to the north, so he rolled up the windows on the pickup and checked the carport to make sure the ones on Megan's car were closed.

He went back inside and used the laptop to check the WunderMap on Weather Underground. The weather forecast had called for thundershowers. The interactive radar showed him that they were moving in their direction. No warnings or alerts were posted, so hopefully it would be a pleasant rainy afternoon. A good day to take the afternoon off and stay inside, preferably right there.

Turning on the television, he kept the volume low and watched a show on the Discovery Channel about sunken treasure in the Caribbean. He was about to go tap on Megan's door when she came wandering down the hall.

"Did you sleep?"

"Yes. You had a good idea. I feel a lot bet-

241

ter. I thought I heard thunder." She paused and looked out the window. "Looks like the weather guys got it right this time."

"I checked the radar. It should be raining in a few minutes. But nothing serious."

"Good. I don't have time to go hiding out in a cellar."

"I should check the one out back. Dalton never used it. One of his duties is weather spotter, so if it's nasty, he's out in the thick of it. The pest control folks come around on a regular schedule. They spray outside the houses and in the cellars. That normally takes care of the spiders, scorpions, and everything else. From spring to fall, I inspect the one at headquarters about once a month anyway. Don't want to make a mad dash to safety in a storm and race right back out again."

"I think I'm glad we never had a cellar. Now I'm not sure I'd want to go down there."

"As long as the creepy crawlies are vanquished, it's okay."

She headed toward the kitchen. "Don't tell me you're afraid of spiders."

He followed and pulled out a chair from the table. Turning it around, he straddled it and rested his arms on the back. "Only the ones that bite, like black widows and brown recluse. It's not like I'm going to faint if I see one."

"Just run the other way," she said with a grin. "Smart man. I'd be waddling along right behind you."

He slapped his palm against his chest. "I'm crushed that you'd think I'd leave you behind."

"There's no way I could keep up with you."

"I'd carry you, silly woman. No fast waddling necessary."

"I don't go anywhere fast lately."

"Nothin' wrong with that. By the way, your cakes look fantastic. I peeked."

"Thank you." She turned toward the sink and stared at it for a second, then met his gaze with wide eyes. "You washed the dishes?"

"Yes, ma'am."

"Thank you."

"Aren't you proud of me?" He gave her an impish smile.

"Yes. Actually, I'm amazed. I assumed you'd never washed a dish in your life."

"Honey, I'm a bachelor." He pretended to pout. "Nobody washes my dishes but me."

"You must fill your dishwasher once a week."

"That's about right."

"So why aren't you out counting cows or fixing a fence or something?"

"It was supposed to rain. No sense starting something where I'd wind up getting wet."

She removed a sealed bowl from the refrigerator. "It's supposed to have rained all week."

"But I knew that today it would. Remember that broken leg I told you about when you were in the hospital?"

She nodded as she dumped the icing from the bowl into the mixer bowl.

"It gets a little achy when the weather changes. Nothing bad, but enough to tell me when a storm is coming in. It's more reliable than the forecast."

"That's what my grandpa used to say about his rheumatism."

Another family member, another clue. "Does he live in San Angelo too?"

"He did part of the time. He passed away shortly before I left home."

"I'm sorry."

"I'm not." She turned on the mixer.

Whoa! Will was glad she didn't see his startled reaction. That said volumes about the man.

She ran the mixer for a minute, turned it off, raised the beater, removed it, and placed it on a plate on the counter. Glancing over her shoulder, she said, "I guess that's an awful way to feel, but I'm being honest. He was as mean as a rattlesnake with a headache."

Will watched as she tore off about a foot of plastic wrap and laid it on the counter. As she scooped a blob of icing from the mixing bowl, he asked quietly, "Did he beat you, Megan?"

She froze with the large spoon of icing poised in the air. A second later, she plopped the icing on the plastic wrap and dipped more out of the bowl without looking at him. "How did you guess?"

"When you got in the truck after the tornado, you said you felt like you'd been beaten up. Something in your tone gave me the impression that you were speaking from past experience."

She rolled the plastic into a cone shape with a long tail and dropped it into a pastry bag, also cone shaped. After pulling the clear plastic through the metal tip on the end of the bag, she snipped it off.

She walked over to the sink, wet a clean dish towel, and wrung it out thoroughly. "We didn't see him very often. Mom stayed clear of him as much as possible."

"He was her father?"

"Yes. He'd come by occasionally just to give us a bad time. It didn't take much to make him mad as a hornet and earn a smack. When I was fourteen, I didn't get him a cup of coffee fast enough, and he beat the stuffin' out of me before my uncle could stop him."

Too bad the old man was dead. Will tamped down his anger. "How bad were you hurt?"

"A black eye, busted lip, and bruises all over. It could have been worse. He knocked me down and was drawing back to kick me when Uncle Riley tackled him."

"I hope he got jail time."

She shook her head. "Not for that. Mom was too scared of him to call the cops. I wasn't hurt bad enough to need a doctor, so it never got reported."

Will tightened his fingers around the top of the chair. *Calm down.* The last thing she needed was to see how angry he could get. He couldn't believe they hadn't taken her to a doctor.

"What did he go to jail for?"

"A month later, he robbed a convenience store and shot the clerk."

"Did he kill him?"

"No, thank goodness. He wasn't hurt badly. A patrol car was going by, and the

246

officers saw it happening. When Grandpa ran out with a bag of money in one hand, his pistol in the other, they were waiting for him. We all figured if he died in prison it would be from a fight, but it was a massive heart attack."

She leaned against the counter and wiggled a spatula at him. "Enough conversation, Callahan. I have to concentrate on this cake, and I can't do it with you sitting there yakking."

"You're going to turn me out in the rain?" He gave her his best sad hound-dog look. As if to emphasize his point, thunder rumbled and rain pounded the tin roof.

"You won't melt." A tiny smile lifted the corners of her lips.

"I might. Since I'm so sweet and all." He stood and tucked the chair underneath the table. "How 'bout if I wander off into the living room and catch up on world events on the laptop. I'll be quiet as a church mouse."

"Do churches really have mice?" She smiled up at him as he stopped in front of her and rested his hands at her waist. Or what used to be her waist.

"Can't say as I've ever seen any at ours. They must be sneaky as well as quiet."

Did she have any idea how pretty she was?

Or that she had a splatter of icing on her cheek? He reached up and gently brushed it off with his thumb. "Icing."

"Are you sneaky?" She lifted a delicate eyebrow.

"Nope. Unless I'm trying to pull a prank on Chance or Nate. Generally, what you see is what you get."

Her expression softened as she searched his face. "I like that."

Leaning down, he brushed a light kiss on her forehead. "Good."

He headed toward the living room, whistling a happy tune.

"Hush, Will Callahan." Laughter tinted her voice.

"Yes, ma'am." But the tune kept running through his mind.

17

That evening they sat together on the couch, their bare feet resting on pillows on the coffee table. Will was surprised but pleased when Megan let him put his arm around her and tuck her in close. The plan was to watch the baseball game, but five minutes after it started, she was asleep, her head resting on his shoulder. He muted the TV so it wouldn't disturb her and halfway watched the game.

His thoughts kept going back to their earlier discussion. Considering her family background, he was amazed that she'd done so well. Striking out on her own had been dangerous, but maybe not any riskier than staying with her mother. As for her grandfather, dying of a heart attack was too merciful.

Resting his jaw against her hair, he breathed the light flowery fragrance of her shampoo. He couldn't quite pinpoint the scent to a particular flower. It was more like a mixed bouquet, similar to something his mom might have sitting on the dining room table in the spring.

Would his wife enjoy putting fresh flowers on the table? What else would she change in his bachelor pad? He liked his house and had done what he could to make it feel like home. But it needed a woman's touch to give it life. Megan's?

His gaze drifted to her round stomach. He could provide well for Megan and her child. She would never have to worry about having a good place to stay, food to eat, or clothes to wear. Sweet Baby could go to the finest college, have a business, or do anything she wanted.

Equally important, she'd have a daddy who loved her and would keep her safe. Something Megan never had. She'd called him a fixer, and it was an accurate description. Was that what he was trying to do? Fix her life? Was he thinking about marrying her for the wrong reason?

What were the right reasons? Love, certainly. But falling in love didn't mean you were right for each other. Jenna had loved her first husband, or thought she did, and he had almost destroyed her. Of course, Jimmy Don was a selfish jerk who loved only himself. Unlike sweet Megan. Even if he hadn't already seen evidence of a gentle heart and caring soul, the love she had for her baby showed him the kind of woman she was.

He straightened his neck before he got a crick in it, and leaned his head against the back of the couch. Friendship, respect, and compatibility were important in a marriage. As was shared faith. That ranked at the top of his list. He had known Jesus and God for as long as he could remember. She met God in a bar ditch beside the road, and she had earnestly been seeking to know him better ever since.

Will had always believed he couldn't marry without love. He still didn't want to, but if all the other elements were there, would it be wrong? Did that automatically doom the relationship to failure? How did you know you were in love anyway?

He'd asked Chance, but he hadn't been any help. "You just know," his younger brother had proclaimed with honest sincerity. Will guessed Chance was right, for himself anyway. Nate wasn't any help, either. He'd fallen in love with Jenna when he was fifteen, and she'd been the only woman for him ever since.

Megan shifted slightly and laid her hand

on her stomach, but she didn't wake up. The baby must be wiggling around again.

Lord, I need some help here. Guidance and wisdom. If he married Megan, it needed to happen before the baby came. This child deserved to have two parents when she was born. He also didn't want to have to adopt her, like Nate had done with Zach. It hadn't been too big of a hassle because Jimmy Don had agreed to it right away. Still, life would be much simpler if his name was on the birth certificate.

Sweet Baby Callahan. Needed a little work. Will smiled and glanced back at the TV. The Rangers had just made a home run, and here he was thinking about baby names. Sure as shootin' his single days were quickly coming to an end.

And that was more than all right with him.

He noticed the Bible and spiral notebook sitting beside the recliner. Megan had bought her own Bible last week. At her request, Pastor Brad had given her some notes and Scriptures to read to help her learn about Jesus.

He felt a little Holy Spirit nudge to see if she had any questions about what she'd been studying.

She stirred, stretched, and tried to sit up straighter. He moved his arm to make it easier for her. "Hi, Sleeping Beauty."

Leaning her head against the couch, she looked up at him. "Have I been out for long?"

"About twenty minutes. A nice little cat-nap."

"Thanks for letting me snooze."

"Sure." Like he was going to make her stay awake. He motioned toward the Bible. "Been studying?"

"Whenever I have time. Not so much the past few days. When I stop working I fall asleep if I try to read."

"I've done that plenty of times. I try to read my Bible when I first get up, but that doesn't always work if I'm still groggy. Do you have any questions about anything you've read?"

"Is it really so simple? All I have to do to be saved is to believe that Jesus died for me? That he paid for my sins by giving his life?"

"Pretty much. You need to believe that he's the only Son of God." She nodded, making him smile. "And that he came back to life, or in Christian parlance, he rose again. That's how he defeated death and gives us eternal life."

"I believe all that." She leaned forward rather clumsily and picked up her glass of water, taking a long drink. When she settled

253

back, she scooted over a bit and turned toward him. "The Bible says that's what happened, and Pastor Brad says the Bible is the Word of God. God's instruction manual to us."

"That's right."

"I know I'm a sinner, and I asked God to forgive me. But don't I have to do anything else? Nothing is free. How do we earn God's love and forgiveness?"

Will took a moment to sip his iced tea, gathering his thoughts as he set the glass on the end table. "We don't have to earn it. Can't earn it. Had you done anything to cause God to save you from the tornado?"

"No. I asked him to save us, begged him to not let my baby die. I sure didn't deserve it, but Sweet Baby was innocent. I'd never had anything to do with God. I'd never prayed in my life." She smoothed the edge of her top where the hem was turned up. "Mrs. Hoffmann believed in him and talked about how loving he was. I didn't know if he was real or just a myth that she clung to. But I had nowhere else to turn." She broke away from Will's gaze, her expression thoughtful, and rested her hands in her lap. "I had no one else to believe in.

"Up until that day on the highway, I'd never had any reason to think God cared about me. Nobody except Mrs. Hoffman ever did, so why should he?" Looking at him again, she took a deep breath. "You've probably figured out that life was tough when I was a kid."

He reached over and curled his fingers around hers. "Do you want to tell me about it?"

She hesitated and lowered her eyes. "The best meals I had were the ones we got at homeless shelters. The only thing I remember Mom cooking was scrambled eggs, when I was five. She showed me how to do it. From then on, if I wanted eggs — or if she wanted them — it was up to me to make them."

Will stared at her. She couldn't be serious. "How did you reach the stove?"

"Climbed up on a chair. Just like I did to wash the dishes. We lived in a low-rent apartment complex for a while, and the manager left a chair in the laundry room so I could put clothes in the washing machine and dryer." Somehow, she managed a smile. "Chairs are handy things."

"Yes, they are." He remembered Jenna standing on a chair when she was little, helping their mom make cookies. She'd even had one at the sink to help with the dishes — back when she thought it was fun.

But his mother or Ramona had always been there to supervise, to make sure she was safe. And to help.

"When I was real little, before I started school, we usually had some cold cereal on hand, but not always milk. Most of the time there were eggs, bread, and margarine because Mom liked eggs with toast and jelly. Sometimes she'd make me a peanut butter and jelly sandwich. Or as soon as I could, I'd make it myself. I ate a lot of macaroni and cheese. A box of it would last a couple of days. And Top Ramen."

"No meat? Fruit and vegetables? No candy?"

"Sometimes she'd get a few bananas, but no vegetables. She hated veggies. She avoided sweets because she was afraid she'd get fat. All she had going for her was her looks. So she rarely bought me candy or cookies. Maybe that's why I love desserts now."

"Or it could be because you make such great ones."

She grinned and moved back around to put her feet on the coffee table again. "Thanks. But if I didn't like 'em, I wouldn't go to the trouble of making them."

"Didn't she have money for food?

Couldn't she get food stamps or something?"

"She did get food stamps. They used to come as coupons, and when you bought something, you'd get the change if it didn't take the whole amount. As soon as she got the new allotment, she'd go to several stores and buy a little something in each one."

"So she could get cash back."

She nodded and absently rubbed the bottom of her left foot with her other one. "Party and beer money. When the state switched to a debit-type card, only the amount actually spent could be deducted from the account. So she'd buy groceries for someone else, and they'd pay her seventy-five cents on the dollar."

"Now I understand why you were trying so hard to make it on your own, even though there was help available." He'd done some checking. The state had special programs to help low-income pregnant women.

"The day of the tornado, I had exactly fifty-five dollars and twenty-one cents to my name. I'd already decided that I had to find a shelter because I had just enough gas to get to Abilene. I'd have to fill up the tank again to look for work. If I didn't find a job within a few days, I would have applied for emergency aid. Either way, I was going to apply for medical assistance. I'd been fool-ish not to do it months earlier. When you insisted on taking me to the hospital, I was embarrassed that I hadn't already done it."

"I know. That made me want to help you even more." He ran back over the begin-ning of their conversation. "Getting back to your question — salvation is a gift. We can't do anything to earn it, but we do have to believe it and acknowledge it, which you've done. I suspect, in your own way, you've already asked him to be Lord of your life."

When she frowned slightly, he tried to explain better. "When you make Jesus Lord of your life, it means that he's in charge. You want to live the way he wants you to, and you trust him to guide you by the Holy Spirit and through what you learn in Scrip-ture. You pray and try to get it right. And when you don't, you ask him to forgive you and you try again. He knows we aren't perfect. He's the only one who was. But he does expect us to keep trying to do what's right and live the way he teaches us to. And love him. That's at the top of his wish list because he loves us."

"I haven't put it in those exact words, but I do ask him to guide me. I want to live the way he wants me to, but I think I have a long way to go."

"Believe me, sugar, so do I. Your heart is right, and you're doing the best you can. That's all any of us can do."

"That's a big relief. I see all of you helping with things at church and in the community, and I was afraid I was messing up because I just sit there like a bump on a log."

"No one expects you to pitch in. You're pregnant, remember?"

She laughed softly. "How can I forget. I just don't want people thinking I'm a slouch."

"I'm no expert on mamas-to-be, but I've noticed that even the ones most involved in church activities cut way down about this point. Their main focus is staying healthy, not getting too tired, and delivering a strong, healthy baby." He slid his arm around her and gently pulled her against his side. "And that's what you should be doing. No more big projects."

"There you go, being bossy again." She slipped her fingers between his.

"You know I'm right." He couldn't resist a little teasing. "As usual."

"I don't buy that as usual part, but I'll admit you were right on the wedding cake. It was scary-close to being too much to handle. I won't tackle another one for six months, at least."

"People will remember it. I have no doubt that you'll have folks clamoring for you to make theirs when you're ready to start up again. That's when small town gossip pays off. You let a few people know you're back in business, and before the week's out everybody within twenty miles will know it. When you put it all together tomorrow, it will be spectacular."

She tipped up her head, looking at him with a happy smile. "It is amazing, isn't it."

"Yes, ma'am." He brushed her cheek with his fingertips, and his heart rejoiced at the soft welcome he saw in her eyes. "And so are you."

Leaning down, he did what he'd longed to do for weeks. He kissed her with all the tenderness in his heart.

18

The next morning in the church fellowship hall, Megan shoved the last of four twisted crystal-like plastic pillars straight down into the second layer of the cake. "Almost there," she whispered. Carefully lifting the separator plate holding the third tier, she placed the small feet on the bottom of the plate into the openings of the pillars.

Turning to Will, she pointed to the four remaining pillars and the top tier. "Your turn."

He took a step back and glanced nervously at the cake. "Are you sure you want big-fingered, clumsy me to do it?"

"I'm not worried. Anybody who can build a little Lego car can handle a plate. Besides, you can reach it a lot easier than me. I'm liable to topple the whole thing if I try it."

"Too short." He nodded sagely.

"And too fat. I'm afraid Sweet Baby will kick it over." As she hoped, he laughed. That

should help him relax and not drop anything.

"Don't worry if you knock off a flower or
stick a finger in the icing. I can fix it when I
replace the two rosettes I broke."

"Okay. Tell me what to do."

"I thought you were watching me."

"I was." He grinned unrepentantly. "You.
I wasn't paying much attention to the
details of what you were doing."

She rolled her eyes and motioned him
closer. "See the little marks on top of the
cake?"

He nodded. "Is that where I put the
posts?"

"Yes. I marked each tier with the feet on
the next size plate before putting the cakes
on them."

"Smart."

"It was in the instructions."

"So? Not everybody reads instructions."

She almost pointed out that was a male
thing, but decided it would lead to a playful
argument. One that probably would be fun
any other time, but she needed to focus on
the task at hand. "Just push them straight
down until they're resting on the plate.
Then set the next plate on top of them."

He picked up one of the plastic pieces and
inspected it. "The foot on the plate fits

inside here?"

"You got it. You learn fast, Mr. Callahan."

"Why, thank you, ma'am," he drawled. He followed her directions, putting everything together precisely.

"Perfect. Now to replace the rosettes that fell off." Using the pastry bag, she squeezed a dollop of icing in the empty spot on the first layer and another on the second. Then she took a spare rosette from the plastic container and carefully stuck it onto the cake. She did the same with the second one. After closing the container, she set it in the box with the pastry bag and all the other things she'd brought along in case she needed them.

"Now, add this to the top. Lindsey's mom saved it from her wedding cake." She handed him the white plastic circular platform with a bride and groom standing arm in arm beneath an arch of tiny silk flowers. It was in remarkable condition. Lindsey loved old things, especially family heirlooms. It was perfect. "Center it and press down a little so the icing secures it."

Suddenly, a wave of sadness surprised her. She'd never have a wedding cake or a fancy wedding. Despite Will's sweet words and his interest, she knew she'd never have a wedding at all. She'd learned long ago that dreams didn't come true. She'd be a fool to allow herself even the tiniest glimmer of hope that this one would.

Will completed the task, caught her hand, and drew her back a few steps to have a good view of the cake as a whole. It was so beautiful, Megan didn't know whether to laugh or cry.

He slid his arm around her waist and gave her a gentle hug. "It really is amazing."

"Thank you." She stared at her creation in wonder. "I did it. I really did it." Smiling up at him, she slid her arm around his waist too. "But I couldn't have put it together without your help. Or your encouragement yesterday. I was about to have a total melt-down."

"See, we make a good team."

"We did on this. Did you bring your camera?"

"Yep. Got it right here." He patted his shirt pocket.

She moved her arm and stepped away from his hold. "I need to clean up the mess before we take a picture."

He reached the cake table before she did and picked up the box with all her supplies. "You wanted this in the kitchen, right?"

"Yes, in case something happens and I need to make another repair before the reception. I'll put the cake boxes in there too. They'll want to save the top tier, and there might be some cake left over."

"Don't bet on it." He followed her into the kitchen. "If a cake is good, some of us aren't shy about taking seconds if there are pieces sitting there. If yours is half as good as it looks, it will disappear pronto. It's the prettiest wedding cake I've ever seen."

"Thank you." She set the cake boxes back in a corner of the counter. "But have you seen many wedding cakes?"

"Seen and tasted." He put her supplies alongside the boxes. "I've been to so many weddings since high school that I'm an expert."

"On weddings or cakes?" She led the way through the door, then walked beside him to the long rectangular tables.

"Mostly food in general, though I could tell you that you don't have a Texas wedding outdoors at four in the afternoon in August, and that nobody needs ten bridesmaids and groomsmen. A normal wedding would be half over by the time everybody gets down the aisle."

"So how many have you gone to?" She moved the groom's cake over a couple of inches so it was centered on its table.

"More than I can count."

Megan looked up, expecting to see that teasing glint in his eye that always made her smile. He was serious.

She didn't know what to say. She had only attended two, both people she'd worked with. What a pitiful statement about her lack of friends.

"There were a few a year during college, and five the summer we graduated. The rest have been scattered out over the years. At the last one, Dalton and I were the only single guys our age there." He stuffed his hands in the pockets of his jeans and slowly looked around the room. "By five o'clock all my buddies will be hitched. Not that it will be all that different. I've been the fifth wheel at most get-togethers for a while now."

"Why don't you take a date?" Surely he had a little black book — or a long list of available women in his cell phone.

He pulled his hands from his pockets. "I haven't dated anyone in two years."

"You're kidding. Why not?"

"Nobody I wanted to go with." He met her gaze. "Until now."

The enormity of him escorting her to the wedding hit her. It would cause a gossip frenzy of major proportions. But that paled against the importance he placed on their relationship. She swallowed hard, then whispered, "Why me?"

"Because I —"

"Aha! Caught you." Laughing, Jenna swept into the room, carrying a box of short vases filled with fresh bouquets to add to the centerpieces on the guest tables. Lindsey and Emily were right behind her with more.

Lindsey spotted the cake and let out a squeal that made Will laugh and shake his head. He winked at Megan. "I think she likes it."

The three intruders practically tossed the boxes on a nearby table and raced across the fellowship hall. For a second, Megan thought Lindsey might plow right into the cake, but she stopped about five feet away, her mouth open in awe.

Tears misted the bride-to-be's eyes. "It's incredible. I knew it would be pretty, but it's even better than I'd expected." She turned and hugged Megan tightly. "Oh, sorry. I shouldn't have squeezed you so tight."

"It's okay. You didn't hurt anybody."

Lindsey laughed and looked at the cake again. "That's good." She walked over to the groom's table and shook her head.

Uh-oh. Megan glanced at Will, spotting a frown. "Did I do something wrong?"

"Goodness, no. It's perfect." Lindsey's smile lit up her face. "Dalton will be so proud of it. Megan, I'm blown away. I should be paying you twice what you asked for."

"Next time I'll up my price." Megan grinned, and Lindsey giggled.

"There won't be a next time. Not for me anyway." Lindsey moved over a step as Jenna and Emily joined her. "But seriously, for this kind of work, you can charge more."

Jenna studied the groom's cake, then turned back to the wedding cake. "I think we've lost our assistant."

"Not for a while." Will crossed his arms, his gaze flickering from his sister to Megan. "No big projects until after Sweet Baby is born, and her mama has fully recovered." How could such a quietly uttered command echo in the large room?

Megan caught an amused glance pass between Jenna and Emily. They clearly expected some fireworks.

"I'm just sayin' what she told me last night. Her decision." He uncrossed his arms and met his sister's grin with an expression of pure innocence. "No pressure from me."

"Not much," said Megan. "But he's right. I don't intend to do anything like this for a while."

"I know a couple of people who will be disappointed after they see these." Lindsey walked over and picked up a couple of vases and bouquets. "But you're being smart. Which is what we need to be. We have to get these set out and start getting ready."

Will checked his watch. "It's six hours until the ceremony starts."

"But only five until the photographer starts taking pictures. We have to hustle."

"We have to add the water," Emily reminded her, plucking the vases from her hands.

"We can do it," said Will. "Y'all run on home."

"Thanks." Jenna gave him a hug. "Just put them on the silver mats. Then take Megan home so she can rest."

With waves and happy chatter, the three rushed out the door.

Will chuckled and picked up one of the boxes, taking it into the kitchen, with Megan tagging along. "See, I'm not the only Callahan who tells people what to do."

"No comment. I'll add some water to these, if you'll bring in the rest."

"Got it covered."

They worked together, filling the vases half full and carrying them out two at a time to the tables. Megan rearranged some of the turquoise and silver ribbons spiraling around the vases. A variety of flowers made up the centerpieces, so no two were exactly alike. When they finished, they stood at one end and surveyed the room.

"Looks good." Will caught her hand and gently tugged her toward the cake tables. "We didn't get pictures." He took several of the wedding cake from different angles and four of the groom's cake. "Now, come over here and let me take some with you and your creations."

Megan shook her head. "No, thanks."

"You can use it in an advertisement some day. To remind people of who you are and what you're capable of. Go stand behind the table."

"I hate having my picture taken, but you have a point." She moved around behind the table and stood beside her masterpiece.

When he called "Say cheese" in a high pitched voice, she laughed and he snapped the picture. "Good one. But let's get a few more." He took two more there and two with the other cake.

"Enough already. Let's get out of here before the caterers arrive."

"Yeah, they might put us to work." Will slid the camera into his pocket and rested his hand at her back as they walked toward the main door of the fellowship hall. "Have I told you that I'm proud of you?"

"About five times. I appreciate it."

"Just tellin' the truth, sugar."

The cautious part of her mind told her to be careful, but she ignored it. She would accept this man's praise and hold it close in her heart.

Later that afternoon, Megan did one last check in the full-length mirror that someone along the way had left in the bedroom. She couldn't see Nate or Dalton hanging it on the wall, though maybe they'd used it to check their appearance before a big evening out.

"I'm going on a date with Will Callahan," she whispered, halfway expecting to wake up any minute. She studied her reflection in the mirror. Would he be pleased at the way she looked?

Jenna had loaned her a knee-length maternity dress she'd kept after Zach was born. Teal chiffon over satin, it was sleeveless with an empire waist and a modest V-neck ruffled bodice. The color was perfect for her, and the style made her feel feminine and pretty despite beginning to look as big as a house. She'd never worn anything so fine.

A pair of black dressy sandals with one-inch heels came with the dress. Normally, they would have been a half-size too big, but since her feet were slightly swollen, they worked fine. Megan decided a necklace would be too much with the ruffles but added some dangling, silver filigree earrings that she'd found on sale the year before. She'd paid only five dollars for them, but they were every bit as pretty as the seventy-five-dollar ones in the fine jewelry department.

"Lord, please don't let me do anything stupid to embarrass Will." Thinking back to that first Sunday at church, her stomach started to churn. "Don't let anyone make snide comments about us being together. Don't let anybody ruin this. Please."

She heard him drive up. He really was treating this as a special occasion, going to the front door instead of the back. Taking a deep breath, she picked up her small black purse, walked down the hall, and opened the door. She stared at him as he walked across the yard.

Will Callahan was a handsome man under any circumstances, but decked out in black dress pants, black boots, crisp white shirt, silver brocade vest, gray and black tie — with a diamond tie tack — the man was heart-stopping gorgeous.

He was also driving a sporty model silver Cadillac.

He stepped up on the porch and let his gaze run slowly over her, whistling softly. When he looked back up at her face, his eyes were alight with admiration. "You look terrific."

"So do you." Surprised that her voice didn't sound all weak and flustered, she opened the door and stepped back. "Come in while I lock the back door."

"I'll get it." He was halfway across the room before she could say anything.

"Thanks."

"No problem. Do you need anything from in here?"

"The apron that's hanging over the chair back. In case I have to work on the cake."

He picked up the apron and strolled back to her side. "It should be okay, shouldn't it?"

"As long as nobody sticks a finger in the icing or knocks off a flower, or heaven forbid, hits the table and knocks it over."

"It will be fine. Mom said Lindsey had assigned a couple of her high school cousins to guard both of them. She was afraid a few of the younger cousins might try to swipe some icing. Guess they did that at her sister's wedding."

"I wish you hadn't told me that."

He made a face. "Sorry. Don't worry about it. They have everything under control." They walked out onto the porch. "You have your keys?" When she nodded, he twisted the lock on the door and pulled it closed.

"Where did you get the car?"

"From my garage." He cupped her arm as they walked down the steps. "I've had it for three years but don't drive it much."

No dates, she thought.

"I couldn't ask you to ride to the wedding in my dusty pickup." He opened the passenger door. "I figure this car will be more comfortable for you from now on."

She turned around to sit down but paused and laid her hand on his chest. "You are such a sweet, thoughtful man."

He grinned and held her hand in place. "Keep talkin'."

"Nope. I don't want to boost your ego too much."

He released her hand, hovering beside her in case she needed help getting into the car. "Some folks think it's highly inflated already."

"Some folks are jealous." She sat down and swung her legs and feet into the car, shifting on the seat. "This is easier to get into than the pickup. But you don't drive it around the ranch, do you?"

"Strictly a road car, even if the roads between here and the highway are dirt." He walked around and got in. "If you want to drive anywhere else on the ranch, we'll have to use the pickup."

"I can still manage it for a while. I enjoy going with you to check the cattle. I love to watch the calves."

"So do I." He fastened his seat belt, as did she, though it was becoming a little trickier to accomplish. Pulling onto the road, he said, "I did some more research on the wind turbine idea. I've decided not to push it with Dad, mainly because I don't want to ruin our view."

"A wind farm has some artistic appeal." Megan studied the pasture as they drove by. "But it can't compare to this scenery."

"I did make some headway with the old man on testing the new grasses."

"How did you convince him?"

A tiny smile hovered on his mouth. "Told him I wouldn't bug him about the wind turbines if he'd let me try it. I also pointed out that if he didn't let me do something with what I've learned, he wasted a whole bunch of money sending me off to college."

She laughed and turned her attention

back to the road. "I'm sure that gave him something to think about."

"Think about is right. He cogitated on it for a week before he gave in."

"Did he say why he's resisted you so much on this?"

"Not exactly, but I got the impression he wanted to make sure it was important enough that I'd keep after him about it. I expect he did some research on his own to see if I knew what I was talking about. Guess I passed the test."

"Negotiating might have made a difference too. Suggesting three things you were interested in but dropping one of them. In real estate it was often good to have some things we could throw away during the negotiation process. It made us seem more reasonable."

"And kept the other party from feeling like they were being run over by a charging bull." Will stopped at the highway and checked for traffic before pulling out onto the pavement. "Good point. I'll have to keep that in mind when I bring up the cattle auction again."

They chatted about ranching all the way to town. If she didn't understand something, he explained it without making her feel dumb. He had a college degree, and she'd never finished high school, yet he treated her as an equal. No man had ever shown her that much respect.

After they arrived at the church, Will slipped on his suit coat before he came around and helped her out of the car. They were early so she could check on the cake, but plenty of people still saw them. Dalton's cousin, Kim, who had made the scene that first Sunday, briefly scowled at her before smiling sweetly at the attractive man with her.

But it was Kim's date that sent Megan's heart rate into hyperdrive. Mike Craig. He was taller and had filled out some, but she had absolutely no doubt who he was. She'd daydreamed about him too much when she was fifteen to forget him. *What is he doing here? Please, God, don't let him notice me.* She took a deep breath and tried to calm her racing heart.

"Guess we won't have to worry about Kim today," Will said quietly as they approached the building.

"Good. Do you know the guy she's with?" Megan was relieved her voice didn't give her away.

"No. Dalton mentioned that Kim had a date, but I don't remember his name. He's Lindsey's aunt's stepson by her third marriage or something like that. They met when the families got together in April for a barbecue. Who knows, maybe they'll make a match." He opened the church door for her. "That happens at weddings, you know."

"So I've heard." She didn't know how Mike had turned out. He'd seemed like a nice guy, if a bad-boy wannabe, when her cousin Josh had introduced them. He'd hung out some with her cousin, but as far as she knew, he never joined in Josh's criminal activities. If the good guy won out over the bad boy, he deserved somebody better than Kim. Preferably someone who lived a thousand miles away.

Thankfully, her foes weren't in the foyer. There would be a big crowd at the wedding. Maybe she could keep from running into him.

Will and Megan visited with a few people before they slipped away to check the cakes. Everything there was fine, with Lindsey's cousins protecting them. The caterers bustled around the kitchen and fellowship hall, finishing the last-minute preparations for the dinner buffet.

As they walked back down the hall to the foyer, Megan excused herself to make a pit stop. She went into the ladies' room and almost collided with Kim. "Oh, sorry."

"Boy, you need a lot of room these days."

I'm not that big! Megan forced a smile. *Don't lose your temper.* "Gaining every day, just like Dr. Cindy ordered."

Kim ran a comb through her hair, which was more golden blonde today than platinum. "I see Will brought the Caddie." She met Megan's gaze in the mirror. "And you."

"That's right. Special occasion calls for a special car. Who's the handsome guy you're with?"

"Mike Craig." Kim slipped the pink comb back into her purse. "He's an oil man from Angelo. Not as wealthy as Will by any means, but he's nice. And he likes me." She snapped the purse shut with a faint grimace and a firm click. "Which is more than I can say for Will."

Kim opened the door, then looked back at Megan with a resigned expression. "You're lucky. Will has always had a soft spot for strays."

19

Walking back to meet Will, Megan tried not to let Kim get to her. The woman's words had been filled with more regret than spite. Unfortunately, they still hit Megan's weak spot. How many stories had the Callahans told about Will bringing home some scrawny dog that someone had turned loose on the highway? He didn't have a pet now. Was that why he felt so compelled to take care of her?

Since more than half of the people attending the wedding knew both the bride and groom equally well, the guests were invited to sit on either side of the church. Chance escorted her, with Will following them, to a pew five rows from the front. Dub, Sue, Emily, Ramona, and Ace joined them a few minutes later.

Soon the church was full. Nate escorted Lindsey's mother to her seat in the front row. Chance came in a minute later with Peg Renfro on his arm and Dalton's dad right behind them. Dalton and Pastor Brad entered through a door beside the baptismal and walked to the center front below the stage.

The organist switched to a different tune, and Jenna came down the aisle, escorted by Nate. As always, she looked lovely in a simple floor-length lavender satin gown trimmed in white lace. Nate was dashing in his black tuxedo. When they reached the front of the sanctuary, they walked up the platform steps together and split off to each side of the stage.

Will grinned and whispered, "He didn't even wear a tux to his own wedding."

Lindsey's youngest sister, who was eighteen and wore an identical gown, came next with Chance as her escort. The bride's middle sister and Dalton's brother finished off the row of attendants.

When Megan heard murmurs and soft chuckles drifting through the crowd, she knew Zach was making his entrance. They turned to see him and Lindsey's two-year-old niece coming down the aisle. Zach looked adorable in his tux. Wearing a serious, determined expression, he held the pillow with the fake rings out in front of him just as Jenna had taught him.

The golden-haired little girl beside him

was an angel in pink organdy ruffles. Every so often, she tossed a few handfuls of pink and lavender flower petals on the carpet. Halfway down the aisle, she stopped and looked around wide-eyed at the huge throng of adults. Zach went a little farther before he realized she wasn't with him. He ran back to her, tucked the pillow under one arm, and carefully took hold of her hand, leading her the rest of the way.

"That a boy," Will murmured with a nod and a bright-eyed smile.

Zach helped the flower girl up the steps and escorted her to her mother, who was Lindsey's matron of honor. Afterward, he ran to Nate.

The organist began the wedding march, and everyone stood, turning to watch Lindsey and her father come down the aisle. The bride was radiant. Her dad's smile wobbled slightly.

After they passed Will and Megan's row, she found herself staring straight into Mike Craig's eyes. Surprise and recognition flashed across his face.

Feeling like a cornered animal, she fought down a jolt of panic and turned toward the front of the church. She barely noticed Lindsey's father kiss the bride's cheek and place her hand in Dalton's.

Running was out of the question, though that was her first impulse. *Ignore him. Brazen it out if he tries to talk, pretend you don't have any idea who he is.* That would have been easy two months earlier. She wasn't sure she could pull it off now. Somehow, being in a church made it that much worse. But she had to. Didn't she?

It wasn't only that he might reveal her identity to Will and the others. That would be bad enough. But if he were still friends with her cousin and told him where she was, it would be a disaster. Josh would tell her mother, and Jackie would find her, demanding money and scheming how they could bilk the Callahans out of more.

Her mind spinning, she observed the wedding in a fog. The only thing that clearly registered was when Zach came running back down the aisle to sit with Dub and Sue. She thought the flower girl's daddy had rescued her from center stage at the same time.

Kim said that Mike was a successful oilman. Surely that meant he had broken ties with Josh years ago. Possibly he wasn't as much of a threat as she feared.

Much too soon, the ceremony was over. Beaming, Dalton and Lindsey walked back down the aisle as husband and wife. The others on the stage followed them out, with Nate and Jenna stopping briefly to take Zach with them. Chance and Nate came back and escorted out the newlyweds' parents. Then they were back, releasing the rows one at a time.

Megan slipped her hand around Will's arm as they stepped into the aisle, earning a smile. Good thing he didn't realize she was hanging onto him because her legs were so shaky. She had to avoid any kind of scene, couldn't do anything that would ruin Lindsey's wedding.

They stopped in the foyer to visit with some friends Will hadn't seen in a while. By the time they reached the fellowship hall, the room was crowded. Dalton and Lindsey had chosen not to have an official receiving line but planned to go from table to table to greet folks during the reception.

Zach spotted Will and Megan and came racing over to meet them, dodging another couple on the way. He'd already shed his coat and tie. Will scooped him up and gave him a hug. "Good job in the wedding, buddy."

Zach rested his arm on Will's shoulder. "Thank you."

Megan smiled at him. Jenna and Nate had been teaching him manners, and he was doing well. "It was good of you to go back for Elizabeth."

The little boy nodded. "I had to help her 'cause she got scared. Mommy said that might happen, so I was 'pared."

"Did it bother you to have all those people looking at you?" asked Will, nodding to his sister across the room.

"Nope. I was up there at Christmas."

Will looked at Megan. "He was in the Christmas play."

"I was a sheep boy."

"Shepherd," Will corrected.

"Yeah. Shepherd." Zach wiggled, wanting down, but his uncle held onto him. "I want a snack."

"We'll have some supper in a few minutes." Will turned to the buffet tables where some of the church ladies were setting out the food. "Can you wait that long?"

Frowning, the little boy shook his head. "Hungry."

"Let's go see if your mom has something stashed away for you."

Megan led the way, weaving awkwardly through a maze of tables and chairs. Will's siblings had picked a table where Nate could put his back against the wall and have a good view of the room. She had noticed that habit before, and Will had explained that it was something left over from the war. Nate was doing pretty well dealing with the PTSD now, but Will warned her not to approach him from behind without calling out a greeting several yards away. More than one guy had been decked after they came up behind him and startled him.

When they joined the others, she smiled at Jenna. "You have a hungry boy."

"I expected that. I hurried in here with him so he could run around a little before it got crowded. He'd stood, then sat, for as long as he could." Jenna took a slice of Colby cheese from her purse as Will set Zach down in the chair beside her. "Will this hold you over?"

"Uh-huh."

"You need to stay in the chair to eat it." Jenna peeled the plastic off the cheese and handed it to him. "Take your time and chew it good."

"Okay."

Megan watched Jenna and her son, hoping that she would do as well with Sweet Baby. She desperately wanted to be a good mother, but she'd never been around one until she met the Callahans. Though Mrs. Hoffmann had been sweet and kind to Megan, she'd never had children. If reading books about child rearing helped, then she should be an expert. The few she'd had before the tornado were long gone, but she'd bought more at the bookstore in Abilene and had devoured them.

Still, she expected nothing compared to experience, unless it was being around someone like Sue or Jenna. Dr. Cindy was right. The Callahans — all of them — were a good support group. She'd learned so much about how a real family worked by simply watching them.

They weren't anything like her totally dysfunctional family, but neither were they perfect. They got tired and grumpy and even argued now and then, particularly Dub and Will. But at the end of the day, or sometimes after a few days, they resolved their differences or silently agreed to disagree. She hoped Will's test pastures were a success and proved to Dub that he knew what he was talking about.

She wished she could be there when those new grasses grew tall and green next year, but by then, more than likely she'd be on her way . . . to somewhere. *Lord, give me enough time with them to learn to care for my baby, to learn how to raise her in a way that pleases you.* She skimmed the crowd but didn't see Mike Craig. *I know I'm selfish and probably in the wrong, but please, God, don't let him give me away.* There was so much he could let slip about her relatives without even meaning to cause a problem.

Pastor Brad offered the blessing, then directed folks to eat whenever they were ready. There were two buffets on opposite sides of the room, set up so people could go along both sides of the tables. The lines moved smoothly, enabling Megan and Will to return to their seats faster than she'd expected.

They dined on prime rib, roasted potatoes, petite green beans, and fresh melon. Megan enjoyed the food, though her worry over Mike distracted her from talk around the table. The room was so noisy from laughter and conversations that she doubted anyone noticed.

After they were finished eating, Will carried their plates to the plastic tubs by the kitchen and picked up two more glasses of punch on his way back. He settled in beside her with a smile. "You doin' all right?"

"Stuffed." She took a drink of the punch and sighed in semi-contentment. Life would be wonderful right then if the ghost from her past wasn't lurking somewhere in the room. Still, if everything blew up in her face in the next few minutes, she had much to be thankful for. The past month with these dear people had been a blessing, and one of the best in her life.

God had given her many gifts since that day on the highway. Her's and Sweet Baby's lives for starters. Forgiveness and salvation. Security and provision for the time being. People who cared for her. She glanced at Will. Perhaps a man who could take her and her child into his heart forever.

But would he love her if he knew the whole truth about her family? She didn't think she'd out-and-out lied to them, though she might have. She'd dodged being totally honest so many times. Was that the same thing?

She decided that if Mike approached her, she wouldn't hightail it to the ladies' room and stay there until everybody left like she wanted to. Nor would she lie about who she was. She'd just try not to go into too much detail and pray he did the same.

Dalton and Lindsey finished chatting with folks at the next table and moved to theirs.

"You want to sit down and rest a minute?" asked Will, getting up and offering Lindsey his chair.

"Thanks." She eased down on the seat, being careful not to rumple her dress too much. "Is that glass clean?"

"Yes." Emily handed it to Dalton, who

poured his bride some water from the pitcher on the table.

Lindsey downed the whole glassful. "That's better. I've talked more in the past hour than I do all day at the bank."

"Have you figured out where he's taking you on your honeymoon?" asked Jenna, who was sitting to Megan's right.

Lindsey leaned toward her. "Lake Travis. Dalton has a friend who has a beautiful vacation house on the lake. It will be wonderful, a whole week to relax and recover from all this in peace and quiet." Smiling, she pushed away from the table. "Mama is giving me the high sign."

Dalton winked at Megan and held out his arm to Lindsey. "Come on, Miz Renfro, showtime."

"Don't you dare smash cake in my face." She hooked her arm through his.

"Me? You're the one who's been threatening to stuff it up my nose."

"Dalton Renfro, you know I wouldn't do that. Though I might smear it around a little." Laughing together, so obviously in love and happy, they strolled to the end of the room.

Dalton's brother waited for them, microphone in hand. "I'd like to offer a toast to the bride and groom. Lindsey and Dalton, may you always be as happy as you are today. May your love grow stronger with each passing year. And may God bless you with much joy and a long life together."

Before people lifted their glasses to take a sip of punch or water, Megan heard many of them softly murmur "amen." What a difference between this wedding, where God was the center of their union, and the other two she had attended, where he was not.

Instead of going right for the knife to cut the cake, Dalton took the microphone from his brother.

"Lindsey and I want to thank each one of you for coming today and for sharing our joy. We're blessed to have so many friends." He grinned at the four tables filled with his family and the ten containing Lindsey's. "And family." He paused a moment as laughter skittered across the room.

"We also want to thank everyone who helped us put on this shindig. Pastor Brad for his wise counsel beforehand and uplifting words during the ceremony. My buds who dressed up in monkey suits to hang out up front with me. And thanks, Zach, for rescuing Elizabeth when she got a little overwhelmed." He gave the little boy a thumbs-up, and Zach gave him one back, making folks laugh again.

"Of course, I mustn't forget the lovely ladies who stood up with my beautiful bride. Also the ladies who decorated and kept the buffet tables, coffeepot, and punch bowl full. I'd also like for you to give a hand to the folks from Mary Lou's Catering out of Abilene for the delicious meal."

During the applause, he passed the microphone to Lindsey, who thanked the organist and the young woman who sang a solo. "I'm sure I'll think of others later . . . oh yes, I can't forget Buds and Blooms for all the beautiful flowers." Lindsey smiled at the florist. "I'm sure y'all wish we'd get on with it so you can have some of the cake, but I have a little story to share with you about this wonderful creation. Isn't it beautiful?"

The applause touched Megan's heart. Most people weren't merely clapping to be polite. Judging by their expressions, they truly appreciated how pretty the wedding cake was.

"Two weeks ago, the bakery that was supposed to make our cakes had a fire and couldn't do them. I called all over the area and couldn't find anyone who would. In case you haven't noticed, there are a lot of weddings in June. Then I thought about my friend Megan. She's new to the area, but she's made some wonderful desserts for functions at the museum, including a cake that was a perfect replica of a patchwork sampler quilt." Several of the locals nodded and sent glances her way. "She saved the day, making both our cakes on terribly short notice. Megan, would you please stand up and take a bow?"

Heat flooded her face. She really didn't want to stand up in front of all these people. Being the center of attention made her uncomfortable at any time. Knowing Mike would be able to pinpoint where she was sitting filled her with dread. But it would be impolite if she refused.

When she started to get up, Will slid her chair back slightly to make it easier. Popping up and back down quickly would have been her preference, but that wasn't possible these days. Still, she stood only for a few seconds, long enough to acknowledge Lindsey's kindness and to raise a few eyebrows when people noticed how pregnant she was.

She sat down, and Will put his arm around her, giving her a hug right there in front of everyone. Her face grew even hotter, but when he left his arm around her shoulders, she didn't pull away.

Amid cameras flashing, Dalton and Lindsey held the knife together and cut the first piece, two chocolate layers with strawberry mousse filling. They fed each other a bite and managed to get most of it inside their mouths instead of on their faces. Then their aunts took over to serve everyone else, two at the wedding cake and one at the groom's cake.

Will and Nate pushed back from the table at the same time. Grinning, Chance was right behind them. "Shall we bring you some cake, ladies?"

"By all means," said Jenna. Emily nodded.

"I want cake too." Zach started to get down from his chair, but Nate stopped him.

"I'll bring you a piece, buddy. You'd better stay here. It looks like we're going to have a stampede, and you might get squished."

"A big one." Zach held his hands wide apart.

Nate laughed and ruffled his hair. "That would be half a layer. Don't worry, you'll have plenty."

Will rested his hand on Megan's shoulder and leaned down. "You want a piece, don't you?"

"Yes. Guess I'd better see how it tastes." She was nervous, but there was no reason to be. She'd made the cakes and fillings before. They would be fine. She hoped. She didn't think she'd left anything out. "If they're cutting the second layer from the bottom — white with pineapple mousse — I'd like to try that. Otherwise, whatever is available is fine."

Less than ten minutes later, Will set their dessert plates on the table.

Before he pulled out his chair, Mike Craig walked up.

20

Stay calm. Act like it's no big deal. Not easy to do when Megan's heart pounded like a jackhammer. Had he purposely waited until Will returned? Was that good? Or bad? The two men shook hands and introduced themselves.

"Dalton mentioned you were dating Kim," said Will.

"We've gone out a few times, though I don't get up this way as often as we'd both like." Mike stepped aside so a woman could walk between the tables. "This sounds a little weird, but I came over here mainly to meet the pretty lady who made the cake."

"You planning on needin' one soon?" Will asked dryly.

Mike laughed and looked down at Megan as she glanced up at them. "No." He nodded politely to her. "Excuse me, ma'am. I know Lindsey said your name was Megan, but I can't get over how much you look like someone I used to know. Did you ever live in San Angelo?"

Will's eyebrows shot up.

"Yes, I did. Hi, Mike. I thought I recognized you earlier, but I wasn't sure." *Liar.* She swallowed hard and managed a semblance of a smile.

His face broke into a wide grin. "I knew it. You're prettier than ever." He focused on Will. "May I join y'all for a few minutes?"

"Fine with me, as long as Megan doesn't mind." His eyes narrowed slightly as he looked at her.

"You'll need to scrounge up another chair." *Please, Will, stay close.*

He quickly put that particular worry to rest. He was already pulling over an empty chair from the table next to them and aiming it at a spot between Jenna and her. Jenna scooted over to make room, and relief washed through her. He wasn't about to let another guy boot him out of his place beside her.

Mike thanked Jenna and Will, and greeted everyone else at the table. Chance and Nate leaned over to shake his hand and introduce themselves and their wives. Then he turned his full attention to her. "What happened to you? All I heard was that you'd taken off."

Will sat down and casually put his arm

around her shoulders. She shifted slightly, leaning against his side. His closeness gave her strength, and the big hand gently cupping her shoulder calmed her. The slight flare in Mike's eyes told her that he didn't miss Will's possessive move, and her response to it.

"My mother was driving me crazy, so I struck out on my own. Went to Austin. I've been there ever since. Well, until about a month ago."

"I could tell your home life was rough." He frowned and shook his head. "I wanted to help you, but I couldn't see any way to do it." He glanced at Will, his lips twisting with regret. "I was twenty-two and she was fifteen."

She figured Will was thinking "jail bait."

Mike looked back at her. "If you'd been older, I would have asked you out."

"If I'd been older, I wouldn't have been there."

He nodded and smiled ruefully. "When I saw you in the sanctuary, I asked Kim about you. She told me about the tornado. Going through that must have been awful. Kim said you're living with the Callahans."

"I stayed with them a few days, but now I have a house of my own at the ranch. I'm working for them." She expected Kim also told him that she wasn't married.

"Good. I'm glad to hear you're doing okay." He paused, his expression thoughtful. "Have you talked to any of your family lately?"

"No. I haven't had any contact with them since I left eight years ago, and I don't want any now."

"I understand."

"I've heard a few things through the grapevine." She kept up with them through various online sites. Public records — weddings, divorces, obituaries, arrests, and court records — told her all she wanted to know.

"I ran into Josh about a month ago at a convenience store." He watched her closely.

"He's back in San Angelo?" That should tell him she knew her cousin had been in prison.

"Yes. He's been back almost a year. He's helping his dad, though I don't know what they're doing. To be honest I was only half listening. I was late for an appointment and stopped to grab a sandwich. The cashier was talking to me at the same time, so I didn't catch everything Josh said. I don't know if they're working for someone else or if they're in business for themselves. There was something about covering his dad's territory and being on the road a lot."

They're rustling cattle! Megan's heart began to pound all over again, and her throat went dry. Her grandfather and Uncle Riley had stolen cattle off and on for a few years. They'd gotten caught and gone to jail when she was in elementary school.

She needed to change the subject pronto. "I talked to Kim earlier. She was bragging on you."

"Tallying up my assets is more like it." When he smiled, Megan caught a glimpse of the mischievous guy she'd once had a crush on. "I took over Dad's oil business a few years back when he decided to retire. We're busier than a boomtown saloon. Lindsey gave me fair warning about Kim, but I like her anyway. I just don't put up with her nonsense.

"Well, I'd better get movin'. I'm supposed to be fetching some cake." He stood and glanced at Megan's round stomach, his expression growing serious. "I hope everything turns out well for you, M.B. Oh, sorry, I forgot." A twinkle danced in his eyes. "I like Megan better."

"So do I." She stood too, and he leaned down so he could hear her over loud laughter from a nearby table. "Please don't tell anyone that I'm here."

"I won't. The best thing you ever did was get away from that bunch."

"You too." She wondered when he'd come to his senses.

"I only hung around because of you."

That was a surprise. "It's good to see you, Mike."

He gave her a little hug and murmured in her ear, "Hang on to Callahan. I hear he's a good man."

As he walked away, she sat down and glanced around the table. Bless Zach's sweet little heart. Totally focused on his dessert, he was the only one who wasn't dying of curiosity about the exchange between her and Mike.

"It really is a small world," said Nate.

"Isn't it?" She picked up her fork, wishing that was the end of it, knowing it wouldn't be.

"There are several folks from San Angelo here, but it's a big town. It's amazing that you'd run into an old acquaintance." Chance ate his last bite of groom's cake. He leaned close to Emily and whispered something in her ear. When she looked across the room, he swiped a bite of wedding cake from her plate.

"Chance Callahan, you stop that." Emily playfully swatted his hand.

"Aw, darlin', you have to share. There's not going to be any of it left, and I wanted to taste it." He turned his attention to Megan. "Jenna's piece had chocolate mousse filling, and Emily's has strawberry mousse. But both of them came from the bottom layer. I watched Lindsey's aunt cut them. How did you do that?"

She laid her fork down without taking a bite. "Because the bottom layer is so big, it's made using half-circle pans. It takes four half-circle cakes for the bottom since each layer is two cakes high. So I used different fillings for each half, then put them together on the plate so they looked like one big round layer and iced them."

"Smart."

"I just followed directions." She picked up her fork again. The white cake with pineapple mousse tasted even better than she'd hoped it would.

"So how did you know Mike?" Chance turned his attention back to her.

"He and my cousin Josh were friends. I met him about six months before I left home."

Will had waited to eat his dessert. If he wondered why she didn't say anything about Mike when they first saw him, he kept it to himself. "So why did he call you M.B.?"

"That's what everybody called me growing up."

"Why?" Jenna finished wiping Zach's face and hands with a damp lavender paper napkin and helped him down from the chair. He immediately ran around a couple of tables to see Dub and Sue.

"Mom was going through a hippie phase when I was born."

"Uh-oh." Will looked down at her, a hint of a smile crinkling the corners of his eyes. "What did she saddle you with?"

"Moon Beam."

"Are you serious?" Emily — and everyone else at the table — stared at her.

"Unfortunately, I am. Thankfully, my first grade teacher took pity on me and called me M.B. from the very first day. All the other teachers followed her lead, so the kids did too."

"Did you change it when you left home?" Jenna asked, giving Nate a smile as he put his arm around her.

Megan nodded. "I couldn't legally change it until I was eighteen, but I told people my name was Megan. My bosses knew otherwise because I had to use my real name on job applications, but they were kind enough not to mention it."

"So when you went to school in Austin,

you were able to start fresh as Megan?" Chance asked, his mild expression not hiding the fact that he was on a fishing expedition.

Will tensed, and Emily glanced at her husband in surprise.

Up until then, none of the Callahans had pushed her for information about herself. She knew Will and Chance were very close. It was natural that Chance would want to look out for his brother.

The noisy people at the table next to them had left. The table on the other side was also empty. No one else would be privy to their conversation. She didn't know if Will had told his family about her mother and grandfather. If he had, and she answered Chance truthfully, it would be another mark against her. How much more would it take to change their kindness to disapproval?

"I never did go back to school, or get my GED. I was too busy working." And trying to survive.

"You were all on your own?" Emily stacked her empty dessert plate on top of her husband's.

Megan knew Emily came from a wealthy family. No one ever actually said so, but Megan put little things together. Did they have any idea what it was like to fend for themselves, to wonder where they'd sleep or when they'd have their next meal?

"Yes. Though I wasn't too proud to ask for help. I didn't want to live on the street. I stayed at a homeless shelter for a couple of months. I had worked before I left and had a little savings. I found a job waitressing pretty fast, but it took time to save up enough to get into a place of my own. My first job in Austin didn't pay too much even with tips, so I worked a lot of double shifts. Later I got on at a large, upscale restaurant and made decent money. But I still worked long hours."

"How did you get into real estate?" Her lack of education didn't appear to bother Chance. That was a big relief.

"One of my regular customers at the restaurant asked me to work for her and a couple of other agents as an assistant. I learned a lot about the business doing their busy work and being a gofer. And I acquired some computer skills by trial and error. The first month I made up advertising flyers, I almost went back to the restaurant.

"I worked mostly days and had weekends off for the first time ever. That's when I took the cake decorating classes. Later, I took some online real estate classes and got my license."

"And you lost some of your free evenings and weekends," said Jenna. "I had a friend in Dallas who was in real estate. She worked all kinds of hours. Do you think you'll ever go back to it?"

"Not for a long time. I enjoyed it, but I wouldn't want to try to juggle it and take care of a child."

"Speaking of your baby . . ." Jenna grinned at her. "What are you going to name her? Sweet Baby is cute for now, but I don't think she'll want to go through life with it."

That gave them all a laugh. "Definitely not. That would be as bad as Moon Beam. I've been thinking about it but haven't come up with anything I really like."

They started tossing around names, some pretty, some outlandish and only meant to make them laugh. She noticed that Will didn't contribute to the banter, which was unusual.

"Is anything wrong?" she asked quietly as the others hooted about a suggestion Nate had made.

"No. Just considerin'."

"Considering what?"

He leaned close, his breath warm on her ear, and he curled his fingers around hers. "How each one sounds with Callahan."

21

On Monday morning, Will tucked the cash for Megan's van in his pocket and watched Dalton's friend drive it away. He'd thought about trying to add to the money somehow, but he decided it wouldn't be a smart move. If Megan ever found out, she'd throw a hissy fit and insist on giving it back anyway.

He wasn't quite sure what to think of her reaction to his comment on Saturday night about baby names. Longing had filled her countenance, followed by regret before she turned away. She barely talked the rest of the evening, claiming she was tired. He couldn't argue with that. She'd worked way too hard all week, and it had been a long day.

After he took her home, she paid him a hundred dollars toward the cost of her hospital bill from the money she made on the cakes. He told her he didn't want it, but she dug in her heels like a cow pulling against a rope. To keep the peace, he grudgingly accepted her payment and scrawled a receipt on a piece of scratch paper.

When he tried to give her a good night kiss, she shied away — which didn't make a lick of sense because she'd thoroughly enjoyed the one on Friday night.

Will concluded that he'd blown it, pushed her too much with the comment about the baby names. She hadn't seemed to mind him putting his arm around her several times at the reception. She'd even welcomed it, especially when Mike joined them.

Fear had flashed across her face when she saw Mike approaching their table. It vanished so quickly Will thought he'd imagined it. But when he put his arm around her, and she leaned against him, she was definitely sending the other man the message that Will would protect her.

From what? Why was she afraid of Mike? When they first saw him, why hadn't she mentioned that she might know him? What could he do to harm her?

Both Lindsey and Dalton thought highly of him. He was a respected businessman, not some lowlife thug. He must have a clean record, or Dalton wouldn't have been happy about him dating Kim.

Likely Megan was afraid her old friend

would tell her family where she was. Since they appeared to be on good terms when he left their table, he expected Mike had assured her that he wouldn't.

Yet, the nagging thought that she might have been afraid of what he would reveal to them — about her — lurked in the back of his mind. Mike had given them one more piece of the puzzle, a cousin named Josh who was back in town. Back from where? And if she'd had no contact with her family, how had she known her cousin had been gone?

Will climbed in his pickup and started it up. What was it she'd told Mike? *I've heard a few things through the grapevine.*

Things she didn't want to mention in front of the Callahans, and Mike had gotten the message.

"Lord, I wish she'd just sit down and tell me all about her family, about her life. I want to get to know her, to understand what makes her tick. I hate getting these chunks that only leave me asking more questions. I'm trying to trust you here, but her baby is due in eight weeks. The way I see it, we don't have a whole lot of time to get this situation resolved."

It didn't help that he hadn't seen her since Saturday night. She missed church for the first time since arriving in Callahan Crossing. She passed on the family get-together to celebrate Father's Day too. His mom thought maybe she was uncomfortable with it since she'd never had a father.

Will believed there was more to it than that. He hoped she'd worked out whatever was bugging her because he intended to intrude on her space whether she liked it or not.

As he drove around to the back of her house, he was surprised to see her standing by the pasture fence, a small bouquet of wildflowers in her hand. He parked the truck under the chinaberry tree and walked out to join her.

She glanced back at him with a smile. "Good morning."

That was a good start. His mood scooted up a notch.

"Mornin', sugar." He stopped beside her and rested his hand lightly at the small of her back. When she didn't pull away, he breathed a little easier. "What ya lookin' at?"

"Grass, birds, and cows way over yonder. Is that a different pasture?"

"Yes. It's hard to see the fence from here."

"So that's why they never come over this way." She looked up at him. "Why aren't

310

there any cattle in this pasture?"

"In the past, we usually had a cowboy living here, so it was for his horses. Since Nate married Jenna, we haven't needed it for a hired hand. That worked out well when Dalton lost his home in the fire. Not only were we able to provide him with a house, but it gave him a place for his horses too. The grass has grown quite a bit after that good rain, so I could move some cattle in here next week if you'd like."

"What do my likes or dislikes have to do with it?"

"Cattle can get noisy if they're upset about something, and occasionally it might be smelly if the wind blows in the right direction. Most of the time here, it blows the other way."

"I'm from the city, remember? I think I might enjoy a few cow moos. It will remind me of car horns."

He chuckled and gave her a gentle squeeze. "A calf bawling for its mama sounds better than a honking horn. Don't tell me you miss all that hustle, bustle, and racket of Austin."

"I did at first, but not now. I really love it here."

"That's what I like to hear." Hearing "I love you" would be even better, but he'd take what he could get for the moment. "Do you want some more flowers?"

"A few more would be nice. I'm to the point where bending over is difficult."

Will laughed and stepped away to gather verbena for her bouquet. "Sweetheart, you reached that point a couple of months ago. I'm surprised you didn't topple over pickin' those." He dodged when she threw a daisy at him, though it didn't come close. Still grinning, he broke off several small branches of the purple flowers and walked back toward her, picking up the daisy on the way.

He handed her the verbena but kept the daisy. "Do you want more? I'll get some from the pasture if you do."

"I ought to make you go through that fence — and hope you get stuck on the barbed wire — but I won't. These are enough." She turned toward the house and started walking. "Did Dalton's friend show up?"

"Yep. He drove off with the van too."

"His offer was better than the others?" She stepped around a patch of grass burrs.

"Not a lot, but every little bit helps." He patted his pocket. "Got five hundred cash."

"That's two hundred more than the salvage company. You did good, Callahan.

Thank you." Her happy smile warmed his heart.

He grinned and flipped one of her curls with his fingertip. "Yes, ma'am, I did. I'm a horse trader from way back. What are you up to today, besides enjoyin' the scenery?"

"I'm going to start on the museum newsletter. I have some new formatting ideas Emily said I could try, so it will be fun. She has a new display set up that we'll highlight."

"The general store one?"

"Morgan's Mercantile. Emily said it was like a general store. I was surprised at all the things the family brought in. Bolts of fabric and lace, shoes, hats, some books, and several different kinds of canned goods. Emily was pretty excited when she found an old unopened package of Arbuckles' Ariosa Coffee in one of the boxes. Something on it indicated it was from around 1885." Laughter danced in her eyes. "I acted happy too, though I still don't know what all the fuss was about. Other than it being old and the date documented. Someone came in, and Emily went off to give them a tour. I never got around to asking her about it.

"I'm not real up on history. Just between you and me, I never found it very interesting, but Emily is changing my thinking on that. She's given me a couple of tours of the museum, plus I hear her talking to visitors. I learn something new each time. She's so knowledgeable and explains things like a story. I used to think history was dull, but she makes it fascinating."

"That she does. I heard my grandparents talk about Arbuckle coffee. It was real popular with cowboys and pioneers because it was already roasted. Before the Civil War, coffee beans were sold green and folks roasted them at home or in a skillet over a campfire. If you burned even one bean, it could ruin the whole batch.

"After the war, the Arbuckle brothers figured out a way to coat roasted beans with an egg and sugar glaze that retained the flavor and aroma. They sealed them in airtight one-pound bags and shipped them all over the country. There are several entries in Grandpa Aidan's record books for a case of Arbuckles'."

"Emily said there were one hundred one-pound bags in a case. Your grandpa must have really liked coffee."

Will smiled and cupped her elbow as they walked up the back porch steps. "He was buying it for the whole crew. They had anywhere between ten and twenty cowboys working for them at various times. The chuck wagon cook constantly kept a pot of hot coffee by the campfire, so they went through a lot of it. The packages came with a stick of peppermint, and the cook used it to get the cowboys to turn the coffee grinder." He opened the screen door and followed her into the kitchen.

"Whoever ground the beans got the candy?" Megan took a glass from the cabinet.

"That's right. Those boys didn't get to town too often, so they didn't have much opportunity to enjoy candy." He watched as she put the flowers in the glass, added water, and rearranged them a bit.

She glanced at the daisy he still held in his hand. "Are you going to keep that one?"

He nodded. "I thought maybe we could sit on the porch a spell and talk."

"Isn't that what we've been doing?" She set the bouquet on the kitchen table, pausing to admire them.

He handed her the money for the van before he forgot it. "We've been visiting. Now I want to do some discussin'."

She stopped by the sink and filled two glasses with water. "Discussing or meddling?"

"A little bit of both."

After handing him a glass, she led the way

back out to the porch and sat down in one of two rocking chairs he'd brought over a few weeks earlier. "This sounds serious."

He smiled, hoping to put her at ease. "Not dirge-worthy serious. Just have some things on my mind."

She sat down, still not looking too happy. "Okay. Shoot."

Thinking of the cash he'd just given her, enough to keep her going for a little while if she took off, he prayed silently. *Lord, don't let me make a mess of this.*

"When we first saw Mike Craig outside the church, did you recognize him?"

She hesitated, then nodded.

"Why didn't you say anything?"

"He was with Kim. Wouldn't she have been thrilled if I walked up and greeted him like a long-lost friend?"

"Good point. I can understand you not wanting to make a scene." He studied her intently. "But why didn't you tell me you knew him?"

"I didn't want to talk to him. It was silly, but I hoped I could avoid him."

"When he approached us at the reception, I saw fear in your eyes. Why?"

"When I left home, he was Josh's friend. I was afraid he might tell my cousin where I am. Then Josh would tell my mother, and she'd be out here faster than a duck on a June bug."

"And she'd try to steal your money and generally make your life miserable."

"Exactly. But she wouldn't stop there. She'd do anything and everything she could think of to get money out of your family. She'd make y'all miserable too."

"We could handle your mother. Dad is a wise man who isn't easily fooled, especially after that incident with our cousin. He also has a lot of contacts in law enforcement and his ever-ready PI."

"If Mom thinks there is any chance of squeezing money out of a mark, she won't give up."

"She's never come up against the Callahans."

"Aren't you smug this morning."

"Not smug. Just confident in my family's abilities. Some people think we're hicks from the sticks because we live out here." He rocked back and forth in the chair a few times. "But the truth is, Megan, Aidan Callahan was a powerful man and a force to be reckoned with. So are we."

"Now you're bragging."

"Just tellin' it like it is. Dad's the head honcho, but he's taught his children well."

He plucked a petal from the daisy. "The

thing is, sugar, I'm falling in love with you."

Off came petal number two. "But I don't really know you."

Petal number three drifted to the porch. "I care deeply for the woman I've come to know."

Petal number four followed it. "But I'm troubled because she hides too many things from me."

He laid the flower on the little wrought iron table between them. "Be honest with me, Megan. No more secrets."

22

Megan couldn't look at him. No matter what she did, she would lose his respect and his affection. Lose him. She'd had such foolish dreams, even though she'd known they could never come true.

Something Pastor Brad talked about in his sermon a few Sundays earlier came to mind. She couldn't remember the exact Scripture, but the essence was that if you took Jesus's teachings to heart and lived by them, then you'd know the truth, and the truth would set you free.

Then the opposite must be true too. If she didn't live by the things she was learning, she would always be a captive of her past, in a prison of her fears.

As the words echoed in her heart, Megan knew what she had to do, what God wanted her to do. She needed to come clean with Will and his family. It might still destroy the good feelings he had for her, but she would no longer be burdened with the secrets.

"I guess the best way to do this is just to lay it all out there." She moved around a little, trying to ease a mild backache. "Everyone in my family, except me, is a criminal."

Will stared at her. He clearly hadn't been expecting that. "Everybody?"

She nodded and began rocking at a slow, somewhat calming pace. "All of my mom's family. At least all of them that I know or have ever heard of. I don't know anything about my dad or his family. Remember when you were telling me about your cousin's boyfriend attempting to rob Dub and Sue?"

"Yes. You commented that the thief must have been a pro. I had the impression that you knew what you were talking about."

"My cousin Josh gave safecracking a try at one point, but he wasn't any good at it. He griped for two weeks because he couldn't find a pro to give him any tips. He's pretty smart — in some ways at least. If he couldn't do it, I figured the man who broke into your dad's safe had to be a professional." She'd always wondered how one crook asked another to share his knowledge. Wouldn't they become competitors?

"Josh is six years older than me. He wasn't good at opening safes, but he was an expert at stealing cars. He started when he was eighteen, stopped when he was twenty."

"Did they catch him?"

"No. The guy he was working for was afraid his luck would run out if he kept it up. He was getting too sure of himself and taking too many risks."

"I assume he didn't find a real job."

"Actually, he did. He worked as a bouncer at a bar for about six months. But he didn't like regular hours or anyone telling him what to do. So he became a burglar. His partner knew security systems. Seemed like they could break in anywhere. Josh thought if he learned to crack safes, they might do better, but they really didn't need it. They made some big hauls anyway. It's amazing how many people don't lock up jewelry and keep cash and extra credit cards lying around."

"Y'all must have had some strange dinner conversations at your house." He thought for a second and added, "Nix the dinner part. Maybe over beer and pretzels."

What he must think of her. But sadly he was right. Discussions of successful thefts and burglaries or planning potential ones had been commonplace whenever the rest of the family was around.

"Option number two, with Josh telling us

about it in great detail. Generally, no one was too keen on sharin' the wealth if there was any. Although Josh bought me some clothes when I was fourteen. It bothered me that he had made the money stealing some lady's diamonds, but it was a nice change to have something new that my mom hadn't shoplifted."

Will stretched out his legs, but the poor man didn't look comfortable. "Is that how you usually got your clothes?"

"No. Most of the time she only took stuff for herself or to sell. I hated her stealing, and I was relieved when she didn't get anything for me. It made me nervous to wear anything she swiped. I was always afraid somebody would know and call the cops.

"One time, when I was thirteen, I saw a pair of earrings I wanted in the worst way. They were on clearance and only cost two dollars, but Mom wouldn't buy them. She pushed me to take them, telling me what a high I'd have when I got away with it. Later I read that a lot of shoplifters do it more for the adrenaline rush than wanting the item. Maybe it explains why she kept stealing even after she went to jail a couple of times.

"I gave in, slipped the earrings into my coat pocket, and walked out of the store.

But I didn't get a thrill out of it. I was really scared, and I felt dirty. I couldn't stand it. It made me just like her, like all of them. I went back to the store a few days later and slipped the earrings back on the rack. I should have told someone what I did, but I was too afraid."

"You returned them, that's what counts. The Lord had his hand on you even then. He gave you a godly conscience when your upbringing should have molded you in the opposite way."

"That's a comforting thought. I've wondered how I could be so different from the rest of my family."

Just when she thought he was beginning to relax, he tensed up again, his forehead wrinkling in a frown. "Mike mentioned that Josh was back in San Angelo. Where had he been?"

"In prison. A couple of years after I left home, he and his partner broke into an electronics store. They disconnected the alarm, but a man taking out the garbage at a nearby restaurant noticed their fake delivery truck in the alley. Since it was 1:00 in the morning, he called the police. They caught them red-handed with the truck almost full. I read about it in the San Angelo newspaper online. Plus you can learn a lot about people through public records on-line."

She paused for a drink of water, then resumed rocking. "His sentence was for seven years, so he got out early. Unlike Grandpa, Josh didn't have a hot temper. His daddy always told him to obey the rules if he got caught. Life would be better, and he'd get out quicker."

Will frowned and sat up straighter. "Had his father been in prison too?"

She nodded and met his gaze. "When I was in the fifth grade, both Uncle Riley and Grandpa were sentenced to two years in a state jail for stealing cattle."

Will jumped to his feet and walked the length of the porch and back. "Mike said they're working together and on the road a lot. Please tell me they aren't rustling cattle."

"I'm afraid they may be. Of course, I can't be sure. It would be totally stupid because Josh has to be on parole." She took a deep breath, releasing it slowly. "It gets worse."

He slumped down in the rocking chair and watched her warily.

"Mike said they're working Riley's terri-tory. I assume he meant the one he and Grandpa used to have. It was from San Angelo north to the Caprock, west to

Odessa and east to Abilene. They bragged about it being their territory, named ranches that they'd hit. Grandpa threatened to shoot anybody who infringed on it."

The area included Callahan Crossing and the Callahan Ranch.

"It makes me sick to think about it, but they may have stolen those heifers from y'all a couple of months ago." If they had, she knew it wouldn't sit well with Will or his dad, no matter how much they liked her.

"We may never know," Will said. "Once the cattle are sold, often it's impossible to trace who took them. Do you really think they're stealing cattle up this way?"

"Maybe."

"Were you even going to tell me?"

"I've been debating it back and forth. Y'all are already watchful about the cattle. I kept thinking that maybe I didn't need to say anything, hoping they weren't anywhere around here."

Will began to rock. She took some comfort that he was moving the chair at a slow, steady pace, not fast and furious. "Cattle theft has increased all over Texas and many other states. Your uncle may have been at it longer than most of them, but he's got plenty of competition. Would he follow up on your grandfather's threat to shoot them?"

"I don't think so. Riley was always the one who stepped in when Grandpa got rough with us. But I've been away from them for a long time. With Josh just out of prison, who knows how they are now."

"What will they do if you run into them in Callahan Crossing? Won't they assume that you'll know what they're up to?"

"Yes. But I don't think they would necessarily believe that I'd go to the sheriff." Looking away, she picked up her glass and set it back down without taking a drink. "I never turned them in before."

"As you said, you've been gone a long time. They won't know where your loyalty lies, especially since you're living here at the ranch and working for us."

Megan frowned. She'd been worrying about the same thing. "They'd have a problem with that, but I don't know what they'd do about it."

"Would you turn them in now?"

"What would I tell the sheriff? My relatives are in town, and oh, by the way, they may be rustling cattle?"

"That would do for starters." There was an edge of irritation in his voice.

Did he think she'd try to protect them? "I can tell him who they are so he can keep on the lookout for them. He'd be able to find out about them easy enough. But he can't arrest them for simply being in town, can he?"

"Probably not, unless they have an outstanding warrant or something. We have to tell the folks about this."

"I know. I need to be honest with them about everything."

"Cut to the chase. Dad is a just-the-facts kind of guy. Leave out the part about Josh trying his hand at safecracking." When Will stood, she did too.

He surprised her by gently pulling her into his arms. "Thank you for being honest with me. Your kinfolk are a bunch of scoundrels, but you're a good person, Megan. Don't ever let anyone make you think you aren't."

"I'm afraid your parents won't agree with you."

"Dad won't be happy about the possible rustling, but he's a fair man. He won't judge you by your relatives. I'll be right there to back you up."

"Will, why would you do that?"

Tipping up her chin gently with his fingertips, he kissed her lightly but with aching sweetness. He picked up the daisy and plucked another petal from the flower. "There, we ended on the right one."

He loves me.

23

To Megan's relief, none of Will's siblings and their families were at the ranch house for dinner. Ace and Ramona ate quickly and left to go to Sweetwater for dentist appointments. Megan helped Sue with the dishes while Will and his dad discussed what work the hired hands needed to do later in the week.

When she and Sue joined them in the living room, she knew from Dub's thoughtful expression that Will had told him she wanted to talk to them. Will sat on one end of the couch, so she sat down in the middle, next to him. Dub was in his big chair, and Sue sat near him on the other couch.

Sue glanced at her son and husband, and asked, "What did we miss?"

"Nothin' yet." Dub searched Megan's face. "Will said Megan wants to tell us about her family."

"Oh." Sue gave her a bright smile.

"Good."

"Not really," Megan said quietly. "I've shared a few things with Will, but I don't know how much he's told you. I'm guessing you know by now that my birth name was Moon Beam Smith."

Dub nodded. "Courtesy of your hippie mama. Reckon it could have been worse. I met a girl once who went by Cosmic Yucca."

"Where in the world did you meet her?" Sue asked.

"One of my army buddies went out with her." He winked at his wife. "Don't worry, honey, the yucca part was an accurate description of her personality."

Sue shook her head and grinned at Dub. "Sorry, Megan. Go on with your story."

Some story. A melodrama with bad actors more accurately described it.

"I don't know anything about my father or his family. Mom divorced him shortly after I was born. My mother doesn't stay with a man very long. She's had three husbands, and I don't know how many boyfriends. Like I told Will, basically she's a drunk and freeloader." She took a deep breath, releasing it slowly. "And a thief."

Dub and Sue exchanged a quick look.

"Mostly shoplifting. And picking pockets." She felt Will tense. Glancing up at him, she grimaced. "Sorry, I should have told you about the pickpocket part."

"Her mother used their food stamps to get party money," Will said, a faint thread of anger in his voice.

Megan knew he meant well and was trying to win their sympathy, but she hadn't wanted to share that embarrassing part of her life with them. It had been hard enough to tell Will about it.

"Did you have food?" Sue's face softened with concern.

"Yes." When Will snorted, she slipped her hand around his and squeezed, hoping he'd take the hint not to elaborate. "There wasn't a big variety, but I didn't starve."

"Barely," muttered Will, causing both Dub and Sue to frown.

"That's all in the past, and not worth fretting over now." She eased her hand away from Will's.

"So you figured you'd be better off on your own and left home," Dub said quietly.

"Yes, sir. But my mom isn't the only problem. You need to know about the rest of my family. Y'all have men like Aidan Callahan. My great-great-grandfather was a cattle rustler and bank robber."

Dub tipped his head slightly, a faint smile crinkling the corners of his eyes. "We had a distant female cousin a few generations back who ran off with an outlaw. Most families can probably find a desperado somewhere in the family tree."

"I don't know of anyone in my mother's family tree that was an honest person." That made their eyes widen in surprise. "When I was in elementary school, my grandfather and uncle went to jail for two years for cattle rustling. Later, Grandpa went back to prison for robbing a convenience store and shooting and wounding the clerk. He died in prison of a heart attack." Dub and Sue were beginning to appear very uncomfortable.

"My cousin Josh used to steal cars. Never got caught. Then he became a burglar. His partner knew all about security systems and alarms, so they were able to break in just about anywhere."

"What do you mean by anywhere?" asked Dub.

"They focused mostly on rich people's homes, but occasionally hit stores. They were caught robbing an electronics store because a restaurant worker spotted their truck in the alley. Josh went to prison for seven years. But he got out early. I guess for good behavior."

"When was this?" Dub propped one boot

up on the ottoman coffee table.

"Five years ago." She could practically see Will's dad running the numbers in his head. He knew she left home at sixteen. "I read about his arrest in the San Angelo paper online and learned of his conviction and sentence through public records online.

"You probably know that I saw an old friend, Mike Craig, at Lindsey and Dalton's wedding. He told me that Josh was back home. Mike and my cousin were friends for a short time when I was in high school. I think once Mike realized what Josh was up to, he stayed clear of him."

Will picked up the story. "Mike told her that Josh and her Uncle Riley were working together, on the road a lot, and covering her uncle's territory."

"Josh didn't say what they were doing," said Megan. "Or if he did, Mike didn't catch it. He was at a convenience store when they ran into each other. They may be working at an honest job, but I'm afraid Josh meant that they're rustling cattle. Maybe in this area."

Dub's boot hit the floor as he sat up straight. "Why do you think that?"

She explained about the territory her uncle and grandfather used to work when they were rustling. "So they may have been the ones who stole your cattle."

To call Dub's expression thunderous was an understatement.

"It's just as possible that they weren't," Sue said softly. "Why don't we have Peters look into it?"

Dub nodded. "What are their names?"

"Riley and Joshua Richmond. I really hope I'm wrong. Uncle Riley wasn't too bad. He'd get legitimate jobs sometimes, but he never stayed with them too long. He did sell some of the things Josh stole though."

"When your cousin was caught, did Riley go to prison too?"

"I don't think so. I couldn't find any records or anything in the paper. It sounds crazy, given how messed up the family was generally, but Riley and Josh loved each other a lot. They would do everything they could to protect each other."

Sue studied Megan for a few seconds. "This is hard for you, isn't it?"

"Yes, ma'am. When I was growing up, Uncle Riley and Josh were the only ones who were ever good to me. But y'all have shown me far more kindness in a month than they did in sixteen years. I owe you, and it's only right to tell you what I know. I hope I'm jumping to conclusions, and they aren't doing anything wrong."

Dub's anger appeared to have eased a little, but not much. "Anything else you want to tell us?"

"My mother's name is Jackie Johnson, unless I missed a recent marriage." She gave them her mother's address. "Peters shouldn't have too much trouble investigating her. Otherwise, I think I've covered the important things." Megan looked down at the coffee table, breaking away from the rancher's gaze. "If you want me to leave, I'll be gone first thing in the morning."

Will drew in a quick breath. "No. Absolutely not." He put his arm around her shoulders, drawing her against his side. "Don't even think about it." He looked at his father with a hard glint in his eyes. "And don't you think about sending her away."

Dub's jaw clenched. "You tellin' me what to do, boy?"

"Yes, sir. I am." Will's arm tightened, and his body tensed. "She stays."

"Will, don't," Megan whispered. "Please." The worst thing possible would be for Dub to tell her to leave. The second worst thing was to cause Will and his father to argue.

Will ignored her. "Megan hasn't done anything wrong."

"Maybe not." Dub stood, glaring at him.

"But you're treadin' on dangerous ground."

Will rose to his feet and flexed his fingers. "I'm not going to let you push her around."

Megan stared at them, fear curling around her heart. Were they going to fight?

"If anybody's pushing her around, it's you." Clearly angry and exasperated, Dub's voice deepened. He took a step away from the chair. "You're the one giving orders, not me."

Megan gasped. *Lord, this can't be happening.* She couldn't help it — she burst into tears.

"Oh, good grief," cried Sue. "Look what you've done. You two quit pawin' the ground and snortin' like two ol' bulls. Behave yourselves. You're scaring Megan."

Will instantly sat down beside Megan and put his arms around her. "Sugar, don't cry. It's okay."

She tried to pull away, but he held her close. "Don't fight . . ." she sobbed. "Don't want . . ." — sniff — "either one to get hurt."

"Aw, sweetheart, we weren't going to hit each other." He rubbed his hand up and down her arm. "I'm sorry. Don't cry."

Dub came over, sat down on the padded leather edge of the coffee table, and handed her a clean white handkerchief. "I don't want you to leave, Megan. Sue doesn't either."

"That's right, honey." Sue sat down beside her husband. "Even if your uncle and cousin are causing trouble, that's no reason for you to leave."

Megan dabbed her eyes and sniffed again. "Are you sure?"

"I'm sure." Sue patted her knee.

"Me too," said Dub. "As for me and Will — we're natured a lot alike."

Sue nodded. "Muscle minded."

Dub slanted his wife a glance and narrowed his eyes, then turned his attention back to Megan. "So we clash sometimes."

"Trying to see who's the biggest buzzard at the carcass," Sue proclaimed with a perfectly straight face.

She succeeded in making Megan smile, whether or not she meant to.

Sue bumped Dub's arm with her shoulder. "Let's go call Peters and whoever else you need to and let these youngsters kiss and make up."

Megan almost choked.

Will grinned and winked at his mother.

Dub looked at Sue, a smile hovering around his mouth, and stood, holding out his hand. "Yes, dear."

Sue took his hand and let him pull her to

her feet. "Son, I hope you're taking notes."

"Yes, ma'am."

After his parents left the room, Will caressed Megan's cheek. "My dad and I argue sometimes, but it never comes to blows. I don't know any family that doesn't have heated disagreements now and then. Even Jenna and Nate or Emily and Chance have their squabbles."

She certainly hadn't seen his siblings and their spouses argue, but she supposed they tried to be on their best behavior around her. Could she ever fit in with the Callahans? She longed to be a part of this loving family, so close to them that they could be totally themselves with her. After today, they'd probably be even more restrained.

"Megan, did you hear anything I said?" Will murmured, leaning closer.

"Yes. All of it." She looked up at him. "I think. Every family squabbles, and I don't need to be afraid if you and your dad get riled up. You won't punch each other."

"That's right. We might yell and bump chests like the old football players we are, but you don't have to worry about us beating each other to a pulp."

"You actually bump chests?"

"Naw, that was a figure of speech. It would hurt without the pads." He focused on her lips. "Are you done talkin'?"

She shook her head. "I know a lot of sayings, but what does muscle minded mean?"

"Strong willed."

"Oh." She wanted him to kiss her, but his parents were in the other room. What if they walked out and caught them smooching? On the other hand, they clearly left them alone for that very purpose, and she was wasting precious minutes. "Okay. I'm done now."

" 'Bout time." Gently tipping up her chin with his fingertips, he proceeded to follow his mama's instructions to the letter.

24

On Thursday afternoon, Will drove alongside Jack's Creek where they had killed off the salt cedar the previous August. The nonnative plant devoured water needed by the pasture grass and had practically dried up the stream in the past few years. Now the creek flowed at a lazy pace. It wasn't deep, but it provided water for the cattle and wildlife.

He didn't like using herbicides unless absolutely necessary. With salt cedar there wasn't any other effective choice. This project had been successful. Parking the pickup, he got out and walked along the creek bank to see if there were any salt cedar sprouts mingled with the native vegetation.

His cell phone rang, surprising him. Though he carried the phone most of the time, there were many places on the ranch without service. Checking caller ID, he answered, "Hi, Dad."

"Have you been by Jack's Creek yet?"

"I'm there now. Still looks good. We can chalk this one up as a success." Will figured his dad had something else on his mind. Normally, he would have given Dub a report over supper. "What's up?"

"I got a call from Peters. Megan's uncle and cousin work for Whiteside Feed Mill in San Angelo, making deliveries to feed stores. Riley drives the truck, and Josh is his helper. Their area covers a lot of her grandpa's old rustling territory."

"Could be just a coincidence."

"Maybe. The only way to know if they chose the delivery area would be to ask their boss, and I'm not ready to do that. If they are living an honest life, I don't want to stir up any trouble for them." The sound of a horn honking came over the phone, telling Will that his father was in town.

"Peters confirmed that they weren't any-where around here the night our cattle were stolen. They were in San Saba watching a softball tournament the Whiteside team was playing in. But I talked to the sheriff and learned a curious thing. Half of the cattle thefts in the past four months in this region have been on Friday or Saturday nights."

"So theoretically, a man could hold down a legitimate day job, Monday through

Friday, and do his rustlin' on the weekend. If he had a place to keep the cattle until he could sell them. Do the Richmonds have weekends off?"

"Yes, they do," said Dub.

Will sighed and rested his foot on a big rock. "So we can't completely rule them out. That's not what I wanted to hear."

"Me either. After I talked to Peters, I stopped by the feed store. I spotted some sacks with the Whiteside logo, so I asked about the company. Norbin says they produce feed for sheep, goats, and wildlife. He has deliveries every couple of months or so. There's no set time. He puts in an order when he's low on stock. He mentioned Riley and Josh in the conversation, said they were a couple of good ol' boys. They were here last Friday."

When Megan was home decorating cakes. *Thank you, Lord.*

Dub continued. "According to Norbin, Whiteside hired Josh to help his dad because Riley had knee surgery a couple of months ago. It's a short-term job."

"But long enough to scout out potential victims." Will started walking back to his truck. "Megan doesn't want to see them or have any contact with her family. I don't blame her. What worries me is if they are

341

rustling, what will they do if they spot her?"

"Exactly. That troubles me too. I don't see how I can ask Norbin when they'll be bringing the next shipment without him getting too curious."

Will grimaced. The feed store owner was the nosiest man in town, and one of the biggest gossips. "If he gets a whiff of anything halfway interesting, he'll snoop it out faster than Peters. Is the sheriff going to keep an eye out for them?"

"Yeah, he pulled up their mug shots, but the photos are old. Especially Riley's. It might be hard to identify him if he comes into town in something besides the company truck."

"It also means he hasn't been arrested for anything in a long time. Maybe that's a good sign."

"Could be. Or maybe he's good at avoiding the law. Peters said he keeps a pretty low profile. His son doesn't. Josh drives a new pickup, has a nice apartment, and has a rep for being a big spender if he goes out for a night on the town. Living pretty high for a man fresh out of prison. He can't afford that kind of life on what he makes at Whiteside."

Will opened the pickup door and climbed in. "So the assumption is that he had some

342

money hidden away from his burglaries, or he's back into crime."

"Peters will keep digging," said Dub. "Maybe he won some money in the lotto."

"That's better than the other two options. Did Peters say anything about her mother?"

"Pretty much the same as what Megan told us. She spent two months in jail last year for shoplifting, and she's been in court-mandated rehab twice since Megan left home. Evidently, it didn't do any good." His dad took a deep breath, releasing it slowly. "Sometimes we forget how fortunate we are. You comin' over tonight?"

"Probably not. I think I'll cook Megan a steak if she's not too tired. It's past time for her to spend the evening at my place." Especially if she was going to be living there soon. "I need to bring her up to speed on what we've learned."

"Good idea. I'll see you in the morning."

Will ended the call, then dialed the museum and invited Megan for supper. He didn't mention Peters's report or anything else they'd learned. Nor did they talk long. She was busy addressing the museum newsletters and wanted to get them to the post office. He needed to finish up some other work, and he knew for a fact that when he drove half a mile farther, his cell phone would be worthless.

After dinner, Will and Megan relaxed in the living room portion of the great room. It was still too hot outside to be comfortable, especially for a pregnant lady whose feet were puffy.

"I feel bad taking your recliner." Megan sat up a bit straighter when he handed her a small plate containing a piece of German butter cake. "But I have to admit I'm enjoying all this coddling."

"Good. You're supposed to. No sweat on the recliner. I'm comfortable here on the couch." He took a bite of the cake, doughy on the bottom, sweet, gooey, and slightly crunchy on the top. "Oh, wow, this is really good."

"Told you." She grinned at him, looking adorably smug. "I got the recipe from Mrs. Hoffmann. It's supposed to be a breakfast cake, but I like it anytime. I'll leave it so you can have it in the morning."

"Thanks. Though it might not last that long. Do you still have some at home?" Since she obviously loved it, he didn't want to deprive her.

She nodded and swallowed. "I put it in two pans, so I could bring you one."

"Even before I asked you to come over.

Nice." Sweet and thoughtful, so typical of her. He still marveled at how well she'd turned out when her family was such a mess. From the things she'd said about Mrs. Hoffmann, he expected the elderly Christian woman had been a big influence on Megan and not only in cooking.

During dinner, Will had told her everything they'd learned about her family. They'd also discussed her working from home the week her relatives were supposed to make the feed delivery. If they could pinpoint when that would be. They couldn't do it forever, but he'd concentrate on the present for now.

After they finished dessert, he said, "There's still the possibility that Riley and Josh are involved in the rustling."

"I know. If they are, they aren't following Grandpa's plan. He took the cattle out of state or to south or east Texas to an auction. They'd be gone for days, sometimes weeks."

"That's the part that has me puzzled. If they're stealing the cattle on Friday or Saturday night, how do they dispose of them and get back to work Monday morning? There are a few auctions on Saturday, but not many. They'd get suspicious if they brought in cattle with different brands.

None of them run on Sunday."

Megan leaned back in the recliner and stared at the ceiling for a moment, frowning thoughtfully. Then she sat upright again. "They could have a single buyer. I'd forgotten about this. When Grandpa and Riley started out, they sold all the cattle to a man near Midland. He'd change the brand, hold them for three or four months, then sell them at the auction or to another rancher for about twice what he paid for them."

Will stretched out his legs, resting his boots on the rustic coffee table. "So they divided the risk."

"Until Grandpa decided they were getting ripped off and started taking the cattle to auctions himself. They made more money on each deal, but they eventually got caught trying to sell some."

"Whether or not your relatives are involved, that's good info to pass on to the sheriff. I'll give him a call in the morning. If Riley and Josh are guilty, what will you do if they spot you in town?"

"Waddle the other way?"

Will felt a twinge of irritation. She wasn't taking this seriously.

"I'll keep my eyes open for the Whiteside truck."

"What if they aren't in the company truck?"

"You're just full of what-ifs, aren't you?"

"Would they hurt you?"

"No." She put down the recliner footrest and got up, a movement that was getting harder for her. Walking around the coffee table, she came over to sit beside him. "If they're involved and they spotted me, they'd beat feet out of town, and probably out of the area. They won't take any more risks than necessary. They'd know I'd suspect what they were up to."

"That's what worries me." He put his arm around her, smiling when she snuggled closer. "I know Riley rescued you from a beating, but do you honestly think he'd just walk away?"

"Yes. He's the one who told me to leave home, to get away before I became trapped in that lifestyle. He wouldn't want to get me involved, either on his side or the law's."

She still clung to the belief that there was some good in her uncle. Maybe there was. Maybe he was working himself up over nothing.

"What about Josh? He's done hard time. Do you think he's still that nice guy who bought you new clothes?"

"I'm sure he's changed, but I still don't

think he'd hurt me. I may be naive, but I think he'd move on to another area. Besides, it's not like he'd be pulling a stock trailer. If they came to town, they'd hide the trailer somewhere. They wouldn't be so obvious.

"In fact, I don't think they'd come to town at all unless they were casing the area, checking to see where the constable and deputy hang out, or if the law officers follow any kind of pattern in their patrols." She made a face. "I'd better watch how I talk around other people. They might think I come from a den of thieves."

"Can't have them getting that idea."

"Especially since it's true. I'm tired of all this. I'm not going to worry about if and when I can go to town. I'm not going to peek around corners or shadows to see if trouble is waiting. No more talk today about my family or rustling or anything awful. I'm not going to fret about it, but trust God to protect me."

That was all well and good, but Will figured God expected people to use good common sense too. "Just promise me that you'll keep your eyes open."

"I promise." She took a deep breath, held out her hand, and made a pressing motion with her thumb.

"What are you doing?"

"Changing the conversation channel to a new subject. Dr. Cindy came by the museum today to see me."

"Why? Don't you have an appointment tomorrow?"

"I was supposed to, but she has to go out of town, so they canceled my appointment. She wanted to know how I was feeling and told me to still go by the lab so they can do a blood test. She also wants me to take some childbirth classes at the hospital. Three of them, one a week, starting in a couple of weeks." She looked up at him. "Do you think Jenna would be my coach?"

"I expect she would. She'd be a good one." He wanted to be there when Sweet Baby was born, to help her through it, to share in the joy and miracle of birth. But he had no right. Yet. "Are you nervous about having the baby?"

"A little, but having y'all to encourage me is a big help. I don't know how I thought I could do it on my own. Dr. Cindy was right. The Callahans are a great support group."

"We do our best." If he asked her to marry him, would she do it? He knew she cared for him. He could see it whenever she looked at him. But how deep was her affection? Did she love him? Would she say "I do" and stay with him forever or only hang around for a while and want a divorce?

He'd thought he might marry without love if friendship and respect were part of the relationship. Now he realized he couldn't. He wanted the whole enchilada or nothing at all. Even if nothing at all would break his heart.

They'd known each other for five weeks. It was enough time for him to fall in love with her. Was it long enough for her to fall in love with him? Or only to need the security he could provide? Right or wrong, he was selfish enough to want her to love him, not his money. He'd bide his time for a little while.

He'd also pray that her cousin and uncle had become law-abiding citizens. And ask the Lord to switch their route so they never came through Callahan Crossing again.

25

The following Tuesday morning, Megan took a pan of soft oatmeal-cranberry cookies from the oven and set it on top of the stove. Listening to the lost and found announcements on the local radio station, she wondered if the three missing chickens had wound up as supper for a coyote or a person.

She transferred the cookies to a wire rack and murmured, "There you go, boys, almost three dozen cookies should keep you happy."

Earlier, Will and Nate had ridden down the road on horseback on their way to round up some cattle and move them into the pasture behind her house. With a wave of his hat, a big smile, and hollering, "See ya after a while," the handsome rancher had barely slowed down as they passed her house.

Glancing around the kitchen, she decided

she'd done enough work for the morning. Beside the cookies, a banana-split cheese-cake sat on the counter to cool. Another was already chilling in the refrigerator, as were the toppings — crushed pineapple, sweetened pureed fresh strawberries, choco-late syrup, toasted chopped pecans, and maraschino cherries. Serving it at the Garden Club luncheon the next day would be easy, simply spoon small amounts of the toppings on each piece.

"Now, Sweet Baby, if the gals on the food committee will quit bickering over the chicken salad, everything will be fine." She had spent almost two hours on the phone the day before listening to complaints and going back and forth trying to settle the dispute between the three women who were making the main salad.

Each one had a favorite recipe they thought should be used, and none of them would give in. Finally, she suggested that they each make whatever kind they wanted. Hopefully, there wouldn't be a ruckus between the attendees over who wound up with what.

Thankfully, the women making the pasta salads and the fruit salads were much more cooperative and didn't insist on using Mama's recipe, Aunt Bertha's, or Grandma

Nelda's.

This was the last social event scheduled at the museum for the next two months, until the Business and Professional Women resumed their monthly meetings in mid-September. By then, Sweet Baby would have made her grand entrance and be about a month old, so Megan didn't know if she would be coordinating that one or not. She hoped she'd be able to resume her duties before the holiday season began.

If she was still there.

How long would the Callahans let her stay at the ranch and work for them? When would they decide she was taking advantage of their friendship and tell her it was time to go? She had no real reason to think they would fire her and send her packing. They'd said they wanted her to stay at least until after the baby was born and she was back on her feet. However, not even their generosity would last forever.

With the money Will had gotten her for the van, plus the six hundred dollars she'd cleared from Lindsey's wedding, and what she'd been able to save out of her wages, she had a nice little cushion put away. If she continued being frugal, she could add another six or seven hundred before the baby was born.

"We'll have to live on some of it after you arrive, Baby, even if I stay here." She put the mixing bowl in the sink and filled it with soapy water to soak for a few minutes. "They won't pay me when I'm not working." Even if they wanted to, she wouldn't feel right in taking it. "I'd like to have a couple of months off so I can spend all my time with you."

Plus she needed so many things for the baby. She'd hit a few garage sales on Saturday and found some footed sleepers and a couple of cute tops and pants, but almost everything else had probably already been used by two or three kids. Nice secondhand things were fine, even ecologically friendly, she thought with a smile. But she didn't want to put her child in anything ragged, faded, or stained.

Sweet Baby wouldn't go to kindergarten and elementary school wearing the kind of clothes Megan had to.

"I'll keep looking. We'll track down some nice things, I'm sure. The right garage sales are treasure troves. Stick with me, kid, I'll teach you how to find the good stuff."

Megan filled a plastic pitcher with water and carried it out front to water her flowers. She'd found four planter boxes in the weathered, wooden barn behind the house.

Will had hauled two of them around the front and put them on either side of the porch steps. He'd put the other two beside the back steps.

Since she'd never grown a flower in her life, she stuck with what the guy at the local nursery suggested. A mix of red, orange, and yellow snapdragons in the back, and red petunias with purple verbena in the front. She loved the vibrant colors of them all. They made her smile every time she looked at them.

The faint bawling of a calf drew her gaze down the road in the direction Will and Nate had gone. She couldn't see the cattle yet because the ground sloped slightly, but the dust floating in the air told her they weren't too far away.

"They're coming, Sweet Baby. We're gonna watch real live cowboys working cattle. Well, I'm going to see them. I guess you'll have to settle for listening to them this time. You're going to hear some new noises." Megan went into the house, set the pitcher upside down in the dish drainer to dry, and came back to the living room to put on her tennis shoes.

She tugged them on, rested each foot in turn on the coffee table, and tied the laces. By the time she finished she was huffing and puffing. She'd mainly been wearing her slip-on sandals, but she didn't want to go trooping out to the fence in open shoes. It was too sandy, and there were too many grass burrs.

Will had come by the evening before and opened the pasture gate. He'd also unlocked the windmill so it would turn and fill the big aluminum stock tank with water. She'd shut off the air conditioners and opened the windows when she went to bed, letting the rhythmic creak of the windmill and soft swoosh as it pumped water into the tank lull her to sleep. It was a peaceful, comfortable sound, one she didn't think she'd ever tire of hearing.

Going out onto the front porch, she spotted Will and Nate herding the cattle up the road. She counted twenty cows and twenty calves. They moved at a slow, steady pace, stirring up less dust than they had earlier, likely because the grass was thicker alongside the road here. Still, she was glad she'd closed her doors and windows as Will had advised.

One cow decided she wanted to go back to where she came from and turned around, trying to slip past Will. Seemingly without any command on his part, his reddish brown horse moved over and blocked the cow's path. Will slapped his leg and yelled, "Yahhh!" The cow spun around and did as she was told.

As they neared the gate, Will nudged his horse to speed up, and they edged around the herd, getting out in front of them. Moving back and forth across the road between the fences on each side, he turned the cattle toward the opening. He and Nate guided them smoothly through the gate. Will kept them moving past the barn and corrals while Nate stopped and closed the gate.

Megan walked around the house, watching Will herd the cattle farther into the pasture. He looked as if he'd been born in the saddle, relaxed but alert, moving as one with the horse. Both he and the horse seemed to anticipate each cow's every move. She glanced at Nate, who was back on his horse and riding to catch up with the herd. He was just as capable and comfortable in the saddle.

But Will was the one who drew her gaze again and again as she made her way over to the barbed wire fence. He was the living definition of tall, dark, and handsome. If he ever decided to make Western movies, he'd be a star. Put him on a horse and let him ride to the rescue, or have him strap a six-shooter on his hip and saunter down the street to run the bad guys out of town. It wouldn't matter whether or not he could act. His legions of female fans would see only a larger-than-life hero.

Just as she did. Was that her fascination with him? Had she made him into the hero every girl daydreamed about? The knight in shining armor. The rich, handsome prince. The superhero who would fight every foe to protect her. The cowboy who lived by the code of honor and justice.

No, she hadn't made him into a hero. He was one.

And she loved him with all her heart, a secret to be closely guarded. Eventually, the novelty of helping a poor, stranded mother-to-be would wear off, and he would turn his attention to someone who was his equal. A woman who was well educated and beautiful, who had impeccable family credentials and old money.

She cautioned herself to enjoy his friendship, nothing more. Then she thought of his wonderful kisses and the loving way he held her, and longing filled her soul once more.

He rode over to the water tank and dismounted, letting his thirsty horse take a long drink. Will tugged off his gloves and stuffed them in his back pocket. He walked over to the tank, took off his hat, and dunked his head beneath the water, washing away the dust. Straightening, he shook his head, sending a shower of water through the air, then swiped his hand over his face. Smoothing his hair back with his fingers, he stuck the hat back on his head, and remounted.

He turned the horse toward her and grinned, trotting over to meet her. "Honking horns delivered, ma'am."

She laughed, adoring his mischievous smile. "If noise starts coming out of those horns, I'm running the other way." His horse had a white streak down its face and one white back foot, a nice combination with the shiny reddish brown coat. "What a pretty horse."

The animal nodded his head, as if thanking her.

"What do you call that color?"

"Chestnut or sorrel. This is Cecil."

"Cecil? I thought horses were named Flicka and Blaze and Star."

"For some reason that I've never figured out, we're a mite more practical. Winston, Bob, Rusty, Clementine, Stubby, and Jack to name a few. We got a little more artistic with the horse Nate's riding. That's Ebony."

Nate's glistening black horse was still

drinking at the water tank. "She's beautiful too."

"Most of them are from our own breeding program, but occasionally we'll buy one to add fresh genes to the pool. Dad's one of the best horse breeders in Texas."

"I expect he's trained you well."

"That he has."

She glanced farther behind him to the pasture. "Looks like the cows have figured out this was a good move. If they aren't munching grass, they're drinking that nice cool water."

Will dismounted and looped the reins around a fence post. Thirty seconds later, the horse began grazing contentedly. "I kept tellin' them the grass was better up here, but typical women, they griped all the way."

"Careful, cowboy, or I won't invite you in" — she glanced at his dirty clothes — "correction, to sit on the porch and have some oatmeal cookies and iced tea."

Nate rode up. "Did I hear something about cookies?"

"Fresh batch, just waiting for hungry wranglers to gobble them up."

"I'm there." Nate swung his leg over the horse and stepped down, tying the animal a few posts away. He, too, had washed his face in the water tank, but she hadn't noticed until now.

"Reckon we're visitin' with the lady for a while," Will drawled, climbing between the wires on the fence. The leather chaps, called shotguns, encased his legs, but she held her breath until he'd cleared the barbs with his back. That lightweight cotton shirt didn't offer much protection.

Nate followed him through the fence. "That was an established fact before we left the corral this morning."

"Nope. I said I was going to stay and visit a while. Didn't say nothin' about you crashin' the party."

Nate's grin didn't hold one iota of remorse. "You didn't say nothin' about cookies, either."

"Come on, Will." Megan turned toward the house. "You too, Cookie Monster."

"Cook-ieee," growled Nate, sounding a lot like the Muppet.

Laughing, the three strolled to the house, the men's jingling spurs playing a little tune. "Y'all are pretty impressive on horseback and handling the cattle." Megan looked up at Will, enjoying simply being in his company. "When did you learn to ride?"

"Got my first pony when I was four."

"Goodness. That's earlier than I'd expected."

"Dad started carrying me on the saddle in front of him when I was two. It was the same with all us kids. Nate was a late bloomer."

"Chance and I decided we were best buddies in the first grade," said Nate. "So I started spending a lot of Sunday afternoons here. Dub taught me to ride too."

Megan knew he had grown up on a farm not too far from the ranch. "So you didn't have any horses at your place?"

"Nope. Just chickens."

"How'd you saddle 'em?" Will asked as he followed Megan up onto the porch.

"Very carefully. Those crazy things peck." Nate leaned against a porch post. "They're my mom's pets. I stayed away from them. Still do."

Laughing at their banter, she opened the screen door. "Y'all relax."

"Sorry I'm too dirty to help." Will peeked past her into the kitchen and frowned. "You've been working hard this morning. Is that the cheesecake you were telling me about?"

"Yes. I didn't make any extra for the family this time, but there should be some left tomorrow. One wasn't enough for the luncheon, but two will be too much. I wanted to finish baking before it gets too hot. I'm done working for the day."

"Good."

"I'll be right back." She went inside and filled a plate two layers high with cookies. Taking them to the door, she handed them to Will. When she stepped outside a few minutes later with a tray containing a plastic pitcher of iced tea, two empty glasses, and a glass of water for her, she was surprised to see all the cookies still there. "Is something wrong with them?"

"We were waiting for you." A teasing smile lifted the corner of Will's lips as he slowly rocked back and forth. She set the tray down on the small wrought iron table between the rocking chairs. "Though I had to caution Cookie Monster to mind his manners."

Nate smiled but didn't rise to the bait. Megan knew very well that he was just as polite as Will. He'd shifted his position to sitting on the porch with his back to the post instead of leaning against it. One foot rested on the porch step.

She filled their glasses and offered them some cookies. After they'd taken a couple each, she set the plate back down on the table and sat in the other rocker. "Help yourselves to as many as you want."

Nate took a big bite, chewed, swallowed,

and grinned. "Are those dried cranberries instead of raisins?"

"Yes. And some pecans for additional protein."

Will finished off a cookie with a smile. Nate was almost done with his second one. Jenna had told her that her husband had always liked sweets, but after he returned from the Middle East, he relished every bite even more, especially something homemade.

"What makes them so soft?" asked Will.

"I think it's because they have milk in them."

He nodded and reached for a third cookie. "Oatmeal, milk, cranberries, and pecans. A homemade power bar. Or breakfast bar."

"I also substituted applesauce for the oil, so except for being a bit high in sugar, they are very healthy."

"Which saves some calories and leaves room for the cheesecake." Nate took a long drink of tea. When Will held the plate out to him, he took three more cookies.

"Actually, the cheesecake is a low-fat version too. I got it from the *Cooking Light* website."

"Careful, woman, or folks will be clamoring for you to start a bakery." Will studied her with a thoughtful expression.

"I'd love it. Though it would probably be

more practical to stick with wedding cakes and other specialties and work from home. Then I wouldn't have the expense of renting a building in town or finding someone to watch the baby."

"Good point." Will finished off his glass of tea. "What are you doing the rest of the day?"

"I don't know. I'm so tempted to go to Abilene and shop for baby things." She rocked absently, the thought zipping through her mind that she should move one of the chairs inside before the baby came. "But I really should wait a couple of weeks and see what I can find at garage sales."

"I don't have anything pressing this afternoon. I'll take you shopping." Will's tone was casual, but she noticed Nate lift an eyebrow.

"You want to go shopping for baby stuff?" What was he up to? Men didn't like to shop.

"It'll be fun, as long as we stop by a toy department somewhere."

"She's having a little girl," Nate said, pushing up to stand. "You can't buy her a football."

"Okay. I'll get her a soccer ball. Zach still has a blast with his, and girls play soccer. But no dump trucks. Not even a pink one."

Confused, Megan looked to Nate for an

explanation.

"Chance is always buying Zach construction equipment toys. Gave him a whole set of toy machinery for his first birthday. Chance had meticulously painted his company's logo on the side of each one."

"He was just showin' off." Will might have been pretending to complain, but there was a note of brotherly pride in his voice. Chance was a good artist, particularly with cartoons and caricatures.

A glint of amusement lit Nate's eyes as he continued. "Will is always giving him cowboy toys. He keeps griping about Chance trying to turn him into a contractor instead of a cowboy. As I recall, all three of us played with cars and trucks when we were kids, but only one of us wound up a builder."

"So the odds are two to one that Zach will become a cowboy." When Will grunted, Megan chuckled. She wasn't sure if he agreed, disagreed, or was merely being obstinate.

"He'll become whatever he wants to," said Nate. "Except a lazy bum. Which is what the Big Boss is likely to call me if I don't get back to work. You comin' with me, Will?"

"You go on. I'll be along directly."

"All right. See you at dinner, Megan.

Thanks for the goodies."

"You're welcome. I'll bring you a bag of cookies."

"Great." Nate walked down the steps and across the yard, his spurs jingling. Instead of going through the fence, he went to the gate.

"I'm serious about taking you shopping, sugar. Do you feel up to it?"

"Yes." She had a feeling he was offering more to keep an eye on her. He was worse than a mother hen when it came to fussing over her. Which was nice, actually. "Do you want to go right after dinner?"

"Works for me." He stood, then surprised her by leaning down and giving her a lingering kiss. "Sweeter than cookies. Though they were mighty good. Thanks."

A little dazed, she murmured, "You're welcome."

"If the cows bother you, say the word, and we'll move them. See you at noon."

She watched him saunter across the yard, through the open gate, and up the fence line to his horse. Anticipation spiraled through her. Will was going to spend the afternoon with her, and she was going to pick up a few things for Sweet Baby. Right now, life didn't get much better than that.

26

Will was like a kid in a toy store, only they hadn't reached the toy section yet. "This one looks the best."

He lifted the bright red combination stroller/car seat down to inspect it more thoroughly. "It's well made. Nice and sturdy." He checked the info sheet. "It will hold a baby up to thirty pounds or thirty inches. That's better than most of the others. Sweet Baby could ride around in this thing a long time."

It was also over three hundred dollars.

"I don't really need a stroller, only a car seat." Which would still set her back almost two hundred by the time the sales tax was added, but it was a necessity.

"Of course you need a stroller. A good sturdy one for a while, and maybe one of those umbrella things for later. We used both for Zach when he was little. Sometimes when I took him for a walk, I'd carry him in the backpack, but he liked the big stroller better, and so did I. Made it easier to show him the horses and cows, or trees and flowers."

He took his little spiral notebook and stubby pencil from his pocket and wrote down the brand and model number.

"Will," she said softly, "I can't afford that."

"Do you like it?"

"Yes, but something less expensive will do fine."

"Nope. This one had the best reviews online. Plus you get a better deal if you buy the two together. Don't sweat it. You concentrate on the little stuff."

He'd been looking at baby strollers and car seats online? She stared at his back as he walked farther down the aisle.

"Oh, man, this is cool." He squatted down to look at a big box.

"What did you find now?"

"A swing. See, you can put the kid in the seat, turn on the music, set it to swing, and then you get to relax. Or go bake something." He read the label. "It has ten different songs, other soothing sounds, and different speeds. It even has a mobile that turns." He looked up at her with the sweetest smile. "And it's all pink and girly."

Out came his notebook. Another notation added.

They walked around the end to the next aisle, and she spotted something she had planned to get. "This I want for sure."

He stopped beside her, resting his hand at her waist. Anyone walking by would assume they were a happy, expectant couple. The thought brought an ache to her heart. "They call it a bouncer, but it actually vibrates and plays music or rainforest sounds. A young mom in my apartment complex had one, and she said it was great. Babies love it, even newborns. It's not big, so you can take it with you wherever you are in the house. Or to somebody else's house. Baby stays happy for a while, and mom's hands are free to do other things."

"In it goes." He pulled a box off the shelf and laid it in the cart.

She started pushing the basket down the aisle, leaving him perusing other gadgets. "I'm going over to look at sleepers."

"Okay, I'll find you."

Fifteen minutes later, he came around the corner with a grin wide enough to swallow a banana sideways. His arms were full of toys, including the promised toddler-sized soccer ball.

"Did you leave anything on the shelf?"

"Sure. I just got anything that looked like fun for a girl up to one year." He carefully laid the pile in the cart. "I figure Sweet Baby will be a fast learner. There's a mat thingy to put on the floor. It has arches over it with fun things for her to reach. Also got some rattles." He rummaged through the pile, pulling out a small package to show her. "Did you know they have ones you can fasten on her feet so they rattle when she kicks?"

"Those are clever. And cute." Almost as cute as he was. He was so proud of himself.

He put the rattles back and picked up a package of pink flowered and light green cloth blocks. "These have different textures and make crinkly noises." He dropped the blocks back into the basket. "I figure even girls like balls, so I found a couple she'll be able to hold pretty soon. And yes, I know she won't play with the soccer ball until she's a year old.

"I only got a couple of musical toys. I expect those can get annoying. But this bear won't." He handed her a sweet-faced, sleeping bear, wrapped in a soft pink blanket. "It plays sounds from a mother's womb, so when you put Baby down to sleep, it will be like she's right with you. If she cries or bumps it, it will play again."

"That's amazing. I hadn't seen it before." She laid the bear in the cart and hooked her arm around his. "You're really enjoying this, aren't you?"

"Lovin' it. What did you find?" He thumbed through the little gowns, sleeper sets, bibs, and burp cloths in the upper shelf of the cart. "You're going to need a lot more clothes than that."

"When did you become an expert?"

"After my sister came home with a little baby and up to her neck in the quicksand of depression," he said quietly. "We all pitched in to take care of Zach and try to rescue Jenna. I know all about rockin' and singin' babies to sleep. Dodging flying food and changin' diapers."

He slid a package of pink and maroon receiving blankets from a hook and tossed them in the basket. "Don't you want more sleepers?"

"I have a package of each one that they have for girls or that can be used for both. I'll look at some garage sales if I need more."

"You don't have any dresses or Sunday outfits. There's some over this way." He motioned to the right. "And booties. She's got to have booties."

They found pretty little dresses — a purple sundress, a light green ruffled one, and a pink and green polka-dotted one with a pink kitten on the front. Will found booties and socks to match all three, which he put in his growing pile.

Watching him pick out tiny lace ruffled socks and colorful booties was so sweet it almost made her cry. "This is enough for now. She'll outgrow things fast."

"Are you tired?"

"Getting that way." Megan rubbed her lower back. "I'll be fine after I sit down for a few minutes."

"Then we'll head for the checkout pretty soon. I saw some benches near there when we came in. If you don't mind, there's a couple of other things I'd like you to look at before we leave this part of the store."

"Okay." What was he up to now?

He pushed the cart slowly so she could easily walk beside him. Down one aisle and over three more to the baby furniture section. Cribs, bassinets, dressers, changing tables, rocking chairs with padded arms. All the things to make a real nursery, but nothing she could afford.

"Will, I don't need any of this. I can share my dresser with the baby. And change her on the bed."

"Hard on your back."

"I can haul in a rocker from the back

porch." When his eyebrows almost touched each other, she said, "You can carry it in for me. I'm sure I can find a secondhand crib, if not in Callahan Crossing then on eBay."

He put his arm around her shoulders, holding her against his side. "Megan, I want to do this."

"Do what? Buy everything from a car seat and stroller to a bedroom set?" She didn't know why it irritated her. Yes, she did. She could never take all of it with her. Or if somehow she managed to, she'd be reminded of him every time she walked into the baby's room or pushed her down the street in the stroller or put her in the car seat.

It would be agony.

His hand tightened minutely against her arm. "I figure your Fairy Godmothers will want to get some of it. But I have dibs on the swing. And on the furniture. We don't have to get anything here, or anything today. We'll look at some other stores if you feel up to it. Whatever you want, I'll get."

He moved around so he could face her, gently resting his hands on her shoulders. "I want to furnish Sweet Baby's nursery, sugar. I don't care if the furniture comes from Walmart or Neiman Marcus. The only thing that's important is that you're happy with it."

Glancing away, he seemed to be trying to make up his mind about something. He looked back at her, tenderness filling his eyes and his expression. "Let me do this for you, Megan, and for Sweet Baby. It means a lot to me."

She couldn't protect herself emotionally without hurting him. "All right. But I certainly don't need anything from Nieman's. Do they even have baby furniture?"

"I don't know. I was making a point."

She turned away — mainly because she had the feeling he was about to kiss her — and scanned the furniture. Some of it was nice, but nothing was quite right. "I don't see anything here that I particularly like."

"Then we'll look somewhere else."

As they walked toward the checkout area, she studied the items in the basket. Amid all those toys, she spotted a nursery monitor he'd sneaked in there somehow. If ever a man was born to have children, it was Will Callahan.

"You're going to be a good daddy."

"Yes, I am." His soft, husky voice washed gently over her, and he put his arm around her, guiding the cart with one hand.

She pointed to all the toys. "But your kids

are going to be spoiled rotten."

"Yes, she will be," he whispered.

Startled, she looked up at him, and he held her gaze, giving her a glimpse into his heart. Oh, how she longed to love him, to spend her life with him. But wonderful things like that never happened to her. It could never be.

Could it?

They found the perfect furniture set a couple of hours later. She would never have asked for it because it was expensive, but Will noticed how her face lit up when she saw it. The white sleigh style crib would convert into a toddler bed and later to a full bed. There was a matching four-drawer dresser and a changing table with open shelves underneath. The set even came with a wide, two-shelf bookcase.

In the same store, Will found a white glider rocker upholstered in soft white. It had padded arms and a padded footstool. Megan found a nice bassinet there too, which was reasonably priced.

"It looks like a good one," Will said as he gave it a shake to see how sturdy it was. "But you can get that one if you want." He nodded toward the most expensive one, which had a tall, elaborate canopy draping over about half of it.

"I like this one best. It's frilly enough for a little girl, and it will convert to a cradle. I don't know if I want a cradle," she said with a little shrug, "but I like having the option. The hood seems like a better idea. A big canopy would just be a West Texas dust catcher."

"Good point." He hauled the box off the shelf and laid it on top of the cart since it wouldn't fit inside. "We can take this with us, and they'll deliver the rest."

After the clerk rang up their purchase, Megan was almost as surprised as the girl behind the counter when Will handed her his debit card. A fifteen hundred dollar purchase out of his checking account, and the man didn't bat an eye.

Maybe a lot of people had that kind of extra cash in the bank, but she'd never had. Yet the Callahans didn't particularly flaunt their wealth. They had a nice home and drove vehicles that were two or three years old. They dressed nicely for church or other community activities, and she expected if Dub and Sue went to some big cattlemen or oil producers extravaganza in Dallas or Houston, they would dress to the nines. But around the ranch, whether working outdoors or in, they usually wore grubby clothes just like she did.

He helped her into the Cadillac and put the bassinet in the big trunk along with the rest of the items that weren't being delivered. She'd been pleased that he'd actually let her buy the sleepers and things she'd intended to purchase in the first place.

As they picked up a roasted chicken and some salads at Miller's Grocery, Megan tried to ignore the whispers because they were shopping together.

She knew some folks still speculated about Will being the father of her baby. And about her being a gold digger who either lured him into sin earlier or was trying to nab the kindhearted man now. Will didn't pay any attention to any of it. She wished she could do the same.

They went to her house and ate supper in relaxed comfort. Afterward, she rested in the recliner, once again thankful that it had been left behind, and Will put the bassinet together.

He woke her up about an hour later with a light kiss on her forehead. She blinked a couple of times and looked over to see him squatting beside the chair.

"Wake up, sleepyhead. Come see."

"Okay." She stretched and yawned before she got out of the chair. She walked down the hall and stepped into the bedroom she planned to use for the nursery. It was empty.

"I put it in your bedroom." Will leaned over her shoulder. "That's where you want it, isn't it?"

"Yes. I expected it to be in here because that's where you were putting it together." She continued to the end of the hall to the master bedroom. The bassinet sat along the wall beside the dresser. He'd taken the tags off the bear and laid it inside on the mattress as if it were waiting for a baby to join it. *How sweet.* "It looks better than the one at the store."

Standing beside her, he laughed and put his arm around her. "It's just like it."

"No, this one is new. The dust ruffle and hood are cleaner. The bear is a nice touch too."

"I thought so."

She could practically feel his smile. "Thank you."

"You're welcome. I enjoyed it."

"I hope you feel the same way after you put the rest of the furniture together."

Will laughed. "So do I. It's a good thing a couple of pieces will be delayed a few weeks." He gently turned her toward the door. "I'd better head on home. I have an early get-up in the morning."

"Earlier than usual?"

"No, but five o'clock is early no matter how you look at it." He followed her into the kitchen.

His cell phone rang before they reached the back door, and he fished it out of the case on his belt. "Hi, Dad." Megan couldn't hear what his father was telling him, but Will's eyes widened in surprise, and he smiled. Big time. "No kiddin'. Yes, sir, that is good news." He met Megan's gaze. "I'll tell her." He ended the call and put the phone away.

"Tell me what?"

"Josh took up writing while he was in prison and tried his hand at suspense crime novels."

"He has plenty of experience to draw from, and he was always good at telling tales. I think he embellished them a lot." She paused, studying his wide grin. "Did he publish something?"

"Yes, ma'am. He must be pretty good because he has a contract with a big New York publisher. He goes by Josh Riley."

"Riley is his middle name."

"They're using his criminal past and prison time as a marketing ploy."

"Did he make the thief the hero?"

Will laughed. "He did. His second book

comes out in August. According to his website —"

"He has a website?" She'd never thought to Google him. "Did Peters get all this from his website?" If so, her cousin could be selling nonexistent books to unsuspecting readers.

"No. I don't know where Peters got the lead, but he checked the publisher's website and found Josh's books online. He even picked one up at Hastings. He'd only read the first chapter, but he said it was good. According to Josh's website, he has a contract for another series."

"Don't tell me, this one is about a burglar." Josh had turned his life around. Amazing. She was happy for him.

"That's right. The next series he's planning is about . . . wait for it . . ." She grinned as he flung out his arm like the ringmaster at a circus announcing the acrobats in the third ring.

"Safecracking," they said in unison and burst into laughter.

"But he failed at that." Megan leaned against the counter. "He must have found his expert while he was in the calaboose."

"You've been hanging around Emily too long."

"I'm typing up some documents from the

early days of the town, thus calaboose. I think it's a cool word." She smiled. "So Josh left the criminal life behind him, except as fodder for his writing. What about Riley?"

"His record is clean. Been working at Whiteside for four years. Doesn't even have a traffic ticket. He bowls on a team every week and goes to church most every Sunday."

"Church?" She didn't think anyone else in her family had ever set foot in a church. "How long has he been going?"

"He started about six months after Josh went to prison. We all deal with guilt sometimes, but I expect he had a truckload of it. He checks on your mom now and then, but Peters thinks he basically stays away from her."

"He should. She's toxic." It was an awful thing to say, but it was the truth.

"Oh, I almost forgot the other good thing. Whiteside changed Riley's job. He's working in the mill now, so he doesn't need Josh to help him. They won't be coming up this way anymore."

"That's a relief. Even if they have straightened out their lives, I don't want to see them." Surprisingly, she didn't feel as adamantly about it as she had ten minutes ago. Interesting. *Are you doing something, God?*

She straightened away from the cabinet and stepped closer to him, resting her hands on his chest. "You should go. You've had a long day."

"No longer than usual, but shopping is tiring." He put his arms around her. "How do women spend all day at it and not get worn out?"

"I don't know. I've never been much for trooping around a mall. I'd rather run in and get what I want and be done with it."

"My kind of woman." Leaning down, he gave her a toe-curling kiss. He raised his head and searched her eyes. "In so many ways." Releasing her, he pushed open the screen door. "Good night, sugar. Sweet dreams."

She stepped out onto the porch as he walked to the Caddie. He pulled away with a little beep of the horn, and she waved until the car disappeared around the house. Sitting in the rocking chair, she watched the cows gather up their calves and settle down for the night. One cow looked around the pasture and bawled. A moment later a little calf scampered from behind some low-lying pale green mesquites and raced across the darker grass to meet her.

The light breeze turned the wheel on the windmill at a gentle pace, pumping more water into the tank. *Creak, swoosh. Creak, swoosh.* The sunset blazed in a riot of pink and gold, backlighting the dark silhouette of a distant mesa on the gently rolling horizon. A mockingbird landed on top of the barn, serenading her with a twilight song.

Megan touched her lips, remembering Will's kiss, thinking of the man. The wonderful, tender, stubborn, loving, sometimes bossy man. As she gazed out across the wide open land, so different from what she'd known all her life, peace filled her soul.

And she dared to dream, even to hope.

27

Six days later, on July 4th, Megan joined the Callahans for the Ranch Rodeo at the county fairgrounds. Teams of working cowboys from ranches in the county and surrounding areas competed in five events that reflected the work they did every day on the ranch.

Will, Nate, Buster, and Ollie made up the Callahan Ranch team. They had won the cattle sorting event with Will and his horse Cecil cutting yearlings — year old calves — out of a herd and driving them across a line. The other team members kept them from rejoining the herd, which wasn't always easy. Will couldn't simply pick one at random. Each calf was numbered, and the announcer called specific ones to be cut from the herd. They won by sorting out the most calves in the specified time.

They came in second in the mugging competition. Ollie roped the yearling, which

Dub said probably weighed close to a thousand pounds. Then the rest of the team grabbed hold of the calf however they could and threw it on its side, tying three feet together so it couldn't get away. They were ranked according to the time it took to complete the task.

"We use this to immobilize an animal if we need to give it medication or treat a wound," explained Dub. "The cowboys have to be strong, experienced, and work well as a team." Which the Callahan Ranch men did.

Not everyone was as successful. One roper missed the calf. Another team got the calf down but didn't get its feet tied before it managed to wiggle up and run away.

"This next event is the most fun," Jenna said, shifting Zach on her lap so she could see around his cowboy hat. He was cute as could be, all decked out in hat, boots, jeans, and a western shirt that matched his daddy's. Except after wrestling cattle around, Nate's shirt was a lot dirtier. "They have to milk a wild cow."

"Do they do that on the ranch?" Megan glanced at her, but her gaze drifted back to Will, who was standing below them, waiting for the event to start. He looked up at her and grinned, holding up a long-necked bottle. "Looks like Will gets to do the milking."

Jenna nodded. "He can run the fastest. Yes, they milk them on the ranch sometimes. Sometimes a mama cow rejects her calf or has an infection, or the baby can't figure out how to nurse. The guys have to milk her or another cow so the baby has something to eat. You noticed I said that the guys do it. Sometimes I feed the baby, but I'm not big enough to help hold the cow."

"The cows don't like it," added Sue. "They don't like it here, either. They're big, stubborn, and uncooperative beef cows, not docile dairy cows. Which makes for some fun."

Megan thought it sounded dangerous, but the Callahans didn't seem concerned, so she kept her worries to herself. Three months ago if anyone had told her she'd be spending Independence Day at a rodeo and wearing a cowboy hat, on loan from Jenna, she would have told them they were nuts. But here she was having a great time, learning some things about ranching, and admiring her man and his expertise. In her uneducated, totally biased opinion, he was the best cowboy out there. Definitely the most handsome.

All five teams lined up, each with one

cowboy mounted and the rest waiting behind the starting line. The cows were turned into the arena, and the riders took off after them. All five riders roped their chosen animal and brought her back across the starting line. Which wasn't particularly easy.

The second Ollie brought theirs across the line, the team jumped into action. Ollie's horse backed up in an effort to keep the rope taut, but the cow turned and he had to move too. Nate grabbed her tail and hung on, digging his heels in the dirt. Buster, the heaviest guy on their team, threw his arms around her neck and hung on. She kept moving for about ten feet, dragging them all, as Will ran alongside her.

"Milk her, boy," roared Dub. "It don't hurt to get dirty." He grinned and winked at Sue.

By then, Nate was sitting on his backside, feet planted, and still hanging on to the protesting cow's tail. Laughing, Buster still hung onto her head. Bending down, Will squirted some milk into the bottle. He took off running toward the finish line — and it turned into a foot race with another cowboy.

The Callahans and the ranch hands' wives jumped to their feet, hollering their encouragement. Megan stood too, with a little tug up from Emily, and hollered, "Run, Will!"

He sped up and sprinted across the line two steps ahead of the other cowboy. Handing the bottle to the judge, Will bent over to catch his breath. The judge slowly poured the small amount of milk on the ground, and the Callahan Ranch folks cheered wildly.

"Whew!" Sue clapped and leaned closer to Megan. "For a second, I thought there wasn't enough milk. You have to be able to pour it out on the ground."

"That puts us in the lead." Dub took off his hat and waved it to the Callahan team. After he sat down and put his hat back on, he winked at Megan. "He should have had you cheering him on in high school. He would've done even better in track."

Her cheeks turned a little pink, but she smiled back at him. It was one of the nicest things anybody had ever said to her. "Thanks. What's next?"

"Bronc riding. It's the last event. They use a standard working saddle and a bucking horse halter with one rein. No professional rodeo rigging is allowed. Even though we use gentler training methods than they did in the old days, a horse will still buck on occasion. Here, the cowboys need them to buck to give them a good score. Only one man per team participates in this event. Will rides for us."

Megan didn't like that idea. She'd seen some saddle bronc riding on television, and it looked a lot more dangerous than trying to milk a big cow, even if she did put up a fuss. "Is he good?"

Dub looked her directly in the eye and nodded. "He's the best. He's won this event every time he's entered. He probably could have turned pro, but he wanted to stay at the ranch."

That was some comfort, but she'd still worry until his ride was over. *Please, Lord, don't let anything bad happen to him.* "How long does he have to stay on?"

"Eight seconds, like in a regular rodeo." Dub swatted at a fly that buzzed by. "Hardly noticeable most of the time, but it can feel like forever on the back of a bucking horse. Worse on the back of a bull."

"You've done bull riding?" Megan didn't know whether to be impressed or think he might have a screw loose.

"Broncs and bulls both in my wild, younger days. I'm older and wiser now."

"In other words, he doesn't bounce like he used to." Sue patted him on the back. "If he did, he'd probably be right in the thick of it."

"Naw, I get my kicks in other ways these days." Dub plucked Zach off Jenna's lap and gave him a growling hug. "Like playing with this guy."

Zach giggled and hugged him back. "You're funny, Papa."

"Yeah, I know, but looks aren't everything."

Zach frowned up at him. "Huh?"

"Nothing. I was just teasin' you. Are you ready to watch Uncle Will ride the bucking horse?"

"Like the one in the corral last week?"

"Maybe. This one may buck more than Blaze."

"What?" Megan asked. "A horse with a real horse-sounding name?"

"We bought this one, and the name came with it. It's an obvious, if tired, choice since she has a white line down her face." Dub glanced toward the other side of the arena. "I reckon that's why we don't give them horse-sounding names too often. Most of them have been used a lot, and all horses are unique."

"So they should have unique names. I like that." Megan wondered if it was easier to name a horse than a baby. She still hadn't come up with a combination of names that she liked.

The microphone squeaked. "Sorry about that, folks," said the announcer. "Minor technical difficulty, but I think we have it fixed. First up in the bronc riding is Will Callahan of the Callahan Ranch. Will has won this event for the past seven years. Today he's riding Thunder."

Sitting on the other side of Emily, Chance groaned softly. "That's the toughest horse here. Hold on, big brother."

Emily shushed him. "You'll scare Megan." She gave Megan a little hug. "He knows what he's doing. He'll be okay."

Megan hoped she was right. Still, she didn't miss the fact that every one of the Callahans, including Emily, tensed when Will climbed over the fence. He straddled the chute, resting one foot on the fence railing and the other on a gate rail. Thunder tried to buck right there. Will and Nate, who was assisting him, got the horse settled enough for Will to ease down in the saddle and slide his boots into the stirrups.

Will nodded, and a man pulled open the gate, then scrambled over the fence when Thunder leaped out into the arena.

The horse kicked his hind feet in the air, and Will leaned back, keeping his balance. Thunder jumped, all four feet coming off the ground. Will hung on and made it look easy. Thunder came off the ground again and twisted a half turn. Will slipped sideways.

"Uh-oh," Chance murmured.

The horse bucked again, and when his hooves hit the ground, he ducked his head low, arched his back, and kicked his back feet. Will flew off, flipped in the air, and landed hard on his back.

Megan gasped and clenched her fists tight. He didn't move. "Please, God . . ." she whispered. Emily put her arms around her.

Nate jumped over the fence and ran to Will, kneeling beside him. Chance bolted down the bleacher steps and vaulted over the fence. He sprinted across the arena while keeping an eye on Thunder. A couple of riders herded the horse out a gate and into a pen. When Chance reached his brother, he dropped to his knees and leaned down to talk to him.

Dub followed Chance, moving down the steps as fast as his arthritic knees would let him.

"Why isn't he moving?" Megan had barely spoken the anguished words when Will waved an arm — feebly, she thought — and a few seconds later Nate and Chance slowly helped him to his feet. Wobbling and with their assistance, he walked out of the arena through a gate someone opened.

Megan desperately wanted to go to him, but she didn't know how to get to where he was. Dub had reached the steps leading out of the stands, but he stopped and turned around, looking at her. When he nodded, she hurried after him as fast as she dared. She thought Jenna, Sue, and Emily were gathering up their things, but she didn't look back to confirm it.

"Thank you," she huffed when she reached Dub.

He took her hand and helped her down the steps. "I figure he'll want to reassure you that he's all right."

"Is he?" She walked as fast as she could, but it must have seemed like a snail's pace to the tall rancher, especially when he was anxious to see about his son.

"He got his bell rung, that's for sure." He guided her along the back side of the arena, past pickups and horse trailers, pens of horses and cattle. She glanced back. Sue, Emily, Jenna, and Zach came around the corner behind them.

"Shouldn't he go to the hospital?"

"Yes. He'll do it too. Or wish he had."

Spoken like a loving father. Megan smiled in spite of her worry.

They found him sitting in the back of one

of the two ambulances on hand for such emergencies. Johnny was taking his blood pressure. *Of course,* she thought wryly. Butch was on the phone with the hospital.

Will was pale and grimaced in pain. When he saw her with his dad, a little light flared in his eyes, then the pain took over.

Chance and Nate stood out of the way but were keeping a close eye on what was happening.

"Why aren't y'all on the way to the hospital?" Dub glared at them all.

"Because your ornery son keeps fighting us on it." Johnny pressed a button on the portable blood pressure machine.

"Just got a bad headache." Confusion drifted across Will's face. Megan had seen the same expression on the trucker's face the day of the tornado. "Did I hit my head?"

"Load him up," ordered Dub. "Will, you let Johnny and Butch put you on that blasted gurney, or I'll haul you up there myself."

"Just wanna go home."

"Son, don't argue with me."

Megan motioned Johnny aside and took his place. She laid her hand on Will's arm.

"Hi, sugar." He leaned toward her — and almost fell over.

Catching him, she rested the side of his

head on her shoulder and caressed his face. "Please go to the hospital. Let the doctor make sure you're all right."

"You come with me?"

"I'll go with your dad. We'll be right behind you."

"Kiss me and make it better?"

Dub about choked, but she didn't know if he was laughing or ready to throttle his son.

"Only after you go to the hospital."

"That's my girl." He sighed softly and closed his eyes.

She looked at Johnny, trying not to panic, and whispered, "Did he pass out?"

Johnny shook his head. "Come on, Will, quit takin' advantage of the situation. Megan doesn't need to hold you up."

He helped Will straighten, holding on to him to keep him from falling over again.

Will let the paramedics help him into the ambulance. He laid down on the gurney with a moan. Johnny guided him onto his side to keep him off the knot on the back of his head.

Butch stepped out of the vehicle. "Definitely got a concussion, but his vitals are okay. I don't think it's real serious, but the doctor needs to make sure. We'll see y'all at the hospital."

The whole family was there by then.

Chance and Nate decided they'd better load up the horses, then they would follow the rest of them to the hospital.

They all were concerned, but no one seemed extremely worried. Megan took some comfort in that.

Jenna and Zach walked with her, while Dub, Sue, and Emily went on to load things in the pickups. Megan looked down at Zach, hesitant to ask Jenna anything about Will. But she needed some reassurance. "Johnny thought he'd be all right."

Jenna nodded. She glanced at Zach as if she understood that Megan was worried but didn't want to frighten the little boy. "He's had concussions before. Two in football and one from a fall on the ice when we were kids. He doesn't seem any worse than he was then."

"That's good to know. You don't seem real worried."

"I'm concerned, but not in a panic." Jenna picked up Zach. "They didn't have to haul him out of the arena on a stretcher, and that's a good sign."

Megan and Chance stood in the emergency room hall outside Will's room. She concluded like everywhere else in town, the Callahans had more clout in the hospital than anybody else. Dub and Sue were in the room with him, along with Dr. Cindy. Jenna, Nate, Zach, and Emily were in the waiting room. Not even the Callahans could — or would — clog up the hallway.

"Butch was right," said the doctor. "It's a concussion. The CT scan doesn't show signs of anything more serious, but you need to take it easy for the rest of the week, Will. No work. Just be lazy."

"Don't know how." He sounded tired.

"Time to learn. Doctor's orders. You'll probably have a headache off and on for several days, maybe even a few weeks. So it will remind you. Sue, someone needs to stay with him for the next twenty-four hours. Wake him every two to three hours until tomorrow morning at about six or seven.

"You probably remember the routine from his football days. Ask him some questions, check his eyes to make sure they're both dilated the same. If he starts vomiting, call me. Also call if his headache, dizziness, impaired balance, or memory loss increases. I want to see him on Thursday, regardless."

"Cindy, did I hit my head?" Will's voice sounded faint to Megan.

"Yes. Do you remember the rodeo?"

"Yeah. Was supposed to ride Thunder."

"You did. Dub, did he make the eight

398

seconds before he was thrown?"

"Yes," Dub said proudly. "Don't know what his score was, though. We weren't paying any attention."

Megan didn't think it was important at this point whether or not he had the highest or lowest score. Though it probably would be to him.

"I got thrown?" Will's voice was stronger.

"Did a front flip and bonked your head in the dirt," the doctor said. "Can you tell me your name?"

"William Charles Callahan."

"When is your birthday?"

"August first. I'll be thirty-three."

"Okay. I'll go ahead and release you. Too bad y'all will miss the fireworks tonight."

"What fireworks?" Will sounded groggy again.

"Do you know what day this is?"

There was a long pause before Will spoke. "Uh, no."

Frightened, Megan looked up at Chance. "Is that bad?"

"Not necessarily. I got a concussion during a football game and didn't remember it was homecoming. I'd just been crowned king at halftime."

"It's the Fourth of July, son." Sue sounded a lot calmer than Megan felt. "Independence Day."

"Oh."

"Tylenol for pain, but nothing else," Dr. Cindy said briskly. "You can put ice on that bump, but you don't have to unless it makes it feel better. The main thing is rest. You got that, Will?"

"Yes, ma'am."

"All right. You can head on home. I'm going out in the hall to tell Megan that you'll live."

"Tell her she's gotta keep her promise."

"Oh yeah?" Cindy switched from doctor to friend. "What was that?"

"Told me if I came to see you, she'd kiss me and make it better."

The minute they let Megan in the room, that's exactly what she did.

Chance watched over Will Monday night, and Megan stayed at his house during the day on Tuesday and Wednesday. He slept most of the time, so she used his computer to work on a project for Emily. She cooked his meals and kept him company when he was awake, often along with one of the Callahans because they kept dropping by to check on him.

Dub came over Wednesday evening as Megan was leaving, so she decided to stop by to see Sue. When she pulled up in the driveway at the ranch house, Will's mom stepped out onto the back porch and waited there until Megan joined her.

"How's he doing?"

"He has a mild headache, but it's not as bad as the one yesterday. He slept for awhile after you left this afternoon, then ate most of his supper."

"That's always a good sign." Sue opened the door for them to go inside. "Would you like something to drink?"

"No, thanks. I'm good." She followed her friend into the living room. When Sue sat down on one of the couches, Megan sat across from her on the other one.

Sue rested her bare feet on the ottoman and studied Megan for a few seconds. "How are you?"

"Okay, now that he's better. I was really worried about him yesterday." She put her feet up on the ottoman, noting that her ankles were swollen again.

"You've taken good care of my boy these past couple of days. Will you always treat him so well?"

The question shouldn't have surprised Megan. Sue Callahan protected her children like a mama mountain lion with cubs.

"Yes, if we're together, but I don't know if

we will be. He drops little hints, makes promises, and does dozens of other things that make me think he really cares for me." She shrugged, trying to keep her voice light. "But he's never told me he loves me, and he hasn't asked me to marry him."

Megan shifted her gaze, scanned the room, and gathered her thoughts. Looking back at Sue, she decided to be as blunt as her friend. "Sweet Baby's father made a lot of promises and did nice things that made me think he truly cared for me too. But he didn't."

"And he broke your heart."

"I thought so at the time." Lately, she realized he'd hurt her pride more than her heart. She hadn't loved him, though she might have someday if he'd been the man she thought he was. Mostly, she hated being taken advantage of and made to feel stupid.

It was a different story with Will. If he walked away, she didn't know how she could bear it. "I know Will is a thousand times better than Ken, but I'm still afraid he's just leading me on. I want so much to hope for a future together, but I'm scared to trust him."

A tiny frown wrinkled Sue's forehead. "Will doesn't lead women on, and he doesn't make promises, even subtle ones, that he won't keep. You can trust him." She paused, her frown deepening. "What about you? Will he wake up some morning and discover that you and your baby are gone?"

"No. The only reason I'd leave is if he decides that I'm not the woman for him."

"Then neither of us have anything to worry about. That boy is head over spurs in love with you." Amusement tinted Sue's smile. "He just hasn't worked up the courage to tell you yet."

"A Callahan afraid of something? I'm not buying that."

Sue laughed. "Those three little words spark fear in the bravest of male hearts. I expect he's just waiting for the right moment."

"Wish he'd hurry up."

"Shall I give him a nudge?"

"Better not." Megan smiled and slowly got to her feet. "But if he doesn't get his act together soon, I might reconsider it."

28

As Sue drove the Lincoln into the church parking lot on Thursday evening, Megan stifled a yawn. She hoped the ladies' meeting was interesting enough to keep her wide awake. It would be embarrassing to yawn while some nice woman was talking.

Will had felt much better today, and Dr. Cindy had agreed that he could ease back into his normal routine. Megan had barely slept since he was hurt. If she'd had her druthers, she'd have stayed home and gone to bed early.

She'd agreed to come to the meeting because Sue said she should, and she wanted to be as active in the church as possible. Which was why she baked a Black Forest cake the night before to help with the desserts.

Jenna and Emily had arrived early because they were helping, so Megan rode into town with Sue and Ramona. After Sue parked

404

the car, Megan handed the cake box to the housekeeper and scooted out of the back-seat.

Ramona eyed the box as Megan shut the car door. "I think I'll pick up some of these next time I'm in Abilene. It sure makes it easy to take a cake somewhere and leave it."

"As if there will be any left," Sue said with a laugh. "You have a round cake and a square box. How do you keep the cake from sliding against the side and smashing the icing?"

"The cake is basically centered on a square cardboard base the same size as the box. I've used one with a round cake plate too, but it's a little trickier. I crumpled up masking tape and filled the corners and also put a piece of double-sided tape beneath the plate to hold it in place."

"Well, I can't wait to see this cake and taste it." Sue opened the outside door to the fellowship hall and held it. Ramona headed straight to the kitchen to leave the cake. Megan stepped into the large room and stopped a few feet from the doorway.

One end of the room had been set up for the meeting, though she thought it odd that the chairs were arranged in a circle. A semicircle or rows would have been more appropriate to listen to a speaker. Then she noticed a long table decorated with a white tablecloth, pink streamers, and a beautiful bouquet of flowers along with small baby things — booties, a bib, a tiny pair of lace ruffled socks, and some rattles. In the corner, a round table was piled with gifts, with even more sitting on the floor. Some were in gift bags, some were wrapped boxes, but all proclaimed *baby* in one way or the other.

Oh, dear. Why hadn't Sue told her it was a baby shower so she could pick up a gift? Then she wondered why Sue or Ramona hadn't brought gifts.

"She's here," called Peg.

Jenna, Emily, Ramona, and two other ladies came out of the kitchen. Everyone else — at least twenty women — ended their conversations and turned toward the door.

Grinning from ear to ear, Jenna called, "One, two, three . . ." and everyone shouted, "Surprise!"

Megan was too stunned to speak.

Sue rested a hand on her shoulder. "Welcome to your baby shower."

Megan stared at her, then she looked at the blur of smiling faces watching them. "I-I don't know what to say." She caught her breath. "I never expected anything like this." It had never entered her mind that they would throw a party for her. No one ever had, for any reason.

"You're part of our church." Jenna joined them. "This is one of our traditions."

"Thank you." Megan smiled at her dear friends and the others. Though she knew several of the ladies, there were some she'd never met. She was astonished to see Kim with Peg. "Thank you so much. I'm overwhelmed."

"Don't be." Emily led her over to a pale green, striped swivel rocker that Megan recognized as coming from Jenna's living room. "You sit right here and have fun. Ladies, if everyone will take a seat, we'll get started.

"We can't have a party without a few games. Jenna, will you give everyone a clothespin?" As Jenna passed them out, Emily continued. "I see by your smiles that most of you have played this game. If you cross your legs, whoever notices it first can steal your clothespin. Right before we have dessert, the one who has the most will get a prize. So clip those pins where they're easy to reach and see."

"Does crossing your ankles count?" Peg asked with a big grin.

"Yes, ma'am. And if you're wearing sandals, don't cross your toes, either, 'cause we'll count that too." Several women laughed. "Now, you know we can't have only one game."

Lindsey began passing out blank sheets of paper and pens.

"Megan hasn't decided on a name for her baby, so we need to give her some suggestions. They can be good ones or funny ones. It's a girl, so come up with both a first and middle name." She waited a minute until everyone had a sheet of paper and a pen. "There are two parts to this game, so you only have one minute to think of a name, beginning now."

Lindsey sat down next to Megan. "Any suggestions?"

"Nope." She had a sheet of paper and a pen, but she didn't plan on writing anything down. She had half a dozen lists at home already. It was more fun to sit and watch everyone else.

"Okay. Did anyone come up with a funny name?" asked Emily.

"Sparkle Plenty," called the pastor's wife.

"Ester Emu." Sue grinned at her.

Emily joined in the laughter. "Good ones. Now, the next part of the game —"

"Do you want to hear the nice ones?" Peg asked.

"We'll collect the papers when we're done

so Megan can take them home and look them over. She might find something that's just right. The second part of the game is to make as many words as you can using only the letters in the names you suggested. You don't have to use all the letters in each word. Whoever comes up with the most words in five minutes wins."

"Oh, good." Mrs. Snyder, the florist, laughed. "I'm glad I picked Victoria Elizabeth."

"That's what I get for trying to be clever," Sue muttered good-naturedly.

"Didn't they tell you what games they were playing?" asked Kim. She looked prettier tonight, more relaxed, happier. Things must be going well between her and Mike. Or between her and some handsome guy.

"No, the sneaky people." Sue wrinkled her nose at her daughter.

Everyone scribbled away, sometimes laughing or showing a friend something they came up with.

Kim looked up, glanced around the room, and hopped up to steal a clothespin from Mrs. Snyder, causing more laughter.

After a few minutes, Megan decided to see what she could do with Sue's Ester Emu. Tums, me, must, steer, rest, meet, rust, strum, tee, use, sue, set, sum, mute, rum, seer . . .

"Time's up."

Megan counted her words and grinned. Sixteen. Not bad, but several people had many more. The winner was Natalie Jones with fifty-six. Natalie was the senior English teacher at the local high school and had taught all three of the younger Callahans. Her husband, Buster, was one of Dub's cowboys. They had lived on the ranch for years.

As Natalie chose a wrapped prize from a large basket, Jenna picked up the pens and papers. Megan wondered how many of the people in the room were connected to the Callahans in some way other than the church. Three ladies were in the Historical Society with Emily and Sue. Another was the family insurance agent. Still another was on the bank board with Will.

Peg Renfro had helped bring Sue's children into the world. Others besides Natalie had taught them in school. The Callahans were woven into the fabric of the town and the church. She doubted there was a single person in Callahan Crossing who couldn't name each member of the family on sight. Most probably knew them personally.

Sue reached over and stole Peg's clothespin.

"Your kids aren't the only ones who are sneaky." Peg wagged her finger at her old friend.

Jenna and Emily took their seats, and a tiny silver-haired woman cleared her throat. Frannie Scott was a museum volunteer, and one of the kindest people Megan had met in Callahan Crossing.

"Megan, I've been asked to share a little tonight. Since I have eight kids, Jenna thinks I know something about raising them," Frannie said with a gentle smile. "They've all turned out well, so perhaps I do. She also knows that I don't spout off for very long, so we'll get to the presents soon." That prompted some light laughter and many nods of agreement.

"Psalm 139 says, 'For you created my inmost being; you knit me together in my mother's womb. I praise you because I am fearfully and wonderfully made; your works are wonderful, I know that full well.'

"God is knitting your precious baby together, Megan. He is weaving together her body, mind, and spirit to make her a whole being, a child created especially for you by our loving heavenly Father.

"I know from our chats at the museum how much you love this baby. I'm certain you'll be the very best mother you can be.

411

Keep in mind that you'll make mistakes. We all do. Seek God's guidance and wisdom every day. Praise him for his goodness and mercy, for the blessing this baby will be to you."

She scanned the faces of her audience. "All of mine were blessings, even if a couple of them were scamps when they were younger, as some of you know.

"Enjoy your little girl. Take time to play with her, to teach her, to love her as only a mother can. Treasure her laughter, comfort her tears, ease her fears." Frannie beamed her a smile. "The Lord has his hand on this child, dear. He has claimed her — and you — as his own. Rest in that assurance."

When the older lady nodded, indicating she was finished, Megan wiped her eyes. "Thank you, Frannie. I'll take that to heart."

"I know you will, dear. Now, Jenna, is it time for her to open her presents?"

"Yes, ma'am, it is." Jenna stood and walked over to the round table behind Megan. "I'll hand you the gifts, and Lindsey will keep track of who brought what."

Kim stole another clothespin. She and another woman — Audrey, maybe? — were in fierce competition for that prize.

For the next half hour, Megan opened presents and passed them around the circle

412

so folks could comment on how cute everything was. Frilly little outfits, sleepers and gowns, bibs and pacifiers. Blankets and a beautiful handmade quilt, sheets and soft baby towels. Onesies and booties, rattles and soft toys. There was a mobile to hang above a crib, fun little toys to fasten onto a car seat or stroller — and the combination stroller/car seat from the Callahan ladies to go with them.

Lindsey gave her a beautiful handmade scrapbook so she could keep track of her baby's firsts and fill the pages with other memories. Ramona had crocheted her an adult-sized multicolored afghan so she and Sweet Baby could snuggle on the couch on cold winter evenings.

Megan handed Lindsey the last gift and looked around the group. "Thank you for all the gifts and for coming tonight. This has been wonderful. I've never had anything like it."

"Kind of like Christmas and your birthday rolled into one," said a lady whose name she didn't remember.

"Even better." Much better. Many years there hadn't been any presents on Christmas or her birthday. Her mom came through with a little something about every other time. Uncle Riley had given her a doll when she was six, but it got lost in one of their moves.

Emily pointed to Kim and Audrey. "Okay, you two, count your clothespins."

Kim tapped each one as she counted. "Eight."

"Eight for me too."

"Good thing we brought extra." Emily held the basket out to Audrey, then Kim, so they could pick their prizes.

Sue thanked the Lord for the desserts and asked his blessing upon them. Megan didn't think he'd zero out the calories despite Lindsey's murmured request after she said amen. Folks bragged on Megan's cake, and she bragged on Lindsey's key lime pie and asked her for the recipe. She didn't get a chance to taste the cheesecake someone else brought.

After the party was over, some of the other ladies cleaned up while the Callahans and Ramona loaded her gifts in the Lincoln and Emily's van.

When they arrived at her house, Will was waiting on the back porch. He strolled out to the car and opened her door, grinning like a possum eatin' persimmons. "Did you make a haul?"

"Boy, did I." Megan took his offered hand and let him help her out of the car. "How long have you known about this?"

"For a couple of weeks." He went around to the back of his mother's car to help carry things in. "Was she surprised, Mom?"

"Very. We actually pulled it off."

"For a minute I thought the shower was for someone else, and I felt bad that I hadn't brought a gift."

"Told ya." Will nudged his sister's shoulder, then turned toward the house with an armload of small boxes. He wasn't supposed to carry anything heavy yet.

"You're right, you warned us," said Jenna. "I'm sorry we made you feel bad, Megan, but we really wanted it to be a surprise. Though I don't think I've ever gone to a shower where the honoree made the dessert. I was afraid you'd get suspicious if I declined your offer."

Megan opened the kitchen door and turned on the light. "It never occurred to me that you might give me a baby shower. I didn't realize that was something the ladies at church did."

"You know, I never thought about telling new folks about the various activities we have." Jenna set some gift bags on the kitchen table. "I'll mention that to our program chairman as something we should cover next year. The ladies' group doesn't meet again until September. We should probably have a brochure ready to give to people."

"That's a good idea." Sue wheeled in the stroller/car seat. "Shall I put this in the bedroom next to the master? I assume you're going to use it for the nursery."

"You assumed right. Thanks."

After all the goodies were brought in, the ladies bade her good night. Will stayed.

"Did you have a good time?" He led her into the living room and guided her down on one end of the couch. "Want a foot rub?"

"That would be wonderful." She kicked off her sandals, propped a throw pillow against the armrest, and lay down. After Will sat down on the end of the couch, she rested her feet on his thigh. When he started gently massaging her feet, she groaned softly. "Oh, my, that feels good. You should become a masseur. I bet the cowboys would love it."

"No, thanks. I'm not about to rub any-body's smelly feet."

"Guess that means mine don't stink."

"No, they don't. Now if you'd been wear-ing tennis shoes, it might be a different story."

"Careful, big guy. It's a straight shot from my toes to your chin."

"Yes, ma'am. I'll behave. Do you want to

ride around the ranch with me in the morning?"

"How early?"

"Pick you up around 8:30. It's nicer to check on the cows before it gets too hot."

"Sure, I'll go." She sighed softly as he gently worked on her arch. "I don't have any work to do tomorrow. Just so you know, as of this morning, all the cows and calves in my pasture were accounted for."

"What did they do, line up along the fence so you could count noses?"

"No. I have a good view of the pasture from the porch. I counted the cows, and at that time of day, all the calves were with their mamas. I usually check them again in the evening. So far I haven't seen any that seem to have any problems. The calves are a hoot to watch. They're even more playful than I thought."

"What's really cute is if there is a little hill or mound of dirt in the pasture." Will held out his hand and helped her sit up and swing her feet around to the floor. "There's always one or two of them that will race around, then storm up the mound and play King of the Hill. Feel better?"

"Much. I'm surprised at how relaxing a foot rub is. Thank you."

"Shall I haul all those presents in here so

I can look at them?"

"Sure. I need to take them out of the boxes and bags anyway. You can help."

Twenty minutes later all the small things were organized into piles on the coffee table. Since he'd had so much fun shopping with her the week before, she wasn't surprised that he got such a kick out of everything.

After they'd looked at the presents, she showed him the names the ladies had come up with.

"Sparkle Plenty? You've got to be kidding." He looked from the paper to her, raising one eyebrow.

"They could be silly or real. Your mom's suggestion was Ester Emu."

He rolled his eyes and studied all the words on the first sheet. "So then they had to find words in the names?" When she nodded, he asked, "Who won?"

"Natalie Jones."

"That doesn't surprise me. She was always doing word puzzles of some kind at lunchtime."

They looked through the suggestions, laughing at the funny ones, discussing the real ones. None of them were right.

"I want one name to be Marie, after Mrs. Hoffmann. She was the kind, loving grandmother I never had." Megan studied the sheet of paper in front of her and pursed her lips. Marie Alexandra? Nope. Didn't work for her. "The one I keep coming back to is Marie Elizabeth."

"Elizabeth is my mom's middle name." His gaze slid her way.

"I know. Do you think she'd mind?"

He tossed the papers on the table. "I can't think of anything that would please her more."

"Then it's settled. Sweet Baby is now Marie Elizabeth. Only that poses another quandary."

"What?"

"Should I call her Marie or Beth?"

He smiled and slid his arm around her shoulders. "How about Mari Beth?"

"Oh, I like that."

But would her last name be Smith or Callahan?

29

Friday morning, Will decided he'd made a big mistake. Not in what he had planned, but in telling his brother and Nate about it.

"You're going to propose to her in a pasture." Chance poured himself a cup of coffee and turned around to lean against the counter, gently blowing on the hot brew.

"At the spring. Where Nate proposed to Jenna." Will started to get another cup of coffee, then decided against it. He was already wired enough.

"It's still in the pasture." His brother was good at pointing out the obvious.

"I didn't exactly propose to her there." Nate chugged the last bit of orange juice in the bottle, annoying Will further. Now he wouldn't have any for breakfast tomorrow.

"That's not the way Jenna tells it." Will picked up the empty jug and rinsed it out in the sink. He'd put it in the recycle bin later.

"Yeah, well, she has her side of the story, and I have mine." Nate grinned unrepentantly.

"I guess marrying her there was easier than gettin' down on one knee in the dirt." Chance looked at Will. "You gonna get down on one knee?"

"Did you?" Will frowned and turned off the coffeemaker.

"Yes, siree Bob." Chance's eyes twinkled with glee. "But I was smart enough to kneel in my living room, not where I might land on a cow pie."

"I'll look first," Will said dryly. He glanced at the clock on the stove. Twenty minutes to go.

"Are you sure you're up to this?" The teasing laughter had disappeared from Chance's face. "You look a little pale. Is your head hurting again?"

"It's all right." Nothing Tylenol wouldn't control when it kicked in. "I'm just nervous as a worm on a hook."

Chance and Nate laughed.

Nate laid his hand on Will's shoulder. "Appropriate. Just remember the gettin' caught part works both ways, for the fish and the worm."

"What if she turns me down?"

"She won't." Chance set his cup on the

table, pulled out a chair, and sat down. "Not because you've got money to burn. She loves you. She was worried sick when Thunder threw you." He glanced at the clock. "You'd better get moving."

Will started for the back door, then turned around to look at them. Neither of them appeared to be in a hurry. "Aren't y'all going to work? Or are you gonna sit there and drink up my coffee?"

"You're not going to drink it." Chance stretched lazily. "I'm in no rush this morning. What about you, Nate? Do you need to hurry off to the job?"

Nate shrugged. When he glanced at Will, his smile was full of mischief. "Naw, the boss is gone a'courtin'. I can take my time."

When Will pulled up in back of Megan's house, she was sitting on the porch. He got out and walked over to her, resting one boot on the bottom step. "Tallying up the cows?"

"They're all present and accounted for."

"Good. You ready to go?"

"Yep." She pushed herself out of the chair and picked up a bottle of water. "Where are we headed this morning?"

"Down by Aidan's Spring." Was there a quiver in his voice? He glanced at her quickly. If so, she hadn't noticed.

He helped her into the pickup, hurried around to the driver's side, and headed down the road. For the life of him, he couldn't think of anything to talk about. She didn't seem to mind.

Because he drove extra slow over the bumps and dips, it seemed to take forever to get to the spring. *No,* he thought ruefully, *it would have seemed like forever if I'd been going sixty.*

"It's such a nice morning, would you mind sitting here at the spring for a spell? We might see a critter or two come to drink." He parked the truck and turned off the ignition.

"I'd like that. In fact, I'd like to look around a little bit. What is that little building? I didn't notice it when we were here before."

"It's the springhouse. Some bushes had grown up and hid it. I cleared them out after we were here." He got out of the truck and walked around to lift her down.

"Careful, I'm getting so big you might strain your back." She grinned when he took his sweet time setting her feet on the ground.

"You're still a lightweight. I'd better hang on to you. The ground is uneven."

"Excuses, excuses." They walked over to

the stone spring-house, stopping on the slight incline above it. "Did they build it from rocks here along the creek?"

"Mostly. I think Aidan and Jack hauled some bigger ones from the base of one of the mesas for part of it. I've never found any rocks that size along here." He opened the old, rickety wooden door.

"Is that the spring?"

"Yes. It provided fresh water, and the springhouse gave them a place to store things that needed to be refrigerated, like milk, butter, eggs, vegetables, and fruit. Though I don't know how many vegetables they really had. The water flows out underneath the building and forms the creek."

Holding on to his arm, she leaned over and peered inside. "How did it work?"

"They put food in crocks, bottles, or maybe a basket for eggs, and set them in the cement trough in the middle. See how the cold water from the spring flows through the trough? It flowed around the crocks or through the egg basket and kept the food cold, even in the hot summer."

"It probably helped that the trees shade it."

"I'm sure it did. There's another one up by the dogtrot. Aidan used water from the windmill to keep it cool, though it didn't work as well as this one."

Though Nate and Chance had only been teasing him, maybe they'd been right. He hadn't brought her here for a history lesson. He shut the door on the little stone building. "Let's go sit on the bench. Maybe a bird will sing us a tune."

Dumb, Callahan.

"That would be nice. I enjoy having the windows open at the house and listening to the birdsong."

Okay, maybe not so dumb.

They sat down and quietly listened. There must have been a dozen birds in the trees around them, and for about five minutes all they did was chirp. Pleasant enough but not as good as a concert.

A sparrow landed above them in the pecan tree and sang a pretty song. Will had always been partial to a sparrow's music, and it calmed his nerves a bit. *Thanks, Lord, for that little blessing.*

"Megan, when we talked a while back, I said I wanted to see if God had something good for us." He took her hand, caressing the back of it with his thumb. "The more I've grown to know you, the more I'm convinced that he sent you here so that we could find each other."

She looked up at him, love shining in her

eyes. "I think you're right."

Oh yeah. She was going to make this easy. "I love you, sugar."

"I love you too, Will. I never knew I could care so deeply for someone."

"Then we probably should spend the rest of our lives together, don't you think?"

He glanced down at the ground to make sure it was clear of rocks and other unsavory debris and slid off the bench, kneeling on one knee on thick grass.

"Oh, Will . . ." she whispered.

He fumbled a little taking the ring out of his shirt pocket. Holding her hand, making sure she could see that big ol' diamond, he asked, "My sweet Megan, will you marry me?"

"Finally," she murmured, her eyes sparkling.

Will frowned. That wasn't even close to the enthusiastic response he'd expected. "What?"

The love of his life laughed, even as her face turned pink, and she caressed his cheek. "Sorry. I was beginning to think I'd have to sic your mama on you to get you to propose. Yes, I'll marry you, my sweet, stubborn, bossy, wonderful man!"

That's what he wanted to hear.

He slid the ring onto her finger, relieved

that it fit, and leaned up and kissed her. She put her arms around his neck and kissed him with all the love she'd been holding back. A half dozen kisses later, he eased back, dropping a light kiss on her nose. "I've got to get up."

Laughing, she released him and held out her ring to examine it. "Wow. Double wow." After he sat down real close to her and put his arms around her, she leaned her head on his shoulder, her hair tickling his chin. "That's one whoppin' diamond, Will Callahan."

"Only the best for my girl. Soon to be my wife." He kissed her forehead. "Speaking of which, the wedding will be soon, right?"

She jumped and put her hand on her stomach. "It better be." She winced and smiled up at him. "Mari Beth approves."

Will looked down at the little foot poking up against her top. "May I?"

"Of course," Megan said softly, taking his hand and guiding it to her stomach. "Mari Beth, this wonderful man is going to be your daddy."

He rested his hand lightly on her stomach, and his little girl touched him, tapping that tiny foot against his palm to say hello.

For the first time in a very long time, tears rolled down Will Callahan's cheeks.

■ ■ ■ ■

When they reached the ranch house an hour later, the whole family was waiting for them. The instant Sue spotted the engagement ring, she cried, "Hallelujah!" and hugged first Megan, then Will.

Everyone else gave them hugs, slapped Will on the back, and offered their congratulations. Zach danced around in excitement and finally asked, "Why's everybody so happy?"

Will scooped him up, holding him on one arm so they could see eye to eye and talk man to man. "Megan and I are going to get married. She's going to be your aunt."

Zach threw up his hands. "Yea!" He looked down at Megan's round stomach and leaned closer to Will. "Mama said she's going to have a baby."

"That's right. A little girl. She'll be your cousin."

Zach nodded, though Will wasn't sure the little guy really understood what a cousin was. He was, however, clearly pondering something. The room fell silent as they waited to hear what Zach had to say. "Ramona said Megan's going to pop soon, so y'all better hurry up and get hitched."

Will roared with laughter, along with all the adults, including his very red-faced bride-to-be and the equally rosy-cheeked housekeeper. He gave Zach a big hug and winked at Ramona. "She's right."

He set Zach down and put his arm around Megan. Smiling at his bride, then his mother and the girls, he laid down the law — as agreed to previously with his betrothed. "We're exchanging our vows two weeks from tomorrow. Pastor Brad already has us on his schedule. So y'all better jingle your spurs."

"We're already ahead of you." His mother pointed to the couch. "Sit."

"Yes, ma'am." Will followed Megan to the couch. "Now, before the steamroller gets moving, just remember that you don't want to squash a pregnant lady." Or a cowboy who'd just as soon skip all the fuss and get married in Pastor Brad's study in three days. He didn't even want to wait that long, but the law required it. "Don't take too long because we need to go get the marriage license."

"Might as well wait to go to the court-house this afternoon." Dub glanced at his watch. "By the time you get to town, the county clerk will be getting ready to go to lunch."

"Did y'all know he was going to propose?" Megan held his hand, squeezing a little too tight. Was she upset with them or just a little nervous?

"He spilled the beans to Nate and me early this morning," said Chance.

"Wanted some tips on how to ask you." Nate picked up Zach and set him on his lap.

"I did not."

"You asked if I got down on one knee." Chance conveniently ignored the fact that he'd mentioned it first.

"After you asked —"

"Boys!" Sue frowned at them. The fact that she included Nate in her motherly chastisement showed that she considered him one of her kids. "We have better things to do than listen to you snip at each other."

"Yes, ma'am." The words came from all three of them, though not quite exactly at the same time. Zach looked at his dad and uncles and grinned. Even the kid knew when his grandma gave a command, everybody obeyed.

His mother picked up a yellow, legal-size pad. "I assume you reserved the church when you talked to Pastor Brad?"

"He said it was available that day, but we didn't reserve it."

"Why not?" His mom held the pen in the air above the pad.

Megan laid a hand on her stomach. "I don't think I should have a church wedding, uh, given my situation."

His mom waved a hand in dismissal. "God's grace is sufficient to cover any situation. If anyone has a problem with it, then they don't have to come." She looked at her list. "The ceremony at four with a catered meal afterward. I assume you aren't going very far away on your honeymoon?"

"We're going to postpone it for a while. The wedding will be only three weeks before Megan's due date, so we want to stay close to home."

When Megan released his hand, he put his arm around her and leaned down close to her ear. "If you're not okay with this, just say so."

"It's sinking in." She looked up at him, a glimmer of excitement in her eyes. "It will be all right."

"Good." That was a big relief. Will knew his mother wasn't about to let her firstborn son get married anywhere other than the church with all the falderal and packed house that came with it.

"We'll call the florist this afternoon. Do you want any particular kind of flowers,

Megan?"

"I like everything, though I'm especially fond of daisies. It would be nice if they were part of the decorations."

Will smiled and rubbed his hand lightly on her shoulder. She had gotten his message the day he plucked the petals from the flower.

"Then we'll make sure they're included. And Emily will call her mother in Dallas and have her find someone to do the cakes."

"Her mom is a high-society mover and shaker," Will said quietly. "She has a lot of contacts."

"And a lot of bakeries that want to stay on her good list," added Emily.

Sue tapped the pen on the pad and focused on Megan. "I know you'd love to make your own wedding cake, but you'll be too busy."

Megan sighed. "It would be too difficult anyway. Lindsey's cake about did me in."

His mother checked her notes again. "You'll need to decide on attendants right away, so the ladies can find dresses, and the men can take care of getting tuxedos."

"That's easy. Mine are right here." Megan pointed to Jenna and Emily. "Only you'll both have to be matrons of honor because I could never choose between you."

"Mine are here too, ornery cusses that they are." Will nodded to Chance and Nate. "My two best men."

"Excellent. Ramona just waved at me, so dinner's ready." Sue laid the pad and pen on the coffee table. "This afternoon, we'll get things rolling while you go get your license. Save all day tomorrow, Megan, so we can go shopping for a wedding gown."

"I don't need anything elaborate." Will helped her up off the couch. "Do they even make wedding dresses for pregnant women?"

"An empire waistline will work perfectly." Emily scooted in and hooked her arm through Megan's. "Of course you need something beautiful and elaborate." She winked at her husband. "You're marrying a Callahan."

30

It turned out that the dress Megan fell in
love with was beautiful but not particularly
elaborate. Sleeveless, with a shallow scooped
neckline, the only decoration on the cham-
pagne silk gown was intricate, exquisite
flowered beadwork around the empire
waistline. Though simply made, she looked
at the price, choked, and put it back on the
rack.

Jenna promptly took it off again and
marched her into the dressing room. The
floor-length gown was a good fit, except for
being too long. The shop seamstress assured
her it was no problem. She had the short-
ened dress to them by Wednesday of the following week.

The Callahan whirlwind — Sue, Jenna,
and Emily — along with some help from
Lindsey, had taken care of every detail for
the wedding, always consulting her but
making sure that she didn't have to do

much of the work.

They had also taken an inventory of what she had for the baby and either ordered or bought everything else she could possibly need. And then some.

Now, she sat in a room at the church, waiting to go down the aisle. The photographer had already taken a gazillion pictures. She'd shed a few tears, and so had Sue. They'd laughed together as they came back in here and touched up their makeup.

Sue had been escorted into the sanctuary. Behind her, the first four rows on one side of the church were filled with Will's extended family on his mother's side.

Megan felt a twinge of regret that there were no relatives on the bride's side. Perhaps someday she would see Uncle Riley and Josh again, maybe even her mother. But not today.

Lindsey, who was acting as the wedding coordinator, handed Megan her cascading bouquet of coral roses. She checked the wide, pearl, fan-shaped clips nestled in Megan's soft brown curls in lieu of a veil. Sue's mother had worn them at her wedding, thus they fulfilled something old and something borrowed. Her gown took care of something new, and a blue ribbon and lace garter hidden beneath it completed the old tradition.

"You're radiant." Lindsey gave her a careful hug. "And happy."

"I am." Happier than she'd ever dreamed she could be. "Two months ago if someone told me I'd be standing here in this beautiful wedding gown, about to marry a handsome, wonderful man, I'd have asked them what they'd been smoking."

Lindsey laughed and opened the door. "God had it planned all along."

"So it seems." Megan walked down the hallway to the back of the church.

Emily and Chance, with Jenna and Nate standing behind them, were lined up to go inside the sanctuary. Emily and Jenna wore coral floor-length silk dresses made with spaghetti straps, a fitted waist, and gently flared skirt. Chance and Nate were handsome in their black tuxedos, despite Chance complaining about having to drag his out of the closet again.

Peg monitored Zach and Sarah Jane, the four-year-old daughter of one of Will's cousins. Both of the children were adorable, with Zach in his tux and Sarah Jane in a bright yellow dress with a big bow in the back. The kids were having an animated conversation.

"Don't get scared and stop before we get

there," Zach said to Sarah. "The last time I had to run back and get the flower girl."

"I know what to do. I've been in a wedding too."

Megan laughed. Another bossy Callahan man. But the little girl was enamored with him and didn't mind a bit.

Dub walked over to meet her. He had gotten all misty-eyed when she asked him to walk her down the aisle. "You're a beautiful bride, Megan."

"Thank you. You're quite handsome yourself." He always was, but like his sons, he looked as good and at home in fancy duds, as he called them, as he did in his everyday western wear.

He held out his arm. "You ready to commit matrimony?"

"Yes, sir. I am." She slipped her hand around his arm, thankful for his solid strength.

"Nervous?" He rested his hand over hers.

"A little."

"You'll do fine."

The music changed and Lindsey motioned for Chance and Emily to start down the aisle. When they were in position on the stage, she prompted Nate and Jenna. Zach and Sarah Jane were next. They made it without mishap, with Sarah Jane tossing the rose petals perfectly.

There was a pause, then the organist hit the opening chords of the "Wedding March," and Dub winked at Megan. "That's our cue, honey."

The church was packed with Will's relatives, church members, and folks from Callahan Crossing. There were also cattlemen from other counties as well as Texas oil bigwigs, including Emily's grandparents, all longtime friends of the Callahans. She heard some whispers and wondered if they were commenting on her very obvious baby bump. A jab of self-consciousness shot through her.

Then she met Will's gaze, and no one else, nothing else, mattered. Could the dear, sweet man's smile get any bigger? His expression any happier?

When Dub placed her hand in Will's, the love of her life whispered, "You doin' okay, sugar?"

She nodded. "Couldn't be better."

She was certain it was a beautiful ceremony, but it seemed she was destined to spend weddings in a daze. She'd missed most of Lindsey's worrying about Mike. She spent most of this one soaking up the love shining in Will's eyes.

Everything went smoothly, as far as she

noticed. The soloist sang perfectly. The unity candle lit on the first try. Pastor Brad shared about the love of Christ, and how God had used a tornado to bring them together. They said their vows, neither of them blowing it, and promised to love each other forever. And Zach and Sarah Jane made it through the whole wedding up on the stage without fidgeting too much.

"Will, you may kiss your bride," said Pastor Brad.

Her husband, her love, gently put his arms around her and kissed her tenderly.

"Ladies and gentlemen, may I present Mr. and Mrs. Will Callahan."

The audience stood and applauded loudly. "It's about time you found your woman," hollered someone. A few others whistled their approval as Will escorted her down the aisle and out the door of the sanctuary.

He took her to the side of the foyer and held her close. "I love you, Mrs. Callahan."

"I love you, Mr. Callahan."

He kissed her again, and when he straightened, he tugged at his tie and grinned. "Man, I'm glad that's over."

"You didn't look nervous." She rested her head against his chest.

"Scared silly."

"Why? You've been in a dozen weddings."

"Yeah, but this is the first time I've been the groom."

"Better be the last time too."

"Yes, ma'am."

They made their way to the fellowship hall. Bouquets of coral roses, white daisies, and trailing ivy in tall clear glass vases served as centerpieces on all of the round tables, which were covered in white linen tablecloths.

A large multicolored floral arrangement centered one long table with a silver punch bowl on each end. Since there were almost four hundred people at the wedding, they had decided to put water pitchers and coffee carafes on each table instead of using the silver tea and coffee services.

Megan figured only the Callahans, with their wealth, connections, and organizational skills, could have pulled it off in such a short time.

Megan loved the cakes, delivered that morning by a prestigious Dallas bakery. The wedding cake consisted of six square tiers covered in smooth white fondant icing, with each layer having a different added design. She knew they were all simple patterns, but put together, they made an intricate and beautiful cake. Two large locking sterling silver hearts decorated the top.

A marvelous three-dimensional, chocolate cake replica of an armadillo centered the groom's table. The CR brand had been nicely painted in white on the critter's shoulder.

Everyone else would simply think they'd gone with the popular armadillo theme and added the brand for a bit of whimsy. To Megan and Will, it was a reminder of a special, fun moment they'd shared the first time he took her riding around the ranch.

Because it was tiring for Megan to be on her feet too long at a time, they chose to sit and let their guests come to them.

Three hours later, all their guests had stopped by to wish them well. Everyone had eaten their supper and cake. The toasts and speeches had been made, and people slowly began to leave.

Lindsey came over to them. "Time to throw the bouquet and make your escape."

"I like the sound of that." Will stood and helped Megan up.

Lindsey picked up the microphone. "It's garter and bouquet throwing time. Single men over here. Single ladies over there. Will, Megan, front and center."

Lindsey handed Megan the toss bouquet, a smaller replica of her real one. She'd wanted to keep the tradition but had also wanted to save her bouquet and dry it. The florist had suggested the replica, saying it was commonly done these days.

Will knelt on one knee. Holding onto his shoulder, Megan rested her foot on his leg, and he slipped his hand beneath her gown, pulling off the garter. Giving her a kiss, he stood, turned his back to the surprisingly large group of single guys who jovially teased each other. He held up the garter over his head and flipped it like a rubber band into the crowd.

A tall, skinny cowboy who appeared to be a few years older than Will elbowed everybody out of the way to catch it. He nodded decisively and muttered, "If I catch enough of these blasted things, maybe it will work."

Trying not to giggle, Megan faced away from the single ladies and heaved the toss bouquet in the air. Will helped her turn around in time to see Kim make a flying leap to catch the bouquet, then do a little victory dance.

Megan glanced at Mike Craig. He watched Kim with an indulgent smile. After she ran back to his side, he gave her a lingering kiss that drew some whistles and cheers. He looked up and caught Megan watching them and winked.

"Shall we go home?" Will asked softly.

Megan nodded. Home. Not simply a house to live in, but a place where she belonged, where they would raise a family and grow old together.

"Good night, everybody. Thank you for being here," Will called as they waved at the remaining crowd and headed toward the door.

Silent praise welled up in her heart. Thanks to a loving God, all her dreams were coming true.

They spent the next two and a half weeks on their at-home honeymoon, opening all the presents, setting up the nursery, and loving being together. It was pure bliss.

Three days before her official due date, they were finishing a big shared bowl of ice cream after supper when Megan gasped.

Will dropped his spoon in the bowl, quickly set it on the coffee table, and took her hand. "Braxton Hicks?"

"I think it felt different." She handed him her spoon, and he put it in the empty bowl. "It's gone now."

But not for long. When the second one hit, Will ran to get his watch. Ten minutes after that, he pulled on his boots and found her sandals.

An hour later, the contractions were coming every five minutes. Will called his mother, who told him to call Dr. Cindy. Dr. Cindy told them to go on to the hospital, and she'd meet them there.

He helped Megan into the Caddie and sprinted around to the other side. Another labor pain hit as he slid into the seat. "Breathe, sugar. Like we practiced. That's my girl." His hands trembling, he fastened the seat belt and started the car. *I'd better follow some of these breathing techniques too.*

"Okay, it's easing up, so breathe deep and let it out slowly. That's it. Relax." He tried to do the same as he threw the car into gear and roared down the road. Thankfully, he'd had Buster grade it two days earlier to give his sweetheart a nice smooth ride to the highway.

A glance in the mirror told him the rest of the family was following them, all except Emily and Zach. They'd decided that Jenna should be available to help during labor if he needed her. Will wanted backup if he messed up somehow.

After they reached the hospital, Dr. Cindy examined her and smiled. "We're going to have a baby."

"Uh, Cindy, we already figured that out." Will kissed Megan's hand.

"But it will be a while. Y'all keep handling

those contractions just the way you are. You make a great team." She patted Megan's shoulder and looked at Will. "I knew that the first time I saw you together. I'll go tell your folks what's happening. Carry on."

And they did — for ten wonderful, scary, tiring, exhilarating, loving hours until Marie Elizabeth Callahan made her grand entrance into the world.

A couple of hours later, Will felt Megan looking at him. "Hi, little mama. What do you need?"

"To hold my baby. You've been hogging her." Megan smiled and patted the bed.

"Tough job, but somebody has to do it. You've been napping." He placed Mari Beth in her mother's arms and picked up the camera. "Smile purty."

"She can't smile yet." Megan tilted the baby so her face would show in the picture and smiled tiredly. "But she's beautiful."

Will pulled a chair over next to the bed. The rest of the family had gone home to catch some rest since they had stayed at the hospital all night. He figured they'd be back before too long. Zach was itching to see his new cousin.

"Beautiful like her mama. And healthy and whole. A man couldn't ask for a more perfect child." He leaned his head against the back of the chair and watched Megan gazing upon her daughter in adoration. "But I'm already worrying about when she hits high school. We'll have to keep the boys away with a willow switch."

Megan laughed. "You wouldn't."

"Well, no, I reckon I wouldn't actually hit anybody. I am, however, realizing the merit of my daddy's tactic when Jenna was dating."

She lightly brushed her fingertip over Mari Beth's face. "What was that?"

"He waited on the front porch until she got home."

"Oh no. Every date?"

"Every single one, even in the wintertime. He tried to pull that stunt the first time Nate brought Jenna home, but Mom wouldn't let him. I thought for a while she was going to make us hog-tie him."

"That would have gone over well." She sighed and closed her eyes for a minute.

When she opened them again, he asked, "How are you, sugar?"

She held out her hand, and he curled his fingers around hers. "Saved by God's mercy and grace, blessed by his love. And yours."

"Amen to that."

A thousand times over.

446

EPILOGUE

On a pleasant summer evening three years later, Dub and Sue sat on the porch admiring their growing family. The boys were engaged in a semi-rousing game of baseball. Zach hit the ball, and it zipped right between Will and Chance. They almost collided trying to get it and missed it.

Zach tossed the bat aside and raced for the dirt clearing they'd designated as first base. Nate, who was playing catcher, stood and cheered him on.

"Run, Zach," hollered Dub.

"He already is," Sue said with a chuckle. "He should do well next spring on the little kids' baseball team. I can't believe our first grandchild will be in first grade in September."

"Does it make you feel old, sweetheart?" Dub searched her face.

"No. It seems like we're starting over, with the sports anyway."

447

Dub grinned and went back to watching his family. "We get to do the fun stuff and skip the parent-teacher conferences, PTA, fussin' at them about homework, and baking cupcakes for class parties."

"Dub Callahan, you never baked a cupcake in your life."

"I said we, meaning you in the cupcake department. And a lot of the other departments too. Look at Mari Beth run to her daddy. Hey, Will, your little girl wants to play ball."

Sue took a long drink of iced tea. "How can such a girly-girl be a tomboy too?"

Jenna had been a lot like her at that age. "I expect it has something to do with living here on the ranch."

Sue turned her attention to where Jenna, Emily, and Megan sat on a couple of quilts beneath a pecan tree, playing with the youngest children. She nudged Dub. "Aren't they somethin'?"

"Who? Our daughter and daughters-in-law, or their babies?"

"All of them."

"Yes, they are. But it's a good thing those girls spaced the babies out a bit, or you'd have been worn to a frazzle." He had to stop and think a minute to remember their ages. Chance and Emily's little boy, Cody, was a year old. Nate and Jenna's girl, Suzie, was seven months. Will and Megan's second child, Charlie, was two months old.

Megan's uncle and cousin had come by to visit the week before to see her and the baby. She'd contacted them six months after she and Will were married. Her mother had gone off to California with a guy in a rough biker gang shortly before that. Both Riley and Josh encouraged Megan not to try to get in touch with her, worrying that it would only lead to trouble and heartache. Megan had taken their advice and let it go, which Dub figured was just as well.

She didn't see her relatives too often, but when they got together, they had a good time.

Sighing in contentment, the rugged rancher stretched out his legs and scanned his land. The houses where his children and grandchildren lived. The barn his grandfather had built. The horse pastures behind the house with the white fence that he and his boys had put together. The ranch had been in his family for 130 years. God willing, it would remain in the family for generations to come.

When he and Sue were gone, the things they'd taught their children, the legacy they'd leave them, would remain. Love of

God, love of family, and love of the land.

Another of his prayers had been fulfilled too. God had chosen the perfect mate for each of them. His children were happy, and that made him happy. God was faithful to keep his promises.

But blessed is the man who trusts in the Lord, whose confidence is in him.

Life was good.

ABOUT THE AUTHOR

Sharon Gillenwater was born and raised in West Texas, and loves to write about her native state. The author of several novels, she is a member of the American Christian Fiction Writers. When she's not writing, she and her husband enjoy spending time with their son, daughter-in-law, and adorable grandchildren.

The employees of Thorndike Press hope you have enjoyed this Large Print book. All our Thorndike, Wheeler, and Kennebec Large Print titles are designed for easy reading, and all our books are made to last. Other Thorndike Press Large Print books are available at your library, through selected bookstores, or directly from us.

For information about titles, please call:

(800) 223-1244

or visit our Web site at:

http://gale.cengage.com/thorndike

To share your comments, please write:

Publisher

Thorndike Press

10 Water St., Suite 310

Waterville, ME 04901